The Cove

Michael Grant

Copyright © 2011 Michael Grant

All rights reserved.

ISBN: 13: 978-1456560324
ISBN-10: 1456560328

LCCN:

DEDICATION

To Elizabeth who has given me a new life.

ACKNOWLEDGMENTS

My undying thanks to Sandi Nadolny who is the most efficient and meticulous copy editor an author could wish for. Thank you for all your time and attention to my manuscript. Your efforts are greatly appreciated. I also want to thank my good friend Bob Mescolotto for his careful reading of the manuscript and for his many cogent suggestions.

CHAPTER ONE

The five men moved silently down the grimy East Harlem tenement hallway lit only by a single 40-watt bulb. But for their purposes, even that was too bright. A hand reached up and unscrewed the bulb, plunging the hallway into darkness. Detective Pete Delaney handed the hot bulb to the man behind him. Lt. Harlan Weber, Delaney's boss, took it without thinking. *"Oh, shit..."* he muttered, bobbing the hot bulb until he finally managed to stuff it in his pocket.

In spite of the tension, Detective Ralph Sanchez, Delaney's young partner, and the two Emergency Service cops—bulky in flak jackets and bristling with a battering ram and shotguns—grinned at the lieutenant's discomfort.

"That wasn't funny, Delaney," the lieutenant hissed.

The lieutenant was seldom right, Delaney thought, but he had to agree, he might have a point this time. They were about to take down two whacked out gang bangers wanted for a triple homicide and there was certainly nothing funny about that. Still, in spite of that, and for reasons that escaped him, he thought it *was* funny. Lately, he was finding everything either very funny or unbearably sad. This, he decided, was funny. Go figure.

The two Emergency cops positioned themselves on either side of the door. Their moves had been carefully choreographed ahead of time and honed to clockwork precision. The battering ram would be used first. Usually one well placed blow was enough to take down these old decrepit pre-war doors. But sometimes the bad guys reinforced the door with steel door jambs and then a shotgun was required to blow the hinges off the door.

Lt. Weber tapped the cop on the shoulder and the man lunged at the door with the ram. There was as loud *crack* and the screeching of tearing wood as the door came away from the hinges. With gun drawn, Delaney pushed the door and scrambled over it before it hit the ground. As he did so, he had a flash memory of those old World War II newsreel movies of soldiers charging off the landing craft at Normandy beach.

In the gloom of the apartment, he saw a figure dart from the kitchen to the living room. By the time Delaney caught up to him, the man had one leg out the window. The detective dropped into a combat stance and pointed his Glock 20 at the perp. *"Back up or you get a new asshole,"* Delaney shouted.

Reluctantly, the man backed out of the window.
"Assume the position."

The Cove

The man, no stranger to the arrest process, dropped to the floor, but he wouldn't put his hands behind his back so he could be cuffed. Delaney knew what the perp was up to. It was just more street bullshit. The unwritten code of the street was that if the cops busted you, you made it as hard for them as possible. He'd seen rookies roll around in the street trying to cuff a perp as the neighborhood howled in delight. But Delaney had the recipe for uncooperative perps. He delivered three sharp punches to the man's kidneys. The man screamed in pain—and his hands shot behind his back.

As Sanchez snapped cuffs on him, Delaney moved into the bedroom to look for the other perp. As soon as he came into the room, he knew he had a problem. A raggedy curtain fluttered in the breeze coming through the open window. That meant either the perp was long gone, or worse, Delaney would have to take on a tedious—not to mention tiring—chase up the fire escape and across God knows how may rooftops. Not for the first time in the last several months did it occur to him that he was getting to old for this shit.

As a reluctant Delaney started toward the window, a closet door behind burst open and a man, covered with assorted gang tattoos and wielding a machete, lunged at him. In a nanosecond, it confirmed Delaney's suspicions: He *was* getting to old for this shit. Only a goddamn rookie would be stupid enough to walk by a closed closet door without checking what was inside.

The machete blade whistled toward Delaney's head. Instinctively he deflected the blade with his gun hand, but the force of the blade knocked the gun from his hand. The man crashed into Delaney and they both fell back on a bed wrestling for control of the knife. The man was taller and heavier than Delaney. And worse–*he was on top.*

Slowly, he forced the blade closer and closer to Delaney's cheek. The man's breath was hot on Delaney's face and he could smell garlic on the man's breath. His biceps and forearms burned from the effort to keep the blade away from him. He knew he couldn't hold him off much longer.

Where the hell was Harlan Weber when you needed him?

The blade touched his cheek, carving out a three-inch gash. The man, sensing that his opponent was weakening, raised his body off Delaney to get additional leverage so he could thrust downward with both hands on the machete. It worked—sort of. The blade carved another gash in Delaney's cheek, but taking his weight off Delaney had made him vulnerable. Delaney drove his knee into the man's exposed testicles. With a grunt of agony the man dropped the machete and rolled off the bed.

Delaney dove for his gun at the same time the man went for the machete. They spun and faced each other from less than ten-feet away.

"Gun against machete," Delaney said softly. "No contest."

The man smirked and dropped the machete. "Okay, you got me." Then he saw the look of intense fury in Delaney's eyes and the smirk vanished. Blood dripped down Delaney's cheek, but he felt no pain, just a strange elation. He continued to point his gun at the man's head while bizarre thoughts exploded in his mind. *What would it feel like to blow this guy's head off? Wouldn't he be surprised? What would he do if I put my gun down and told him to go for the machete again?*

Before he could entertain anymore weird thoughts, Weber burst into the room.

"*Delaney*—!" He, too, saw the strange look in the detective's eyes, a look he'd seen before but still scared the hell out of him. "What… what are you doing?"

Like a machine Delaney pivoted toward the lieutenant and trained the gun on him; his eyes burning intently. Weber blanched and backed toward the door, unsure of what Delaney might do.

There was a long, tense moment of silence, then Delaney grinned. "Just making an arrest, Lou."

He spun back toward the man. "You're under arrest, sir. Did I tell you that?"

The man shook his head warily. "You are one crazy motherfucker."

Without warning, Delaney stepped forward and slammed his gun into the side of the man's head and he went down like a dead tree.

Once Delaney saw that everything was under control, he slipped out of the apartment. The last thing he needed now was meaningful dialogue with his young pain-in-the-ass boss, who was book smart, but common sense challenged. What did Texans say about a guy like that? *All hat, no cattle.* But Weber had seen him slip out and gave chase.

Delaney hurried down the stairs as uniformed cops and EMS paramedics hurried in the opposite direction.

Weber, pushing the cops aside, shouted, "He was unarmed—"

"I didn't shoot him." Delaney dabbed his cheek with a bloody handkerchief.

"You wanted to."

"There's nothing in the Penal Law about thought crimes, Lou."

Weber caught up to Delaney in the foyer and spun him around. "I got the feeling you wanted to kill me, too."

Delaney looked at him for a long moment. "I couldn't do that, Lieutenant. You're my superior officer and it's against department policy."

Delaney banged through the doors and came out on the stoop. The street was filled with radio cars and ambulances and flashing red lights.

"I want you in my office in ten minutes," Weber said.

Delaney grinned at two cops standing on the stoop. "Thanks for stopping by, fellas. Anybody got the time?"

"Ten after twelve, Pete."

"No shit. Hey, I'm on vacation."

He skipped down the steps and started up the block.

"You're a crazy bastard, do you know that Delaney?" Weber shouted after him.

Delaney waved over his shoulder.

"One week," Weber continued to shout at the retreating figure. "You got one week to come back squared away."

Delaney waved again.

Ten minutes later, the detective was in his beat-up '88 Honda parked around the corner from the station house. He reached into a cooler in the back seat, popped the tab, and took a long slug of cold beer. He studied himself in the rearview mirror. The gashes had stopped bleeding, but he looked like shit. "Well, you dodged the bullet again you lucky bastard," he said aloud.

Oddly enough, he didn't sound at all pleased.

CHAPTER TWO

    When viewed from the air, Crater Cove resembled a flooded bowl with one side eaten away by the relentless pounding of eons of Atlantic storms. Locals with vivid imaginations claimed the cove was the remains of an ancient volcano. Still others insisted the cove had been created by the impact of a giant meteor. The more prosaic truth was that Crater Cove, like dozens more dotting the jagged New England coastline, had been formed by the scouring action of glaciers.
    The new day's sun—barely ten minutes old—splashed an orange-red glow on the pine-covered cliff overlooking the cove's rocky beach. An old man, dressed in ragged cutoffs and a baggy sweatshirt, waded into the shallows and threw a stick onto the mirror-like water. His young Golden Retriever, never tiring of the daily game, boisterously splashed into the water after it.
    While the dog paddled toward the stick, the man shielded his eyes from the low-level sun and squinted in admiration at the only sailboat in the cove—a beautiful thirty-seven foot yawl bobbing at anchor. The dog bounded up onto the beach, shook the water off his coat and deposited the stick at his master's feet. Just then a gentle breeze rippled across the still waters. The dog lifted his head, sniffed the air, and with a low growl turned abruptly toward the direction of the sailboat. A moment later, the old man caught the same scent and staggered backward, repelled by the unmistakable odor of decaying flesh.

With blue lights flashing and siren blasting, a four-wheel drive jeep sped down the dirt road leading to the cove and skidded to a stop. Deputy Clint Avery, a lanky, sandy-haired young man, bolted out of the vehicle even before the vehicle had stopped rocking.

"I got Bobby Collins on his cell phone, Chief," he shouted breathlessly as he half-fell, half-slid down a sand dune. "He's the closest. Ought to be here any second."

Police Chief Tony Brunetta adjusted his broad-rimmed Stetson to shield his large, inquisitive eyes from the sun and continued to study the sailboat anchored a quarter-mile off the beach. Without turning, he said to the old man standing next to him, "Mr. Kiley, when did you first see the boat?"

"Oh, I guess about three mornings ago, Chief."

"And you haven't seen anyone on board?"

"No, sir. Me and Baily are here just about every morning and we don't stay much more than a half hour. I figured they was late sleepers. Them cruising sailors are a peculiar bunch."

The wind had died down and Brunetta could smell nothing except the usual pungent reek of mussel shells and sea grass. "You sure about that smell?" he asked. "Sometimes whales and dolphins beach themselves," he said hopefully. "They make a helluva stink."

The old man shook his head vigorously. "Chief, back in forty-two, I spent six days and six nights on Guadalcanal. The smell of death is a smell you don't never forget."

Tony Brunetta, a retired New York City Police homicide lieutenant, knew exactly what the old man was talking about. "No, you don't," he muttered to himself softly.

He heard the high-pitched whine of an outboard and shifted his gaze to the inlet opening. A clamming skiff came into view and headed directly toward them.

Bobby Collins, excited about the prospect of getting involved in real police work, flashed a wide grin that revealed a large gap where his front teeth used to be. He nudged the bow up on the sand and threw a line to Avery.

Brunetta nimbly jumped on board and turned toward his newest deputy who was about to throw the line back. "Clint, what are you doing? Get on board."

Avery's eyes widened. "Me, Chief? I figured—"

"Come on. It's time you saw something dead besides road kill."

As the skiff approached the sailboat, Avery nervously licked his lips. What do you figure happened, Chief?" he asked in a voice pitched high with nervousness.

"Don't know, Clint. Maybe there's an old timer on board. Maybe he had a heart attack."

Avery exhaled in relief. "You think so?"

Brunetta intently studied the approaching sailboat looking for anything out of the ordinary. "We'll see," he said softly.

As they pulled alongside, Brunetta cautioned the two men not to touch the sailboat. As he stood up to grab the lifeline, he was hit by the full impact of the putrid stench. Involuntarily, his head snapped back, but not before he caught a glimpse of dark maroon smears on either side of the companionway.

He sat down wearily and motioned Collins to turn off the engine. The engine coughed into silence and the water lapping against the side of the boat was suddenly very loud. It was a pleasant sound and Tony Brunetta wished he could sit there and listen to it for the rest of the day.

"It's a homicide," he said finally. "Collins, tie onto that cleat and don't touch anything else."

The ashen faced young clammer nodded, no longer grinning.

Brunetta pulled himself on board, being careful not to step on the rust-brown footprints on the deck. He looked down at his deputy who had turned the color of the cove's green water and felt sorry for the young man. Ones first introduction to violent death was never a pleasant one. But then again, when was it ever?

"All right, Clint," he said in a quiet, reassuring tone. "Come aboard nice and easy. There's a lot of blood stains. Try not to step on them. And Clint, take off your hat." It would be tight quarters below and he didn't want his deputy knocking his hat off, grabbing for it, and stomping all over the crime scene.

Avery handed his brand new chocolate-brown Stetson to Collins and climbed aboard.

"*Jesus H. Christ!*" the young deputy muttered, covering his nose with his hands.

"It'll be worse down below," Brunetta said. "Breathe through your mouth."

Brunetta slid the hatch open and squinted down into the cabin's gloom, but he could see nothing. The other hatches were closed and the window curtains had been drawn. He wished he had rubber gloves. In the year he'd been the police chief of Haddley Falls, there had been no need for them—he didn't think there would ever be a need for them. Wasn't that the whole point in taking this job?

"We're going down," he said to his deputy, who was staring transfixed on the darkened cabin below. 'Remember what I said, Clint. Don't touch anything."

Deputy Avery mumbled a reply through his cupped hands.

Tony Brunetta inhaled a lungful of the warm fresh sea air and slowly descended the five steps into hell. The smell of death was a smell he'd grown used to in his fifteen years as a homicide detective and then homicide squad commander. But it was a smell that had finally driven him out of the city to Haddley Falls. Now, the smell that he had run away from enveloped him like a living, malignant presence.

It took a moment to realize the buzzing wasn't coming from inside his head. Swarms of flies, guided by an invisible, but powerful beacon of scent, had come to lay their eggs in decaying flesh.

Avery looked over Brunetta's shoulder. "*Sweet Jesus!*" he gasped. "There's *two* of 'em, Chief."

With a cold, professional intensity, Brunetta's trained eyes swept the cabin interior, his brain registering and processing the dozens of bits and pieces of information that might be meaningless now, but might prove to be important later.

The faces of the two victims—a man and a woman—had the same peculiar expression that most people who die a violent death have—a flat, vacant look of acceptance in the eyes offset by the terror in the twisted mouth. But there, the similarity ended. Every victim dies for a specific reason. Why were these two people murdered? That question, Brunetta realized unhappily, was one that he would have to answer.

The woman, apparently in her late forties, lay sprawled in the port bunk. There was a deep black gash on her forehead and her bikini top was wrapped around her throat. The bottom half of her suit had been cut away and her legs were splayed wide in an obscene pose. She'd been sliced from breast to pubic bone, exposing a dark glistening cavity.

In the starboard bunk the man, probably in his early fifties, was on his back, his mouth open in a silent shriek. His throat had been slashed and his chest, half-covered by a pajama top, was caked with blood from multiple stab wounds.

As always, the homicide investigator's first question popped into Brunetta's head. *Why were these people murdered?* A robbery gone bad? Not likely. The man was wearing a Rolex. Judging from the condition of the bodies, that left another possibility. A sex-ritual killer. *Jesus.*

Before he could further dwell on that unhappy scenario, he heard a strange gurgling sound behind him. He turned and saw Avery with a handkerchief up to his mouth.

"Chief...I... think I'm gonna be... sick..."

Brunetta's face displayed no emotion but there was a hard edge in his tone. "Clint, you throw up on my crime scene and you're fired." He spun the deputy around and pushed him up the companionway.

As Avery stumbled up the steps, Brunetta yelled after him, "And make sure you throw up over the side."

A few minutes later, Brunetta came up on deck and greedily filled his lungs with clean fresh salt air. The sun, climbing into a brilliant cobalt-blue sky, promised a postcard perfect day, just the kind of day that the Haddley Falls Chamber of Commerce prayed for. But, now, such a beautiful day seemed obscene in light of the horror that lay in the cabin below.

When he'd been the commanding officer of Bronx Homicide, he'd had the full resources of the New York City Police Department at his disposal, including trained detectives, forensic technicians, and the services of a forensic lab second only to the FBI's. But that was last year. Now, all he had was ten deputies – all unskilled and unprepared to deal with the complexities of a double homicide.

Brunetta looked down at a pasty-faced Clint Avery, who was draped over the side moaning softly, and was grateful for one thing. At least his deputy hadn't puked on his crime scene.

CHAPTER THREE

Pete Delaney steered his battered '88 Honda Civic off the Interstate exit and cast a baleful glance at the temperature gauge which was slowly climbing toward "H."

"Don't do this to me you sonofabitch," he snarled in a tone that was known to strike terror in the hearts of hapless prisoners. He turned into a convenience store to restock his cooler and give the radiator a chance to cool down.

Two beers later the temperature gauge was back to normal and he pulled out onto the single lane road. Doing his best to follow the written instructions, which had gotten soaked from a spilled beer, he worked his way east toward the coast along a series of secondary roads. An hour later, he came to a road sign and slowed down to read it.

WELCOME TO HADDLEY FALLS
EST. 1687
POP: 5,458 (AND STILL GROWING!)

Delaney quickly calculated that even with a five percent murder rate it worked out to two hundred and seventy homicides a year! A piece of cake. No wonder Tony took the job. He slammed his hands on the steering wheel. "Asshole"—he reminded himself aloud—"forget the job."

He'd promised himself he would not think about the New York City Police Department or homicides or courts or his pain-in-the-ass boss. He had five days to do what he had to do and then none of it would matter.

He sucked down the remainder of his beer, crushed the can, and tossed it over his shoulder where it landed with a clunk on top of a dozen other empty cans.

As he turned onto a placid tree-lined street, he recalled the first day he and Tony Brunetta met almost twenty-one years ago. Delaney, along with three hundred other anxious and self-conscious recruits, milled about the lobby of the auditorium in the Police Academy waiting to go inside. Even then, Tony Brunetta stood out in the crowd. He wasn't tall—maybe five-ten—and, except for a pair of large, expressive eyes that made him look more like a poet than a future cop, fairly ordinary looking. But there was something about him—maybe the fact that he looked a lot older than most of the men and women in the group—that drew people to him. There was actually a small line in front of him as confused recruits asked him a multitude of questions. Delaney was amused—and intrigued. This guy was a rookie like the rest of them, yet he exuded a remarkable self-assurance, as though he'd been a cop all his life.

Delaney waited for the line to disappear and then approached. "Hey. You have an extra pen? I left mine home."

Brunetta handed him a pen. "Some cop you're gonna make. How're you gonna write tickets without a pen?"

"I'm not," Delaney said. "I'm gonna be a detective."

Brunetta's expressive eyes studied Delaney. "Oh, yeah? Me, too."

Just before lunch a lieutenant with a big belly came out on the auditorium stage and glared out at the timorous audience of young men and women. "You're almost police officers now," he growled. Almost every one of them self-consciously patted the unfamiliar shield in their pants pocket to reassure themselves that they indeed had been sworn in and issued a silver police officer's badge. But NYPD cops never called it a badge. It was called a *shield*. "But you're *probationary* police officers," the lieutenant continued, "and we will be watching your conduct very carefully. You screw up and you're outta here."

For the next fifteen minutes he reviewed an extensive list of dos and don'ts. The last don't was a prohibition against frequenting bars while on duty.

Delaney and Brunetta had lunch in a faux English pub three blocks from the Police Academy. Brunetta didn't want to go there, but Delaney convinced him that they were in civilian clothes and no one would recognize them.

Over a couple of beers and charred burgers they got to know each other. Brunetta was thirty-one, married with a two year-old daughter. After college he'd gone to work for Merrill Lynch. It took him ten years to come to the conclusion that he didn't want to spend his life crunching numbers.

Delaney's story was less dramatic. He was twenty-one and single. One night after a long night of bar hopping, he and four friends made a bet as to who could get the highest mark on the police entrance exam. Delaney, the only one of the four to pass the test, collected two hundred dollars.

During the course of their nine months in the Police Academy, they became close friends. Both were fierce competitors, but fortunately in different areas. On Graduation day Tony Brunetta marched up to the podium to receive the trophy for the highest academic scores, and Pete Delaney collected the trophy for physical fitness.

Brunetta made detective two years ahead of Delaney, but Delaney caught up and they worked as partners for the next three years. Their yin and yang personalities drove their bosses to distraction, but it made them a great team. Where Brunetta was methodical, thoughtful, and tranquil, Delaney was impetuous and quick with his hands. The meticulous Brunetta handled the paper work, but it was Delaney's instincts that frequently led to the breaking of a case. The partnership ended when Tony passed the sergeant's exam. Four years later they were reunited in the Manhattan Homicide Squad. But now, Tony Brunetta, a lieutenant, was the commanding officer and Pete Delaney, still a detective, was the subordinate. He drove his old friend crazy, but with all his faults and rough edges, Brunetta put up with him because he was the best detective he'd ever seen.

Now, Delaney glanced uneasily at the beautiful panorama of trees and mountains enveloping him and wondered if he'd made a mistake in coming up here. The great outdoors made him nervous. Born and raised in Brooklyn, he felt a lot more comfortable surrounded by bricks and asphalt. The only outdoors he'd been exposed to was Brooklyn's Prospect Park where there were more muggers than trees.

Delaney glanced at his temperature gauge with satisfaction. Now that he was back on relatively level ground, it had stayed midway between the H and C. Still on the outskirts of Haddley Falls, he turned onto a stately tree-lined Elm Street which led directly into the heart of town. Both sides of the street were lined with elegant, gingerbread Victorian homes with wrap-around porches filled with colorful hanging baskets of geraniums. Hung above the front doors of B&Bs were signs with names that the owners hoped would entice tourists with images of a blissful vacation: *Ocean View*, *Sandy Haven*, *Pine Crest*. Delaney noted that every house had a NO VACANCY sign posted; mute testimony to the health of the tourist industry in Haddley Falls.

While he was stopped at a traffic light, a homeless man, pushing a shopping cart piled high with clothing and boxes, crossed in front of him. The light turned green and Delaney continued on his way, but he kept watching the bum in his review mirror. By training, Delaney was attuned to the out-of-the-ordinary and the bum's presence was jarringly out of place in this picture postcard setting. *What's he doing here?*

On impulse, he made a U-turn. By the time he got back to the intersection, the man had vanished. Delaney made a right turn and less than three blocks off Elm, he found another face of Haddley Falls; one he was sure the Chamber of Commerce tried to conceal from the tourists.

There is a bleak sameness to rundown neighborhoods whether it's New York, Chicago, or a small town like Haddley Falls. The only difference is scale. Each has its hardcore unemployed standing on street corners looking for a way to make a quick score, bars with dirty windows and loud jukeboxes, abandoned cars, and too many overflowing garbage cans.

Delaney drove by a clump of idle men standing in front of a bar called the Flotsam. He'd been in enough ghetto neighborhoods to know the men milling about out front were waiting to score drugs. Above the bar were windows covered with cheap curtains and lopsided Venetian blinds. Not a geranium pot in sight.

As he got to the crest of the hill, the temperature gauge started rising again and he pulled over to give the old Honda a breather. While he was waiting for the radiator to cool down, he sat on a stone wall and lit a cigarette. Across the street was a row of redbrick attached houses built in the nineteenth century when New England was a thriving industrial area.

Below him stretched a valley dominated by an ugly, sprawling redbrick factory whose twin smoke stacks belched black smoke into the clear blue sky. A sign said it was the home of TALBOT MEATPACKING, INC. He'd seen the familiar brand in his local supermarket, but he had no idea the plant was located in Haddley Falls, now under the care and supervision of his best friend, Tony Brunetta.

Suddenly, Delaney spotted the homeless man far below him. The old man stopped in front of an old shack on the edge of a clearing and began unloading the contents of his shopping cart. Apparently, this is where he lived.

With the temperature gauge back to normal, Delaney started back down the hill, acutely aware that he was putting off meeting his old friend. But he didn't know if it was because he afraid of what he was going to tell Brunetta or what Brunetta was going to tell him?

As he got closer to the center of the town, he began to see more and more tourists and the types of businesses that attracted them—antique shops, craft shops, and quaint clapboard houses that had been converted into charming little six-table restaurants.

A short, stocky police officer dressed in a neatly creased brown uniform with a large American flag patch on his right shoulder was directing traffic. Delaney pulled up beside him. "Officer, could you direct me to the police station?"

The double-chinned cop studied Delaney from behind mirrored sunglasses. "You a reporter?"

"No," Delaney answered, surprise by the question, not to mention the hostile tone.

The cop took off his brown Stetson and wiped his bald head with a handkerchief. "Two blocks to Main. Hang a left. It's the big beige building on your right."

The front of the single-story police station was blocked by a dozen double parked state and local police vehicles. Delaney was puzzled. *Tony had said Haddley Falls was a quiet town.*

As he approached the front desk, the receptionist, a harried woman in her late sixties, was on the telephone. She hung up and peered at him over thick tortoise glasses. "Yes?" she snapped.

That's *two* who could use a little sensitivity training, he thought. "Pete Delaney, I'm here to see the chief."

"Chief Brunetta is very busy. He isn't seeing anyone."

"I'm a personal friend. He's expecting me."

"I'll see if he's available," she muttered, not at all impressed.

While she was on the telephone, Delaney watched a handful of harried deputies and clerical people grabbing at constantly ringing telephones. It reminded him of a fundraising telethon. Over in the corner two uniformed State Police officers stood in animated conversation with a local lieutenant and a sergeant. For a small time police department there was a helluva lot of activity going on.

The woman hung up. "Down the hall and turn right."

Before he had a chance to say thank you the telephone rang again. She rolled her eyes and snatched it up.

Delaney walked through a door marked CHIEF. Tony Brunetta was on the telephone and Delaney was surprised at his appearance. He'd expected to see a tanned, relaxed man. Instead, Brunetta, whom he hadn't seen since the retirement party a year earlier, looked drawn and tired. In fact he looked worse than he did when he had the pressure-cooker job as the Manhattan Homicide Squad commander. Brunetta cupped his hand over the receiver and said to a deputy walking out the door, "As soon as the forensic people get here, let me know."

A moment later he hung up, came around the desk and grabbed Delaney in a bear hug. It was a habit that even after twenty years still embarrassed Delaney. In the beginning he'd complained, but Brunetta had laughed his protests away, saying uptight Micks didn't understand demonstrative Wops.

Delaney extracted himself from Brunetta's embrace. "I thought retirement was supposed to add years to your life, Tony. You look like shit."

Brunetta smiled wanly. "Thanks, buddy. It's good to see you, too." He motioned to Delaney to sit down and flopped down in a battered leather chair and studied his old friend. It was his turn to be shocked by Pete Delaney's appearance, but he said nothing. His friend had gained a little weight and it had given his face an unhealthy, puffy look. It was mid-summer, but from Pete's pallor it looked as though he'd been living in a cave. A bar was more like it. Delaney was a man with no hobbies and only one vocation—homicide investigation. Squad rooms, courts, and saloons were his only hangouts, none of which provided the restorative powers of sunlight and fresh air.

He pointed at the two gashes on Delaney's cheek. "What happened to you?"

"Cut myself shaving."

"You shaving with a Samurai sword now?"

Delaney grinned. "Actually, it was a machete."

Even though he'd been out a year, Brunetta was still the homicide squad's unofficial father confessor and he'd been disturbed by the stories he'd been hearing about Delaney. It had taken two months worth of telephone calls to finally coax his old partner to come up here, away from the city, DOAs, and unrepentant murderers.

Brunetta ran his hands through his thick salt-and-pepper hair. "Pete, you're not gonna believe this. I got a double homicide this morning."

"No shit. You'd better get someone out there to subtract two numbers from that population sign by the interstate."

"That's not funny. This is a resort town and tourists are very fussy about going someplace where they might be murdered."

"I can understand that. Bad enough you get murdered. You shouldn't have to pay for the privilege. Maybe the Chamber of Commerce could offer a rebate if you get whacked before your rental time is up."

"Pete, you're still the same warm, sensitive human being I remember."

Delaney lit up a cigarette. "So how did these two get done? Fence war? Cattle rustling?"

"You smoking again?"

"Yeah."

"Since when?"

"Since a while."

Delaney held the cigarette between his teeth and in a poor imitation of Humphrey Bogart, said, "So tell me, kid, whaddaya got?"

As Brunetta described what he'd found at Crater Cove, Delaney's amused expression gave way to a look of intense concentration as his professional mind began to sort and analyze what he was being told. Brunetta had seen the look often, but he didn't want to see it now. The last thing Pete Delaney needed now was another homicide to think about.

When Brunetta finished, Delaney said, "Where's the boat now?"

"Secured in dry storage at a marina. I'm waiting for the State Forensic Unit."

"So what do you think you've got?"

Brunetta shrugged. "Ritual killer?"

"You do a background on the DOAs?"

"In the works. All I know so far is that the late Mr. and Mrs. Paul Eccles lived in Toms River, New Jersey."

"Maybe there's something there—big debt, drugs."

"I hope so. I damn well don't need this."

"How about the autopsy?"

"Not done yet."

Delaney looked at his watch. "It's been five hours, Tony. How many DOAs do you get around here?"

"The county coroner is a drunk and he's missing in action. I have my deputies out looking for him."

Delaney stared at Brunetta in disbelief. "Two people get capped and you have to set up a dragnet to find the ME? Tony, what are you doing in this Mickey Mouse job?"

"I didn't plan to come up here and investigate murders. I planned to spend minimum time chasing poachers and boat thieves and maximum time hunting and fishing. Until today that's exactly what I've been doing, and— What the hell are you laughing at?"

"You come all the way up here to commune with squirrels and you get a 'double.' *That's* funny."

Brunetta grunted. "Maybe I'd think so too, if I weren't the punch line."

"Can your deputies do a homicide?"

"Not a chance. I have a road lieutenant, a clerical sergeant and eight road cops. My deputies are either young kids waiting to go onto the State police or old timers waiting for retirement."

Delaney jumped out of his chair. "Brunetta, this is your lucky day."

"Why—? Oh, no. You're on vacation."

The truth was Brunetta had considered using Delaney's talents, but from what he'd been hearing, Pete needed a rest more than he needed a good detective.

Delaney sat on the edge of Brunetta's desk. "You need help and I'm the best goddamned homicide detective in the country."

"And a modest one, too. Thanks, but no thanks. You're on vacation."

"Will you stop saying that? If I don't help you, who will?"

Brunetta shrugged. "Beats the hell out of me. This is all new to me. I'm guessing the State Police. But, enough of this." He stood up and grabbed Delaney in another bear hug. "Pete, it's good to see you."

Delaney, missing his friend more than he cared to admit, gingerly patted his back. "Yeah, you old bastard, it's good to see you, too."

The mayor of Haddley Falls was sixty-seven year-old Royce Gardiner, a tenth generation resident in a town that considered fifth generation residents newcomers. He was also the senior partner in Gardiner, Rice & Mayhew, the most prestigious law firm in Hancock County.

Gardiner, a careful man who left nothing to chance, had personally designed his oak-paneled office to ensure that it was just the right size for a senior partner. It was small enough that frugal minded New Englanders wouldn't think it ostentatious, yet large enough to convey to one and all that this was the domain of a very powerful and influential man.

With his long white mane and bushy mustache Gardiner went to great lengths to cultivate the look of a simple country lawyer. But as a long trail of bloodied and dazed big city lawyers discovered—usually too late—he was anything but. Behind those mild blue eyes and grandfatherly appearance, was the lightening-quick mind of a ruthless negotiator who gave and asked no quarter.

There was only one man in Haddley Falls to whom Gardiner deferred and that man was sitting on his leather Chesterfield couch in his office glaring at him.

Now, with his thumbs tucked into his plain black suspenders—he liked to call them braces—Gardiner was in the process of employing his considerable powers of persuasion to convince Jonathan Talbot that his was the only sensible solution.

"We have got to get the State Police in here right away," he said in his most reasonable tone. "The quicker they solve these terrible murders, the quicker we can get this town back to normal."

Puffing on a large Cuban cigar, Jonathan Talbot, a trim, athletic fifty-year-old, blew a line of blue smoke toward the ceiling. "Not a good idea, Royce."

"We have no choice, Jonathan."

"What about Chief Brunetta?"

"Impossible."

"Isn't he a former homicide detective?"

"Yes, but he doesn't have the wherewithal to—" Gardiner stopped. It suddenly occurred to him why Talbot wanted to keep the state police out. "You're concerned about how this will impact on your Secretary of Commerce appointment, aren't you? That's what this is all about."

Talbot grinned, showing even white teeth. "You're very perceptive, Royce."

Gardiner ignored the sarcastic tone. "What on earth could your appointment have to do with these murders?"

Talbot stood up to study a map of New England, circa 1790, hanging over the fireplace. "For a lawyer you can be very dense, Royce. It's not about the murders. Allow me to connect the dots. The state police work for Governor Emory. You know the level of animosity between us. He'll use these murders as an excuse to send in his lackeys so they can look under every rock until he finds something to use against me."

"So you're proposing I keep the State Police out to protect you?"

Talbot's gray eyes became hard. "Not just me, Royce. The state cops will be asking a lot of questions and turning over a lot of rocks. There's no telling what they'll uncover."

Gardiner heard Talbot's threatening tone and paled. "Perhaps you're right, Jonathan. But what if Chief Brunetta can't find the murderer?"

"Does it matter?"

"Of course it does," Gardiner snapped. Talbot's smug, patrician smile irritated him. It was true that Talbot came from a wealthy and influential family, but they'd been here for less than a hundred years. That didn't give him the right to be so uppity.

"There are only two things we have to concern ourselves with," Talbot said. "One, keep the state police out and two, keep this investigation quiet. Brunetta can deliver on both counts. Besides, we can control Brunetta. We can't control the state police."

"Jonathan, I'm telling you he can't investigate these murderers by himself."

Talbot waved a dismissive hand. "We must be pragmatic. Those dead people—outsiders I might remind you—are of no consequence to us. If Brunetta doesn't find the murderer, so be it. It wouldn't be the first time a homicide went unsolved. Let him close out the case so the town can move on. That's what's important."

Gardiner was shocked by Talbot's callous tone, but he was a pragmatist and he had to admit Talbot had a point. Why turn the town upside down for a couple of outsiders? Besides, Brunetta was a trained homicide investigator. Why shouldn't he handle it? Gardiner could think of only one major obstacle. "I don't think we have the authority to keep the state police out."

Talbot crushed his cigar in an ashtray. "My lawyers have already researched the provisions of the town's charter. The state can't come in unless we invite them in."

The Mayor needed only a moment to decide. Talbot was right again. There was no telling what unpleasantness the state police might dig up. In his role as counsel to most of the influential people in the town, he was keenly aware that there were skeletons hiding in very important closets that should not see the light of day. "All right. Brunetta will handle the investigation."

As Talbot started for the door, he said, "I suggest you call Chief Brunetta in right away and give him the ground rules."

When Brunetta came into Gardiner's office, the mayor was seated at his desk. Behind him was an antique oak roll top desk that had once been the busy workplace of Gardiner's great-grandfather, the founder of the firm. But now it was used to display an assortment of photographs of Royce Gardiner's children and grandchildren.

"You wanted to see me, Royce?"

"Yes." Gardiner stroked his bushy mustache. Something he did when he was stressed. "Terrible business these murders. Anything since I spoke to you earlier?"

"No. I've contacted the Toms River Police Department and the New Jersey State Police. I expect to hear back from them tonight or tomorrow. I've also sent faxes to the state and local police departments inquiring about murders with a similar MO."

"Has the autopsy uncovered anything?"

"It hasn't been done yet. I can't find Dr. Bynum."

Gardiner's blue eyes flashed. "Arthur Bynum is a drunken fool."

"And he shouldn't do this autopsy," Brunetta said.

"He's not that bad when he's sober," Gardiner quickly corrected himself.

"He has no experience with homicides, Royce. The State Police have a couple of experienced pathologists on staff. I suggest we use them."

Gardiner stuck his thumbs in his suspenders. "Tony, we're not going to use... outsiders to investigate these murders."

Brunetta looked at Gardiner in disbelief. He knew New Englanders, especially the good people of Haddley Falls, were insular by nature, but this was ridiculous. "Royce," he said evenly, "we're talking about a double homicide."

"Yes, of course. But you have experience with this sort of thing and you have deputies. Surely some of them can help you with the investigation."

"Goddamn it, Royce. We're not talking about a three car pileup on the interstate. Two people have been murdered. I need the best people and the best technology we can get."

He saw a fleeting glimpse of helplessness in the mayor's eyes and realized that this wasn't Gardiner's idea. But who's was it? One thing was for sure. There was no point arguing with the mayor.

In a quiet tone he said, "I'll see what I can do."

CHAPTER FOUR

It was just after eight when Tony Brunetta pulled the 4X4 into his driveway and turned off the engine. His small, but comfortable, New England salt-box house, situated on a quarter acre of heavily wooded land, was a far cry from the Bronx tenement where he'd been raised. He took in the house with its weathered cedar shingles, the lush trees and shrubs surrounding his home and, in spite of the residual anger from the meeting with Royce Gardiner, he gave thanks, once again, for his good fortune. Even after a year he still appreciated coming home to this tranquil setting.

As Brunetta walked into the living room, Delaney, his eyes slightly glazed, waved a half-finished scotch glass in the air in salute. "The ace homicide investigator returns. Have you solved the crime yet?"

Rosemary Brunetta, Tony's petite wife, came out of the kitchen. She was blessed with magic genes that slowed the aging process to a crawl. At fifty, she didn't look much older than the young black-haired girl in the wedding photo on top of the fireplace mantle.

She gave her husband a kiss. "How's it going, hon?"

She and Tony exchanged a brief, troubled glance. "I see you two have started happy hour without me," he said. "I didn't know we had scotch in the house." In fact, the day before, as a precaution, he'd collected all the liquor in the house, packed it in a box and stuffed it in the back of the garage.

Rosemary ran her hand through her short, black hair and tried a smile. "Pete brought a bottle. Wasn't that thoughtful?"

Brunetta saw the troubled expression in her eyes. "Yeah. Very."

He took his gun belt off and collapsed into a recliner. He'd been on the go since six and he could hardly believe that the homicide had happened just this morning. It seemed like he'd been working on it for a week already.

Rosemary massaged the back of his neck. "How'd the meeting go with Gardiner?"

"Not good."

"Can I get you something?"

"I'll have some of Pete's scotch."

She went to the kitchen and Delaney sat down next to Brunetta. "So what's the latest on the Haddley Falls crime of the century?"

"This isn't a joke," Brunetta snapped. "Two people have been murdered. Even in this backwater town we take that seriously."

Delaney was jolted by the angry tone. Tony seldom flew off the handle unless something was really bothering him. "Hey, I'm sorry, pard—"

"You know what your trouble is, Delaney? You think everything is one big joke."

A chastened Delaney put his hands up in surrender. "Okay, I'm sorry. I didn't mean to break your chops."

Brunetta saw the hurt in his friend's eyes and cursed himself. Pete Delaney didn't need anyone else dumping on him. "No, I'm sorry, Pete. It's this homicide... They want me to handle it. Goddamn it, I don't *want* to handle it. I've had enough."

There was a long, awkward pause, then Delaney's flashed his lopsided grin. "Hey, Tony," he said softly. "Are we gonna spend the next four days apologizing to each other or what?"

Brunetta laughed and the tension was broken.

Rosemary came out of the kitchen and handed Tony his drink. "Dinner is served."

Over dinner Rosemary steered the conversation away from the murders. If the men realized it, they didn't let on and went along with it. Half way through dinner Delaney poured himself another scotch. "So tell me, Rosemary. How do you like being so far away from home?"

"I miss Betty and the kids."

"Do they ever get up here?"

"They spent last Christmas here with us. It was wonderful. Snow on the ground, a roaring fireplace. It was like something from a Currier and Ives Christmas card."

"Sounds great. How come I wasn't invited?"

Brunetta was trying his best not to get angry at Delaney, but with every glass of scotch Pete was downing it was getting more and more difficult. "I did invite you," he said, hacking into his steak.

Delaney raised his glass. "That's right you did, old buddy. I must have been busy."

Tony looked him in the eye. "Yeah, it must have been a two-for-one night at the local gin mill."

Delaney's face reddened and he lowered his glass. "Naw. It had to be at least a three-for-one to miss such a great event," he said quietly.

Rosemary shot her husband a murderous glance and they finished dinner in silence. Then Rosemary said, "Why don't you guys go inside. I'll clean up."

Delaney thumbed through a *National Geographic* while Brunetta glared into an unlit fireplace. Finally, Delaney tossed the magazine aside and said, "I think I'll go back to the city tomorrow."

"Why?" Brunetta asked, startled by this unexpected announcement.

Delaney straightened a doily on the arm of the couch. "Maybe it wasn't such a good idea coming up here. Besides, you have your hands full. I'll just be in the way."

Brunetta studied the multicolored hook rug glumly. Since he'd come home he'd been taking out his anger and frustration on Pete. In the old days they could—and did—insult each other all day and it didn't bother either one of them. But these weren't the old days and neither he nor Pete was as flexible as they once were, especially under these circumstances. He wished he could take back that cheap shot about the two-for-ones.

"Pete, these homicides are stirring up a political hornet's nest. You gotta stay, buddy. I may need some good advice. Okay?"

Delaney patted the doily. "Okay, pard," he said. But there was a note of reluctance in his tone.

Brunetta jumped up. "Good, let's have a drink."

When he returned with the two scotches, Delaney said, "I'm curious. How the hell did you find Haddley Falls?"

Brunetta chuckled. "I got my job through the *New York Times*."

"I'm surprised they hired an outsider."

"It was a fluke. At the time there were two warring factions on the town council and they couldn't agree on a local candidate. So, I was a compromise. First time in the history of the town they went outside the state for a police chief."

"The pay has gotta suck, right?"

"They threw in this house. With what they pay me, my pension, and a free house, I'm living pretty good."

Delaney took a sip of scotch and made a face. "Christ, Brunetta," he said, holding the glass up to the light, "there's enough ice in here to sink the Titanic."

"Quit bitchin'. It's a warm night. Ice melts fast."

Delaney grunted. "So what do you *do* all day when there aren't double homicides?"

"Mostly stroke the movers and shakers. There's a lot of rich people in this town and they require a lot of TLC."

Delaney shook his head in disbelief. "Better you than me. What's the hot crime?"

"Off season it's bar fights, poaching deer out of season, kids stealing cars for joy rides. Tourist season is busier. We get a lot of traffic accidents, burglaries, stolen boats, cars."

"This afternoon I got a look at your town's dirty laundry. "The Flotsam looks like a real bucket of blood."

Brunetta frowned. "It is. Drugs, pros. It's a fringe group hangout—a few locals, but mostly kids who come from the big cities to drop out."

"The townies give you a lot of flak about it?"

"Not as long as the skells stay in their part of town. What the upstanding people of Haddley Falls don't see doesn't hurt them."

Delaney slid back on the couch and grabbed his head with both hands. "I don't know how you do it. I'd go outta my mind here."

Brunetta laughed. "That, my friend, is because you have no hobbies. I, on the other hand, like to hunt and fish. I couldn't have picked a better place to settle down."

He stood up. "Come with me." They went outside to the side porch. Darkness had descended and the only sound was a chorus of crickets and a lone whippoorwill. "Pete, what do you smell?"

Delaney took a deep breath. "Nothing."

"Exactly. That's what fresh air smells like. Notice—no carbon monoxide, no sulfa, no gun powder, no burning rubber."

Delaney was unimpressed. "Yeah, it's terrific." He waved his empty glass. "Can I have another drink?"

After she finished the dishes, Rosemary came out on the porch and joined them, but after a while the two men started telling war stories, most of which she'd heard before. Around ten o'clock, she excused herself and went to bed.

With growing anger and apprehension, Brunetta watched Delaney knock down one scotch after another. The drinks, which Delaney had insisted on making himself after Brunetta's unsuccessful attempt to water them down, contained little ice and plenty of scotch. When he decided that Delaney was mellow enough to talk, he asked the question that he already knew the answer to. "So how come you finally decided to come up here and see me?"

Delaney swirled the liquid in his glass. "Who could resist fresh air that doesn't smell like anything?" When Brunetta didn't respond, he shifted uncomfortably. "I needed to get away from Weber," he said softly.

"How is the new squad commander?"

"He's a thirty-five year-old college graduate, dresses like he fell off the cover of *GQ*, and talks like a college professor. There's only one problem. He's in charge of the best goddamn detectives in the NYPD and that dopey bastard couldn't find sand in the Sahara desert."

"It's not his job to find perps," Brunetta said gently. "That's the job of the best goddamn detectives in the NYPD."

"You weren't that way, Tony. Even after you became a boss, you were still a pretty good detective."

Brunetta smiled. Delaney never could resist a dig against bosses. "That's because I worked with the best goddamn detectives in the NYPD," he said.

Delaney stared out into the inky blackness for a long while. "If Weber would just mind his own business," he said finally, "we'd all be better off."

"He breaking your chops?"

Delaney took a slug of scotch. "Big time."

"Why?"

"He doesn't like my ties."

"Pete, don't pull my chain."

After a long pause Delaney said, "He says I'm drinking too much."

"On the job?"

"You know me better than that. Sometimes I come in after a long weekend and I'm a little hung over."

"You still stopping off after work?"

Delaney grinned. "Do New York taxi drivers wear turbans and run red lights? You remember how it was. A little attitude adjustment after a hard day at the office."

"Pete, we're not kids anymore. When you're young the body can handle that kind of abuse."

Delaney's eyes flashed in the darkness. "What the hell are you talking about? I'm only forty-two and you're fifty-two. You talk like we're ready for the great squad room in the sky for chrissake."

"All I'm saying is as we get older we don't bounce back like we used to."

Delaney went on as though he hadn't heard. "Weber would be a better boss if he drank more. Loosen up his tight ass. Do you know what he orders the few times he does drink? *Daiquiris*! The pussy drinks *daiquiris* for chrissake." Delaney shuddered. "Tony, I'm telling you they don't make detectives like they used to."

"Ever think of getting out?"

Delaney's eyes locked on Brunetta's and there was a hint of desperation there. "What would I do?"

"There's more to life than investigating homicides."

"Like being the marshal of Haddley Falls?"

"There are worse things."

Delaney swirled the amber liquid in his glass. "Yeah, I guess there are," he said, remembering why he'd come up here.

He slid down on the couch, put his feet up, and closed his eyes. "I just thought of something, Tony. You haven't had a murder here in sixteen years. The day I show up you get a double. You think I'm a carrier or what?"

Within minutes he was asleep. Brunetta took the half empty glass out of his hand and put in on the table. Then he sat back and stared out into the blackness beyond the trees, recalling the long conversation he'd had with Lt. Weber the day before. The new squad commander wasn't quite the ogre that Delaney had made him out to be. He'd told Brunetta he was concerned with Delaney's drinking, especially after the latest incident. So concerned that he was thinking of putting him in the "program."

The department's alcohol rehabilitation program, which had saved many cops from that long, slow slide to oblivion, was a good one. But Brunetta knew that his friend wouldn't be able to handle the humiliation of having his guns taken away from him. He'd begged the lieutenant to hold off until he had a chance to talk to him. The squad commander reluctantly agreed, but he said he intended to watch Delaney very carefully when he got back. If the problem was still there, Pete Delaney was going to go into the program or out of the job.

Brunetta wanted to help, but he was troubled by how much Pete was drinking. And now these murders had intervened, cutting into the time he'd planned to spend with Pete. Sitting in the darkness, watching his sleeping friend, he wondered what, if anything, he'd be able to accomplish in the next four days. He got up and threw a blanket over Pete. "It's a pleasant night," he said softly. "Maybe the fresh air will do you some good."

When he slipped into bed, Rosemary was still awake. "He finally go to sleep?"

"Yeah."

"Tony, I'm sorry. I couldn't stop him. He came in and the first thing he did was make himself a drink. I couldn't—"

"I know, Rosemary. It wasn't your fault. And I didn't help by breaking his chops when I came home."

"That's not like you. What happened?"

"I guess it was seeing him half gassed on top of my meeting with Gardiner."

"Want to tell me about the meeting?"

"No."

From his tone she knew it was best not to pursue it. "Pete doesn't look good."

"No he doesn't."

Rosemary heard the concern in his voice and felt for her husband. Tony's true vocation was helping people. Even though that particular trait sometimes drove her to distraction, it was one of the things that she loved about him. As a young cop he was always giving money to bums or young mothers who'd been abandoned by their husbands. She finally had to put a stop to it by pointing out that a young cop's salary barely paid for his own family's needs. Still, she suspected that he'd continued the practice, albeit on a smaller scale. Later, when he became a detective squad commander, she had to get used to telephone calls at all hours of the day and night from his cops—and sometimes their wives and girlfriends. He'd spend hours on the telephone doling out advice about everything from gambling to the practice of birth control. Rosemary kidded him that he should have been a priest, but after they'd make love, he'd nibble on her ear and whisper, "Still think I should have been a priest?" And she, blissfully contented, would tug at his hair. "No, it would have been a terrible waste of a great talent."

Rosemary flung her arm over his chest and pulled herself closer. "What are you going to do? I know you planned to spend time with him, but now... I heard him talking about going back to the city. Maybe he should."

He put his arm around her. "No, I don't want him to go back yet. Pete's not himself. I've seen him in a bad way before, but I've never seen him like this. I can't put my finger on it, but I don't like the feeling I'm getting."

"Have you ever seen him drink this much before?"

"Once. Right after Kitty and Peter died. It was bad. He bounced along the bottom for a long time, but eventually he stopped feeling sorry for himself and snapped out of it. Well sort of. He went from being an out and out alcoholic to merely a problem drinker."

"What do you think is wrong?"

"He's always been a hard charger, but now, I don't know. There's a kind of desperation about him and it's got me worried." Brunetta stared at the ceiling. The light of a half-moon was just enough for him to see where the ceiling was beginning to peel. He made a mental note to paint the room as soon as the homicide investigation was over.

"Every homicide cop comes equipped with his own tolerance level," he continued softly. "The day you reach that level you say, 'That's it. I don't want to look at another dead human body ever again.' It doesn't have to be a particularly gory or horrible murder. You just decide you've had enough. For me it was that prostitute on Canal Street, gutted by her pimp because he didn't like the color of her dress." He stiffened involuntarily at the memory. "He was a big bastard. Head shaved and an ear full of gold loops. He shook his head at the memory. The guy was absolutely indignant. *'I tol' her not to wear that dress, but she dissed me. What else was I supposed to do?'* Just before I punched him off the chair, I said, 'You could have asked her to change.'"

Rosemary, who was resting her head on his chest, felt his heart beat quicken and squeezed him reassuringly.

He was quiet for a moment and then continued. "Homicide cops must have a sense of humor to insulate themselves from what they see every day," he said in the tone of a boss lecturing a neophyte detective. "It can be sick humor, but it's gotta be there. He's gotta be able to laugh. When my cops stopped laughing, I knew they'd reached their tolerance level. Some realized it and got out. The others I transferred. They didn't like it, but I probably saved their lives."

She kissed his cheek. "At least you had the good sense to know when you'd had enough," she said softly. "Is Pete still laughing?"

"Yeah, but there's a desperation in it that I don't like."

"How are you going to get him to talk about it?"

"I won't. I can't. He'll have to bring it up himself and it's not going to be easy. We've been friends for a long time, but he still has little pockets of private thoughts that he keeps from me. Maybe even from himself."

After Rosemary dropped off to sleep, Brunetta remained awake for a long time wondering what he was going to do with Pete. He'd planned to take some time off and do some fishing and sightseeing with him. Eventually, he knew, he'd open up.

But now, the homicides had changed everything. He couldn't let Delaney go back to the city in his condition, but given the limited time he'd be able to spend with him, what could he hope to accomplish? He finally dropped off to sleep without answering that question.

CHAPTER FIVE

The next morning Pete Delaney woke up with the sun shining in his eyes and what sounded like a half million birds chirping in the trees outside. Disoriented for the moment, he sat up quickly.

A bad mistake. The dull axe of a hangover headache smacked him between the eyes. Groaning, he lay back down, but it was too late. He'd started a cerebral thunderstorm that would only be appeased with a gallon of very strong coffee. He got up and stumbled into the bathroom to shower and shave. When he came out of the bathroom, he smelled bacon and eggs and his stomach did a three-sixty.

He came into the kitchen and Rosemary looked up from the stove. "How're you feeling, Tiger?"

"Not so hot. I think I'm allergic to all this fresh air."

"Think that's it, huh? Sit down. The bacon and eggs will be ready in a sec."

Delaney swallowed hard and gently lowered himself into a chair. "Nothing solid for me, Rosemary. Just coffee."

She poured the coffee. "Too bad you can't take this intravenously."

"Funny, Rosemary. That's very funny. Where's Tony?"

"He left hours ago."

"What time is it?"

"Ten-fifteen."

"Why didn't he wake me? I wanted to go with him."

"A hand grenade couldn't have awakened you, Pete. Besides, you're on vacation."

Delaney, steadying the cup with both hands, took a sip of the black coffee and prayed for speedy relief. "I wish you guys would stop saying that. I don't *do* vacations."

That wasn't completely true. In his previous life—when he still had a family—they used to go on vacation every year; dude ranches, resorts–even the Bahamas once. The best part was seeing the world through the eyes of his young son, who never tired of asking questions. But that was a long time ago. Now, his vacation time trickled away one day at a time; usually Mondays when he needed an extra day to recover from a weekend blowout.

Rosemary poured herself a cup and sat down across from him. "You're going fishing," she said with a mischievous smile.

Delaney started to shake his head, but stopped abruptly. The motion had started a spike-studded medicine ball rolling around inside his cranium. "No," he said, careful to keep his head still. "I am not going fishing."

"Yes, you are. Tony will be very upset if you don't."

Delaney poured another cup with a shaky hand. Very little splashed onto the table. "I don't have a fishing pole."

Rosemary wiped up the spill. "Tony has plenty."

Delaney tried another tact. "Rosemary, the last time I went fishing, I hurt myself."

She looked at him over her cup. "How old were you?"

"Ten."

"I think it's safe to say you'll do better now that you're all grown up."

"Rosemary—"

"Pete," she said firmly, "you're going fishing and that's that."

Ten minutes later he was standing in the driveway getting a quick primer on how to let line out, set the drag, and bait the hook. When she was certain he understood how to use the tackle, she walked him to the car. He stood in the driveway with the apprehensive look of a boy about to go off to his first day of school. "Where am I going again?"

"The pier at the end of Main Street. You can't miss it."

Deputy Clint Avery came into Brunetta's office waving a handful of papers. "Chief, these faxes just came in from Toms River PD and the New Jersey State Police."

Yesterday, Brunetta had been sure that his newest deputy would quit as soon as he stopped throwing up, but once he'd gotten over the shock of his first homicide scene, he was fine. In fact, he'd taken a proprietary interest in "his" homicide and even hinted to

Brunetta that maybe he should be assigned to the case full time in civilian clothes.

Avery had been a decent wide receiver at the State University, but not good enough for a shot at the pros. Brunetta had picked him because he had that college "can do" attitude. He was new and he made a lot of mistakes, but someday he would make a good cop. Brunetta would have gladly granted his young deputy's wish, but unfortunately neither Avery, nor any of the other deputies, was capable of investigating this case. He would have to do it himself.

Brunetta was reading the Toms River report, when he was aware that Avery was still standing there looking at him. "Is there anything else, Clint?"

"No, sir." Avery looked longingly at the report in Brunetta's hand. "I was just thinking maybe you wanted me to hang around until you finished reading those reports."

"That's okay, Clint. I'll call you on the radio if I need you."

"Okay, Chief." Avery tried not to hide his disappointment. "I'll be on the air."

Brunetta was pleased by the speed with which this information had been sent and the reports from both agencies were surprisingly complete. But perhaps that was because Brunetta had called a friend in the NYPD who knew someone in the New Jersey State Police. As usual, information flowed much quicker when the informal fraternal brotherhood of the law enforcement community was invoked.

It took only a handful of type written pages to sum up the lives of Paul and Samantha Eccles. They were well off–he owned a small electronics plant in New

Jersey. Credit check showed few outstanding debts; the biggest, besides his mortgage, was a $24,000 loan on the sailboat; something he could obviously afford. Mr. Eccles was a pillar of the community: past president Chamber of Commerce, member of the Rotary Club, the Lions Club, the Kiwanis, and annual coordinator of the United Way drive. Hobbies were boating, golf, and tennis. No known enemies.

    Mrs. Eccles had been a special ed teacher in the local high school, Red Cross volunteer, 2009 chairwoman of the annual blood drive. Hobbies were boating, golf, and archery. Brunetta read that again. *Archery? Who the hell does archery?* No known enemies.

    They'd been married for twenty-five years. A thirty-day cruise, destination Nova Scotia, was part of the celebration. Two grown children: a twenty-four-year-old son, single and living in New York; and a twenty-one-year-old daughter, a senior at Bucknell.

    As Brunetta read on he grew more and more discouraged. There was nothing in these reports to offer a clue as to why these two people had been murdered. He threw the report aside and went to stand by the window overlooking Main Street. Life went on in Haddley Falls and it was business as usual. Streams of slightly glazed tourists in garish shorts and too-tight tank tops wandered up and down the sidewalks. Fortified with the requisite ice cream cones, they streamed in and out of gift shops and antique stores, blissfully unaware that only a couple of miles from here, in a peaceful cove, two people had been horribly murdered.

    And Tony Brunetta had no idea why.

The highest point of Main Street was in the center of town. From there it began a gradual descent to the edge of the bay. Delaney, surprised at the level of bustling activity in the harbor, was seeing yet another face of Haddley Falls. He made his way around a line of cars waiting to board a ferry destined for someplace called Crab Island. The name didn't seem like a very appealing location for a picnic, but it didn't seem to bother the hordes of laughing ice chest-laden tourists who clambered on board.

After considerable effort he found a parking spot three blocks away from the waterfront. Two marinas bracketed the ferry slip and each had its own elaborate, nautical-motif outdoor restaurant where clusters of tourists sat under gaily colored umbrellas advertising Perrier and Heineken, while they drank a colorful assortment of exotic drinks all of which seemed to feature umbrellas and flags.

In front of the restaurants, more than a hundred boats of all sizes and descriptions bobbed at their slips in a maze of finger piers. The smallest boat Delaney saw was an eighteen foot runabout; the largest, an impressive ninety foot ship complete with a helicopter perched on the fantail.

Each of the marina docks had a section where the charter fleet was berthed. According to the professionally lettered advertising signs nailed to the pilings, tourist anglers had a choice of blue fish, porgies, tuna, and even shark. Most of the slips were empty. Clearly, business in Haddley Falls was booming.

A hundred yards to the left of the ferry slip were two parallel piers jutting out into the bay. The newer of the two, a broad expanse of concrete and steel, was jammed with tourists; mostly elderly men shuffling back and forth between two or three poles while their wives sat on folding chairs reading best-selling novels.

Delaney strolled out to the end of the pier, peeking in buckets as he went. The catch was paltry. Across the way, on the old pier, a dubious pile of weathered planks supported by rotting pilings, a handful of locals dressed in baggy chinos, torn tee-shirts, and grimy baseball caps were fishing. Delaney went to investigate and saw that every bucket was full of fish. *This*, clearly, was the spot to fish. Following Rosemary's instructions, he baited the hook and lowered the line into the dark green water.

When he remembered, he listlessly jerked the line the way the other fishermen did, but it didn't seem to make any difference. He'd been here for over two hours and he hadn't caught a damn thing. Obviously Rosemary had given him a defective pole. Everyone on the pier was catching fish except him. He hadn't even gotten a nibble. Well, strictly speaking that wasn't true. His hook had been stripped several times but he hadn't *felt* anything.

He seriously considered going to a fish store and buying a fish, but decided against it. For sure Rosemary would know what he'd done. Besides, the only fish he liked was salmon and he didn't know if you could catch salmon off a dock.

To fight the boredom and tedium, he'd been thinking about the murders and had come up with several questions for Tony. He'd come all this way to escape murder and it had followed him anyway. He'd been kidding when he'd suggested he was a carrier, but maybe people who wallowed in murder for a living were carriers.

The Cove

He looked up at the blazing sun and licked his parched lips. This morning, as he was staggering into the bathroom, he'd sworn he'd never take another drink, but it was nearing one o'clock and the sun was frying his brain and a powerful thirst was threatening to close his windpipe. He'd been hoping to find a kid to send to the store for a six pack, but so far, *he* was the youngest guy on the pier.

An old man, standing twenty feet down the rail, reeled in another fish and tossed it in a bucket that was so full tails were sticking out the top.

"Nice fish," Delaney said.

"Yep," the old man said, puffing on a salty curved pipe.

Delaney, licking his lips, eyed the cooler next to the bucket. He knew there was beer in there. He'd watched the old guy knock one down. "Hot day."

The old man threaded another worm on his hook. "Yep."

"I don't suppose you'd know where I could get a cold beer around here?"

The man jerked his thumb over his shoulder. "'Crost the street. Supermarket."

Jesus, Delaney thought. *This guy talks like a human twitter*. He'd seen the market and had already decided that it would take too long to go inside, get the beer, and wait on line. By the time he got back someone would have walked with his – *Tony's* – fishing pole. "Too far," he said to the man.

The old man squinted through a swirl of pipe smoke. "Too fer?"

"By the time I get back someone could swipe my gear."

The old man puffed thoughtfully. "You're from New York City ain't you?"

"How'd you know?"

"Just a guess."

Delaney felt a sharp tug on his line. "*Whoa*! I think I have something." The fish, feeling the sting of the hook, raced for open water. The reel clicked rapidly as the line spun off. Delaney yanked on the pole but nothing happened. "What the hell—?"

"Star drag's too loose," the old man announced.

"What the hell is a star drag?" Delaney shouted.

The old man pointed to the side of his reel. Delaney found it and twisted it both ways until the line stopped paying out. "All right, you sucker," he muttered. "Come on in. You're invited to dinner."

As the fish got closer to the pier it put up a real fight, dragging Delaney along the pier while the other fishermen frantically reeled in their lines to avoid getting tangled up with the crazy tourist. Finally, after a few more zigzags, the fish tired and Delaney was able to reel him in.

"Wow!" Delaney yelled. "Look at the size of this monster." He noted with some satisfaction that his fish was bigger than anything the old guy had caught.

The man, puffing on his pipe, came over to look. "Good size catfish."

Delaney beamed. "Yeah. Big. Good eatin'?" Jesus! He was beginning to talk like the old guy!

The man puffed on his pipe thoughtfully. "If you're a cat and you ain't too particular."

Delaney was crestfallen. "You mean people don't eat these?"

"Nope."

Delaney looked down on the fish gasping for air. "You sonofabitch," he muttered. Then to the old man: "You got a cat?"

"Yep."

"You can have the fish."

"He don't eat no catfish."

Delaney nudged the fish back into the water with the toe of his shoe. It hit the water with a splash. Then, with a flash of silver, it was gone. As he watched it swim away it occurred to him that he was wasting his time here. He wasn't a fisherman, he was a homicide detective. "That's it," he muttered, reeling in his line. "Time to go to work."

As he was leaving he said, "Hey, pop, have a nice day."

Just then a fish hit and the old man's pole bent in a U. "Yep," he said, calmly and reeled in another one.

CHAPTER SIX

Tony Brunetta wasn't surprised when Pete Delaney came barging into his office. He was surprised that it had taken him so long. He sat back and put his feet up on the desk. "How was the fishing?"

Delaney flopped into a chair. "Listen, Brunetta, no more playing social director. Okay? You almost had another homicide on the pier."

Brunetta suppressed a smile. "Who?"

"Some old bastard who caught a lot of fish and wouldn't give me a cold beer."

"I guess I should be grateful you didn't mug him."

"Let's get something straight. I'm not going to be sent off to camp anymore. Got it?"

"I was just trying to make your stay here as pleasant as possible."

"Do me a favor. Don't do me any favors. If you think—"

The telephone rang, interrupting his tirade. By the time Brunetta got off the phone, Delaney had cooled down and was looking out the window at the crowd of tourists. "Hey, Tony, when these tourists come to town do you issue them the weird clothing or do they bring their own?"

"They bring their own. Outside of Halloween season I wouldn't know where to find stuff like that."

Delaney continued looking out the window and said, "Tony, I want to help you with this investigation."

Brunetta had been expecting this, but he still wasn't sure how he should handle it. Under normal circumstances he would have jumped at the chance to have Pete help. But there were a couple of problems. For openers, the people here resented and distrusted strangers. Hell, he'd been the police chief for a year and some of the townies still looked at him funny. Then there was the drinking. After last night, Brunetta seriously doubted that Pete could stay sober long enough to be of any real help.

"Pete, I'd love to have you help out, but there are legal complications. You're not a town employee and—"

"You're the sheriff for chrissake." Delaney turned away from the window. "Deputize me. I see it in movies all the time."

"I'm not a sheriff and I have no authority to deputize anyone."

"Okay, I'll volunteer my services."

"I don't think so."

Delaney came over and sat down on the edge of Brunetta's desk. "Tony, I'll go nuts doing nothing for four more days."

"Okay, let's play it by ear. You can work with me, but you'll have no official authority. And the first time you get out of hand, you're out. Understand?"

"Spoken like a true boss."

"Pete—"

"It's a deal."

Looking a lot happier than he did when he'd first come into the office, he slid onto a chair. "So what's been going on since I've been doing the Old Man and the Sea?"

"The two Eccles' kids were in here about an hour ago."

Delaney saw the pained expression in Brunetta's eyes and wished he'd been here to talk to them instead. Brunetta always had a hard time dealing with the victim's family. "How'd it go?"

"The son held up fairly well, but the daughter went to pieces when I told them I couldn't release the bodies until after the autopsy."

"The autopsies haven't been done yet?"

"No."

"Why not?"

Brunetta shrugged. "I still can't find the coroner." He slid the faxes across the desk. "This is what I got from New Jersey."

When Delaney finished reading the report, he said, "Too bad. I was hoping Eccles was dirty. It would have made a whole lot more sense. So where does that leave us?"

"Square one." Brunetta stood up. "Come on."

"Come on where?"

"Crater Cove. I have some divers out there looking for the murder weapon. Let's see if they found anything."

Brunetta and Delaney pulled up in the four-wheel jeep and from the top of the dunes watched the activity in the cove. Three volunteer divers in black wet suits were working from an eighteen-foot Boston Whaler. From the beach the divers looked like seals as they bobbed to the surface, oriented themselves and sunk back down into the olive-colored water.

Brunetta and Delaney slid down the dune and approached a uniformed lieutenant. Delaney recognized the tall, barrel-chested man from the first day he'd been in the police station. He'd seen him talking to a state trooper.

Brunetta made the introductions. "Walt Turner, say hello to an old friend of mine, Pete Delaney."

The lieutenant had a turned-down mouth that gave him a perpetual sneer and the kind of heavy-duty beard that required constant maintenance. He clamped down on Delaney's hand in a vice-like grip. Delaney got the distinct impression that the lieutenant was trying to show how tough he was, but Delaney wouldn't bite.

"Anything yet, Walt?" Brunetta asked.

Turner scowled. "No. They've been diving all morning. You ask me, it's a waste of time."

Delaney caught the implied criticism and hostility in the man's tone and bristled. First the old man at the pier and now this guy. He was running short of patience with these country bumpkins. "Waste of time, Lou? How do you figure that?"

The lieutenant's sneer became more pronounced. "Because you'd have to be pretty stupid to throw the murder weapon in the water right next to the boat."

Delaney scratched his chin as though he were pondering the second law of physics. "Let me see if I got this right. You're saying that a murderer–in your *professional* opinion–can't be stupid. Am I paraphrasing that correctly?"

"He might be stupid, but he wouldn't be *that* stupid."

Delaney smacked the side of his head. "You know, that's absolutely amazing. You have this rare ability to distinguish degrees of stupidity in a murderer you've never met."

The lieutenant's sneer gave way to uncertainty and wariness. Delaney continued. "I don't know why we're wasting our time watching these guys splash around in the water. With your amazing insight, maybe you'd like to tell the Chief *who* this guy is and *why* he did it and *where* he is so he can go arrest him."

"I don't know who he is," the lieutenant snapped. I just said he wouldn't be that stupid to—"

"Toss the murder weapon in the drink. Yeah, yeah, I heard you the first time. Lou, can I ask you a personal question? How many murders have you solved? Not counting cows, pigs and road kills."

The lieutenant's face had turned a dark red, but Brunetta wasn't worried about him, he was worried about Delaney. The look in Pete's face said he was about two insults away from decking his lieutenant. He put his arm around Delaney and pulled him away. "Come on, Pete, I want to show you something."

As they walked away, Brunetta squeezed Delaney's neck. "What's the matter with you? Not ten minutes ago you promised me you'd behave."

Delaney pulled away from Brunetta's grip. "The guy's a moron. If brains were dynamite he couldn't blow that ten-gallon Stetson off his head."

"Pete, Pete, why must you always be a bull in a china shop?"

"How can you have an asshole like that working for you? The closest he ever got to a homicide investigation was watching *Law and Order*."

"Walt Turner is not a happy man," Brunetta said patiently. "He was supposed to get my job."

"Well that's tough shit. You won, he lost. Why don't you just fire his ass?"

"Small town politics. Nepotism is epidemic in Haddley Falls. Turner is related to half the townies. I don't sweat it. Guys like Turner come with the territory."

Delaney stuffed his hands in his pockets. "Hey, it's your police department."

Delaney was quick to anger, but just as quick to let it go. They'd walked about a hundred yards down the beach when he stopped and kicked the ground. "There's something puzzling me, Tony."

What's that?" Brunetta asked, hoping Delaney's legendary instincts were finally coming to life.

Frowning in concentration, Delaney knelt down and smoothed the sand with his hand. "How the hell do you draw body outline chalk marks on sand?"

As he darted the clam shell that Brunetta threw at him, he spun and stopped short. Through the dense tree line, up on a cliff overlooking the cove, he saw what looked like a medieval castle. "What the hell is that?"

"Sanborne castle. Home of Whittier Sanborne III."

Delaney climbed up the dune for a better look. "Who is he?"

"One of the movers and shakers in the town. Big bucks. Family money from lumber."

"Who else lives there?

"Just his son, Andrew, and some house help. The wife left him years ago. He never remarried."

"How old is the son?"

"I think early twenties."

"What's he do for a living?"

"Nothing. I understand he's retarded."

Delaney spun around. "Retarded as in *slow* or retarded as in *homicidal maniac*?" He made a slashing motion with his hand.

"I've never seen him. Sanborne is a very private man and he's very touchy about his son. Keeps him hidden away. I understand his retardation was the result of a childhood accident. Anyway, I've never heard anything bad about him."

"Tony, no one ever heard anything bad about Jeffrey Dahmer either until he ate a half dozen people." Delaney scrambled down off the dune. "You telling me you haven't interviewed the people who live in that house? Pal, you've been away from the real world too long. I ought to tear up your homicide investigator's union card."

Brunetta turned away from Delaney's mocking expression to look out at the divers. "Sanborne is an upstanding citizen," he said. "I'm sure he would have come forward if he'd seen or heard anything."

Delaney caught the evasive tone in Brunetta's voice. "Tony, that's bullshit. What's going on here?"

Brunetta started walking back toward the jeep and Delaney followed. "You don't understand small town politics."

Delaney wouldn't let Brunetta off the hook that easily. "So that means that a mover and shaker like Sanborne is off-limits?"

"No."

"Let me tell you something, pardner. I'd interview the Pope if I thought he could shed some light on a case. And so would you at one time."

Anger flashed in Brunetta's eyes. He wanted to tell Delaney that he didn't know what he was talking about, but he had to admit Pete was right. If he was going to solve this murder, he couldn't let small-town politics get in his way. Maybe he'd made the right decision letting Delaney in on the case after all. He could be a pain in the ass, but he was just the kind of reality check he needed. "Come on," he said. "Let's go interview some people."

As they started walking again, Brunetta said, "I might as well fill you in on the whole picture. Do you promise to remain calm?"

"I will have the patience of Job."

"To understand what goes on around here, you have to understand the dynamics of this town. There are two major problems. One, there are some people in this town who have secrets and they're scared to death that this murder investigation might expose them."

"Hey, murder happens. What's the second?"

"Rich or poor, everyone in this town is interconnected through social or economic ties and these connections can go back generations. It's a symbiotic relationship. The rich need the poor to service them, and the poor need the jobs. Haddley Falls is a tourist town and it can't afford to take a hit on its reputation as the most laidback coastal resort town in New England."

"Okay, so get the state police in here ASAP and wrap this thing up," Delaney said.

"That's what I told the mayor, but he vetoed the idea. He wants me to handle the investigation."

"I got it. He can't control the state police, but he can control you."

Brunetta stopped walking and his eyes took on a hard edge. "That's what he thinks. And to tell you the truth and I'm ashamed to say it, I was ready to roll over for him. But you know what? I like this job and I like this town, but I'll be godammed if I'll cover up something just because it might be damaging to someone's reputation."

"Way to go, Tony. So who's gonna do the forensics?"

Brunetta started walking again. "I got Gardiner to agree to use the state police for photos, prints, and blood work."

"So basically you're stuck with a double and no help."

Brunetta patted Delaney's cheek. "I got you, babe. If you're as good as you claim, maybe we can wrap this up before you go back to the city."

Delaney flicked his cigarette out into the water and nodded toward the lieutenant who was standing on the beach with his arms folded, watching the divers. "I just might do that. Just keep farmer Brown out of my hair."

As they were climbing the dune to the jeep, they heard a shout and turned around. One of the divers was holding something over his head. A minute later he waded ashore and handed a tire iron to Brunetta, who slipped it into a clear plastic bag.

"Think this could be the murder weapon, Chief?" the diver asked.

Brunetta examined it. After several days in the water he doubted that the lab would find any traces of blood, but it was worth a shot. He'd learned a long time ago that evidence, no matter how insignificant, was all part of the puzzle. You never knew what was important or wasn't until you fit all the pieces together. "I don't know," he said noncommittally. "We'll see."

Delaney moved next to the lieutenant, who was intently peering at the tire iron. "Funny," he said to no one in particular, "you just never know how stupid some people can get."

Brunetta shot him a warning glance. "Come on, Pete. We have some people to talk to."

CHAPTER SEVEN

Delaney stepped out of the jeep, glanced up at the intimidating stone towers of Sanborne castle and whistled softly. "Isn't this where Dr. Frankenstein used to live?"

Brunetta, who wasn't in the mood for jokes, grunted and rang the bell. A young woman in her early twenties opened the door a crack and peered out. She was attractive in spite of her mousy brown hair and lack of makeup. Her eyes widened at the sight of the uniformed Brunetta. "Yes?" she said in a small voice, "Can I help you?"

I'm Chief Brunetta and this is Mr. Delaney. Is Mr. Sanborne home?"

"No, he's not."

"We're investigating those two murders in the cove. May we come in?"

At the mention of the word murders, she narrowed the door opening by an inch. "Oh, we don't know anything about that."

Delaney flashed his best I-just-want-to-talk-to-you-and-you-have-nothing-to-fear smile and stepped toward her. "It'll only take a minute." Intimidated, she opened the door wider and stepped back.

The inside of Sanborne castle was even more impressive than the outside. The center foyer was thirty-feet square with a forty-foot curved-beam ceiling. Beyond, a wide center staircase led up to a massive stained-glass window on the second floor landing. Delaney half-expected to see Clark Gable sweep down the stairs with Scarlett in his arms. The sunlight, defused by the multicolored glass, bathed the interior in soft blue, green, and gold hues, creating an atmosphere not unlike a cathedral. Delaney, resisting the urge to whisper, said, "Is anyone else home, Miss—?"

"Crown. Madeleine Crown. Just Andrew and Jeff."

"Jeff?"

"Jeff Wallace is Andrew's physical therapist."

"And you are...?"

"Andrew's tutor."

Delaney nodded, glad that he didn't say what he'd been thinking. Calling a tutor and prospective witness a housemaid didn't come under the heading of getting off on the right foot.

Brunetta said, "Miss Crown, we'd just like to ask—"

"Madeleine, who are these people?"

A muscular man in his early thirties appeared from a side door. He had the dull-normal look of an athlete whose blood supply favors the muscles at the expense of the brain. Delaney sized up the big man and decided that Andrew had to be trouble if someone this big was needed to handle him. Andrew immediately jumped to the top of his mental list of prime suspects.

"Hi, Jeff. Pete Delaney," he said, turning on his smile. "And this is Chief Brunetta. We just—"

"Madeleine, Mr. Sanborne said no one is allowed in the house without his permission."

Looking at Madeleine Crown's plain, shapeless dress and unattractive flats, Delaney had already concluded that she probably didn't have a real high opinion of herself and putting up with a bully like Jeff Wallace wasn't helping her self esteem.

The flustered girl blinked rapidly. "I'm sorry, they—"

Delaney felt sorry for the girl and responsible for her breaking the rules. "Hey, pal," he said softly. "Chill out. We're the police, not Amway salesmen."

Brunetta saw Wallace was studying Delaney as though he were measuring him up for a sucker punch and stepped between them. "As we explained to Miss Crown, we just want to talk to everyone about the murders in the cove."

Jeff furrowed his brow. All this was too taxing for him to follow. "You guys have a warrant or anything?"

"No."

Wallace opened the door. "Then you gotta go."

Delaney took a step forward. "Listen, pal—"

Brunetta grabbed his arm. "Let's go, Pete. I'll make an appointment with Mr. Sanborne."

At the door, Delaney said, "You live here, Jeff?"

"Yeah."

"The dungeon?"

Wallace ran his hand across his buzz cut in frustration, not sure if this guy was putting him down or not. "No. Upstairs."

"Then you probably have a view of the cove. We'll talk again. Have a nice day."

When they got back into the jeep, Brunetta angrily yanked the vehicle into gear. "For chrissake, Pete, will you stop pushing your weight around. You're not dealing with city skells."

"What'd I do?"

"Do you live in the dungeon?"

"Tony, if that guy is a physical therapist, I'm the lead dancer with the Joffrey Ballet."

Brunetta laughed out loud at the thought of Pete Delaney in a tutu. It was impossible to stay mad at Delaney for any length of time. "I think you're right. He's gotta be a caretaker."

"What does that tell you?"

"Andrew needs a *lot* of care."

"Right. Who's number one on your list?" Delaney asked, starting the list game they always played at the beginning of an investigation.

"Andrew Sanborne." Brunetta felt his stomach tighten. If he was right, he was going to really earn his pay. "Who's number two?"

"Jeff Wallace. Did you see the arms on that guy? Strong like bull."

Brunetta recalled the scene in the sailboat cabin. Whoever did that was strong and mean. He hadn't seen Andrew yet, but Jeff Wallace seemed to qualify on both counts. He started the engine. "Pete, I have an assignment for you when we get back."

It took Pete Delaney less than two hours to find Arthur Bynum in a rundown motel eight miles out of town. It wasn't hard. He'd simply asked himself a question that none of Brunetta's deputies had thought to ask themselves: *Where would I go if I wanted to get away from it all and drink in peace?* The ninth motel he called said there was a man registered who fit the description of Dr. Bynum.

The Road Way Motel's clientele were semis and pickup trucks. Obviously not the type who stayed in those cute Victorian B&Bs he'd seen on Elm Street

Delaney listened at the door to room seven and heard the sound of a radio playing. He knocked.

A short, gaunt man in his early sixties, wearing a wrinkled white shirt and baggy black slacks, opened the door. The ravages of drink and excess had taken their toll on his face, but behind the wrinkles and pasty complexion, Delaney saw a sensitive and intelligent face.

"Dr. Bynum, I presume?" Delaney said.

Bynum rubbed his red-rimmed eyes. "You the delivery guy from the package store?"

"Afraid not. Chief Brunetta has been looking for you."

"I don't want to be looked for." Bynum tried to slam the door, but Delaney pushed his way into the room.

"Hey—"

"Recess is over, Doc. Get dressed. You have a couple of autopsies to perform."

Bynum rubbed his three day old beard. "Who... who the hell are you?"

"Name's Delaney. I'm working with Chief Brunetta."

"Tell him you couldn't find me."

"Can't do that."

Bynum slumped down onto the bed. "I can't do these autopsies," he said in a voice raspy from too much booze and cigarettes. He held up his shaky hands.

Delaney had already noticed the tremors. If it was his call, he'd never let this pathetic drunk near a patient, not even a dead one. But it wasn't his call. "Doc, I'm not asking you to do a heart transplant. These people are dead already. You can't hurt them."

While Bynum put his shoes on, Delaney studied the room. He'd holed up in rat nests like this himself– rooms that reeked of stale tobacco, the sour smell of alcohol, and pungent body sweat. The frail doctor struggled to tie a knot and Delaney saw a glimpse of himself. He shuddered and opened the door.

"Come on, Doc. We have to see Chief Brunetta."

"I heard about those murders, Mr. Delaney." Tears welled up in the doctor's eyes. "That's why I ran away. I can't do these autopsies."

Delaney studied the frightened little man and felt sorry for him. Something in his life had taken him to this state. Delaney didn't know what it was, but even if he did, he would never judge him.

"I know a good medical examiner in the city," he said softly. "I'll put you in touch with him. He'll tell you what you have to do. Just stay sober." As soon as he said it, he realized that was what a lot of people had been saying to him for a very long time. It sounded so easy – *stay sober* – but he and Arthur Bynum knew how hard that really was.

When Delaney came into Brunetta's office, Deputy Avery was there.

"The coroner is outside," Delaney said, heading for the coffee pot.

Brunetta nodded. "Good. I'll see him in a minute." He turned to his deputy. "Clint, you know Jeff Wallace? He works for Mr. Sanborne at the castle."

"Big guy, crew cut?"

"That's the one."

"I stopped him once for speeding."

"You give him a summons?" Brunetta asked hopefully.

"No, sir."

"Why the hell not?"

Avery nervously brushed a strand of long blond hair away from his forehead. "He was driving one of Mr. Sanborne's cars. I wasn't sure..." His voice trailed off.

"Okay, okay." Ignoring the smirk on Delaney's face, Brunetta continued. "Clint, here's my problem. It calls for a little stealth. I need Wallace's date of birth. How would you go about getting it?"

"I suppose you don't want to ask him?"

"You suppose correctly."

"It'd be on his license," Avery offered.

"Right. How would you get a look at his license?"

"Stop him and ask for it."

"We don't want to make it too obvious."

"Wait for him to commit a violation?"

"That's good. I want you to hang out on the road from the castle to town. If you get a chance to stop him, do it."

Avery looked puzzled. "What kind of violation should I stop him for?"

Delaney handed a cup to Brunetta and sat down. "How about mouth breathing while operating a motor vehicle."

"Use your own judgment," Brunetta said. "You'll think of something."

"Is he like a suspect, Chief?" Avery asked.

Brunetta studied his earnest new deputy. If he was handled the right way, he could turn into a good cop. If not, he'd become another drone, just going through the motions. Brunetta wanted the young man to become a good cop, even if it meant that someday he'd move on to a bigger police agency. "Right now, everyone is a suspect except the late Mr. and Mrs. Eccles."

As the deputy was leaving, Delaney said, "Do you know Miss Crown? She works at the castle too."

"Oh, yeah, I've seen her around town."

"Does she own her own car?"

"Yeah. I checked her out a few times."

Delaney saw the deputy redden and smiled. "Hey, that's one of the few perks of being a cop, Clint. You get the chance to stop good looking babes. Do you have her license plate number?"

"No, sir."

"Well, when you get the chance why don't you jot it down for us."

Clint Avery's eyes widened. "Is she a suspect, too?"

"Like the Chief said. Everyone's a suspect."

After the deputy left, Delaney said, "You're still the same, Tony. Never miss an opportunity to teach a new recruit something. You should have been a school teacher."

"These kids don't know a helluva lot about police work. If I just tell them what to do all the time, they'll never learn anything. Besides, they feel better about themselves when they come up with their own answers."

"You're right, pard. I just wish I had your patience."

Brunetta grunted. "Me, too. Ask the good doctor to step in."

Thanks to the five cups of coffee Delaney had poured into him, Arthur Bynum looked a little better than he did when Delaney had found him in the motel room. He sat down shakily.

"We've been looking for you since yesterday," Brunetta said calmly.

Bynum ran his hand through his unruly hair. "I know. I had—"

"It's not important. I have two distraught kids who want to bury their parents and they can't do that until you autopsy them. How about tomorrow morning?"

Bynum nodded, uncertainly.

"Remember, this is a homicide autopsy, Doc. A regular autopsy ends with the signing of a death certificate. With a homicide autopsy, it's only the beginning. You may be able to tell me how and why these two people died. Hell, you may even be able to tell me who did it. Are you up to it?"

"I think so," Bynum said, sounding not at all up to it. "Mr. Delaney gave me the name of a medical examiner in the city. I'll call him for consultation."

"Good." Brunetta put his arm around the doctor's bony shoulder and walked him to the door. "Get a good night's sleep."

After the doctor left, Brunetta turned to Delaney. "You do good work."

"Tony, this is pathetic."

"I don't make the rules around here."

"What if he takes off again?"

"I've assigned a deputy to watch his house. If Bynum tries to leave the house before tomorrow morning, I told the deputy to lock him up."

Delaney shook his head in dismay. "And Haddley Falls looks like such a nice town."

"It used to be," Brunetta said with a hint of genuine nostalgia.

Delaney thumbed through the in-basket looking for any new information on the homicides while Brunetta put in a call to Sanborne's office. He wasn't there and Brunetta left a message to call him. When he hung up he said, "Anything in the basket?"

"Yeah. The Daughters of the American Revolution are having a cake sale next month. They're requesting a SWAT team to cover the judges. It's to be held in—"

"*Pete*!"

Delaney tossed the paper back in the basket. "Nothing. There's nothing there."

The clerical sergeant stuck his head in the door. "I checked our files, Chief. No record of a Jeff Wallace."

Brunetta looked at Delaney. "Then it's up to Clint."

Around six o'clock, just as they were leaving, the telephone rang. Brunetta listened for a moment and hung up. "The mayor wants to see me."

Delaney saw the look of concern on Brunetta's face. "Think it has anything to do with our visit to the castle?"

"Probably."

"How about I go with you?"

Brunetta cringed. "Absolutely not." He put his arm around his friend's shoulder and moved him toward the door. "You've done enough for one day. Go back to the house and relax. I'll see you later."

When Brunetta pulled up to the mayor's office he saw Whit Sanborne's Mercedes parked in the visitor's spot. Now he knew for sure what this meeting was going to be about.

Royce Gardiner was seated at the head of the polished cherry-wood table in his conference room. Whittier Sanborne III, a colorless, dour-faced man of fifty-five with thinning black hair which he combed straight back, was seated at the other end.

Brunetta took a seat half-way between them. Sanborne and Gardiner were two of the wealthiest men in town and Brunetta respected them for that. But he'd made himself a promise when he took this job that he would never let money or power intimidate him. He didn't need the job that badly.

"Good evening, gentlemen," he said with a smile.

A scowling Gardiner tucked his thumbs in his suspenders. "Chief, Whit is very upset about what happened today at his home. "He—"

"Chief Brunetta," Sanborne, interrupted in a clipped New England accent, "I'd like you to explain the...*invasion* of my home this afternoon."

Brunetta exhaled slowly; a trick he used to keep his temper under control. "I went there to *interview* people."

Sanborne took his wire-rimmed glasses off and wiped them furiously. "Interview or interrogate?"

"This is a murder investigation, Mr. Sanborne. I intend to interview anyone who may be able to shed light on the case. Your home is in direct view of the cove. Someone in your household may have seen something."

Gardiner assumed a conciliatory tone. "Now, Tony, we can certainly appreciate the process involved in a criminal investigation. And of course we encourage you to leave no stone unturned." Brunetta had to force himself not to laugh at the hypocritical mayor. "However, from what Whit tells me, you and another man appeared at his home and were extremely rude to his employees."

Brunetta silently cursed Delaney. "Mr. Sanborne, if there was a misunderstanding, I apologize."

"Well," Sanborne said, mollified, "as long as we don't have a repeat of that kind of behavior again."

Brunetta silently promised himself he would never bring Delaney back to that house. "You have my word," he said. Then added, "When would be a good time to stop by the house to interview your staff?"

Sanborne's thin smile vanished. He thought he'd disabused the chief of that notion.

"Well, Whit?" Gardiner asked impatiently. "The Chief's a busy man. Give him a time."

Brunetta masked his surprise at Gardiner's petulant tone. It was at moments like this that he got a rare glimpse into the pecking order among the town's Brahmins. Over the past year he'd used these occasional breaches in their carefully cultivated facades to determine who the real power in the community was. He knew that

Royce Gardiner deferred to Jonathan Talbot. Now he knew that Whit Sanborne deferred to Royce Gardiner

"I'll have to check my schedule," Sanborne said reluctantly. "My secretary will call your office, Chief." As he stood up to leave he turned to Brunetta. "Who was that man that was with you today?"

"Pete Delaney, a good friend and a homicide detective from New York. He's here on vacation for a few days and offered to help out."

"What about the state police? They—"

Gardiner broke in. "A decision has been made to handle this investigation ourselves."

"Why?"

Gardiner's soft blue eyes turned hard. "Whit, I'll fill you in when this meeting is over."

Unable to attack Gardiner, Sanborne turned his fury on Tony Brunetta. "That man has no business being involved in this investigation."

"I need all the help I can get," Brunetta said evenly.

"Of course you do, Chief." Gardiner flashed a sudden smile that unwary opponents often took for sincerity. "It's admirable that Mr. Delaney is willing to help us in our hour of need, but you know how xenophobic we New Englanders can be."

Brunetta knew he was supposed to agree with the Mayor, but he was in no mood to roll over. "Pete's only going to be here three more days and I am going to use his expertise."

Gardiner caught the adamant tone in Brunetta's voice and wisely decided not to pursue the matter. After all, what harm could the man do in three days? "All right, Chief, but I'm counting on you to keep him in line."

It was after one in the morning by the time Brunetta got home. Rosemary met him at the door. "Were you with Gardiner all this time?"

"No. A real messy accident on the Interstate between an out of state SUV and an oil truck. The SUV missed his exit and attempted to back up. The oil truck slammed into him."

"Any one killed?"

"A passenger in the SUV was seriously injured." He shook his head in disgust. "Every time there's an accident involving goddamn tourists, they all say the same thing. 'I'm not from around here.' Like they don't have traffic signs where they live."

Rosemary knew he was upset. Normally he wouldn't have let something like that bother him. She linked his arm. "Come into the kitchen, hon. I'll make you something to eat."

She retrieved the left-over ham from the refrigerator. "How'd the meeting with Gardiner go?"

Brunetta popped open a can of beer. "Sanborne was there."

"I heard about this afternoon. You in trouble?"

"No, but Delaney is barred from Sanborne's house."

"He keeps it up, he'll be barred from the whole town."

Brunetta rolled the can between his hands. "Sanborne is hiding something."

The Cove

"He's protective of his son. Imagine if Betty had been retarded? It must be a terrible burden."

"I'm sure it is, but that's no excuse for stonewalling me."

Rosemary slid his sandwich in front of him. "What's the point of talking to the son? What would a twenty-year-old retarded man know about those murders?"

"Right now, Andrew Sanborne is my prime suspect."

Rosemary, who was straining to open a jar of mustard, stopped. "My God, how can you say that? You've never even met him."

"Exactly." He playfully tickled her under her chin. "Maybe he's seven feet tall with hair growing out of his eyeballs."

She slid the jar across the table. "I can't open it. Don't be ridiculous, Tony."

Brunetta popped the lid. "So why does Sanborne keep him hidden? There's one thing I do know. The mysterious, unseen son lives in a big house overlooking Crater Cove. He could have snuck out of the house, swum out to the boat and hacked up those two people."

Rosemary shuddered at the possibility. "God, I just hope it's your sick, wild imagination."

Brunetta bit into the sandwich. "So do I, babe. If Andy did it, it'll tear this town wide open. I'll probably be looking for a new job."

"That wouldn't be the worst thing that could happen," Rosemary said quietly.

Brunetta gave her a sharp look. "We're only here a year. I've told you it takes time to get used to it."

"I'm trying, Tony."

He wasn't in the mood to rehash that argument right now. "Where's my delinquent buddy?" he said, changing the emotionally charged subject.

"On the porch couch. Out like a light."

"Drunk?"

"As a skunk."

"Where'd he get the booze? There was less than a quarter bottle last night."

"He bought another one."

Brunetta threw the sandwich down. "What am I gonna do with that guy?"

"What *are* you going to do with him?"

"I don't know. I guess he'll spend the next couple of days with me as planned."

"How? If you're busy—"

"I'll put him to work."

"Can he handle it?"

"Better than he did fishing."

Rosemary smiled. "He told me all about his adventures on the pier. I wish I could have been there to see it."

"Yeah, me, too." He pushed the half-eaten sandwich away. He wasn't hungry anymore.

Rosemary ruffled his hair. "Come on, hon. Let's go to bed."

"Okay. But first I'd better check on him to make sure he hasn't fallen off the couch and broken his damn neck."

Delaney was lying flat on his back, snoring loudly. Brunetta looked down at his friend with a mixture of sympathy and anger.

Rosemary peeked over her husband's shoulder. "Looks kind of peaceful, doesn't he?" she said.

Brunetta spread a light blanket over him. "Yeah, a regular baby."

"I'd better get him a pillow. He'll wake up with a stiff neck."

"Let him. Maybe a stiff neck and a head-banging hangover is just what he needs."

Rosemary paid no attention to her husband. While he was in the bathroom brushing his teeth, she got a pillow from the spare room and tucked it under Pete's head. He never stopped snoring.

CHAPTER EIGHT

As Delaney came through the door, Brunetta glanced at the wall clock. "*Ten-fifteen*? Good thing I'm not paying you," he said, masking his anger with a grin.

Delaney grunted and went directly to the coffee pot. Then, fortified with a cup of hot black coffee, he sat down very slowly, being careful not to jar his brain anymore than necessary.

"The Johnny Walker Drum and Bugle Corps practicing between your ears again, Pete?"

"Yeah," Delaney muttered into his coffee cup. "I think the dirty bastards added an extra bass drum. Why didn't you wake me this morning?"

"I did."

"I don't remember. What'd I say?"

"Go fuck yourself, Brunetta."

Delaney grunted. "You know better than to take my first response seriously."

"Sorry, buddy. One wake-up call per person."

Delaney steadied the cup with two hands and peered at Brunetta through bloodshot eyes. "Anything new?"

"Nope. Until we can eliminate Andrew and the physical therapist, I think we should go on the assumption that we're dealing with some kind of ritual-sexual killer."

"Okay." Delaney waited expectedly. Brunetta was being uncharacteristically obscure. "And—?"

Brunetta peered into Delaney's blood-shot eyes, trying to judge how he would react to his proposal. "I want to put another boat in Crater Cove for the night."

"A decoy?"

"Yep."

"See if the killer will strike again. Not a bad idea. Who do you have in mind?"

"You."

Delaney almost spilled the hot coffee on his lap. "*Me*? You're outta your mind."

"You're perfect for this assignment."

"I don't like boats."

"Why?"

"Because."

"Because why?"

"Because I can't swim."

Brunetta hooted. "*You*? Ace homicide investigator? Can't *swim*?"

"I don't recall ever having to *swim* to the scene of a murder."

"It's not like I'm asking you to row a boat to Europe. You'll be in a big boat and you'll never be out of sight of land."

Delaney glared at his ex-partner. "Remember Bobby Hampton from Ninth Avenue? He offed his old lady in a five gallon bucket. You don't need a whole lot of water to drown, my friend."

"You'll wear a life vest."

Delaney screwed his face up in disgust. "Oh, that's a great idea. How would *you* like to duke it out in a small cabin with a knife-wielding maniac while wearing a bulky life vest?"

"So you're telling me you don't want to do this."

"That's what makes you a great detective, Tony. You're so perceptive."

"I need you, buddy."

"Use your deputies."

"It's tourist season. I can only spare one."

Delaney thought for a moment. "He a good sailor?"

"She's the best."

"*She*? You have female deputies?"

"One. JT has been on vacation and just came back to work this morning. I already talked to her and she's game."

"*JT*? Let me guess. She drives a pickup full of blood stains from last year's hunting season and she owns an albino, mutant, foaming-at-the-mouth mastiff."

Brunetta smiled slyly. "Wrong."

Delaney interest was piqued. "Yeah? So what's she look like?"

"Why do you want to know?"

"I wanna know, that's all. *If* I decide to do this, I don't want to spend a long night in a tiny cabin with someone who looks like the bride of Frankenstein."

Brunetta pointed a warning finger. "This is business." Then he sat back and shrugged. "Actually, it doesn't matter. You hit on her, she'll beat the crap out of you."

Delaney suddenly had a vision of a hefty Wagnerian soprano wearing horns and VW hubcaps for a chest plate. Before he could say there was no way he would go on this trip, Brunetta picked up the telephone. "Charlie, would you ask JT to step in here?"

Deputy JT Bryce walked in and Delaney's mouth dropped open. She was tall—almost as tall as he was—with skin the color of burnished bronze. And she was beautiful.

Suppressing a grin, Brunetta said, "JT, say hello to Pete Delaney."

She studied Delaney with big round eyes the color of emeralds. "Wow," she said, flashing a set of dazzling, white teeth. "It must have been one helluva party last night."

"So they tell me," he muttered, sinking back into his chair and wishing he weren't hung over.

"I've been telling Pete about the plan," Brunetta said. "But"—he paused— "he can't do it because—"

"*Tony*," Delaney said in a loud voice that made his head hurt. "What I said was—"

"What exactly did you say?" Brunetta asked, thoroughly enjoying his old partner's discomfort.

"What I said was—" He paused to rub his temples, trying to think of something intelligent to say, but that damn drum and bugle corps was making it hard to think clearly. "I said we have to make sure... that we... that we look like tourists and not like a couple of cops on a stakeout."

JT flashed a bemused smile. "Mr. Delaney, I didn't plan on wearing my uniform on the boat."

"No, of course not. Please, call me Pete. What I meant was we have to look like... you know, regular people." He winced inwardly. He was sounding like a tongue-tied dolt.

A small smile played around the corners of her mouth. "What do 'regular' people look like?"

"You know, tee shirts, bathing suits—" He remembered seeing barbecue grills attached to the railings of sailboats in the marina and added, "I guess we should cook something."

"Good point," Brunetta said, trying not to laugh out loud. "Is that your *only* reservation, Pete?"

Delaney shrugged elaborately. "Yeah, that's it." He'd made up his mind. It was worth the risk of drowning to spend one night on a sailboat with her.

"Then it's a done deal." Brunetta said. "JT, where's the boat?"

"About ten miles up the coast. My friends are away for a couple of weeks and they said I could use it anytime."

"*Whoa!*" Delaney snapped forward in his seat and the sudden motion activated the bass drum section. "*Ten* miles? I thought we'd leave from one of the marinas in town."

JT looked at him curiously. "Mr. Delaney— Pete, we can't leave from a town marina. Somebody might recognize us."

"Isn't there some place *closer* to start from?" he asked, panicked by the thought of a ten mile ocean voyage.

"There's no harbor between Crater Cove and where the boat is moored."

Brunetta said, "JT, the problem is that... well, Pete isn't a real good swimmer."

Delaney saw a flash of pity in those beautiful green eyes and wanted to strangle Brunetta.

"And I guess you've never been on a sailboat?" she asked.

"Actually, no." He saw her bite her lip. "Is that a problem?"

"Well, you have to be... careful on a sailboat." She tried to imagine single-handing the boat with a non-sailing, non-swimming, and not very bright man on board.

He sat on the edge of his seat. "*Careful.* Do sailboats fall over a lot?"

"No, nothing like that. But there's a lot going on—swinging booms, hauling sheets, trimming sails, that sort of thing." She saw the bleak expression on his face and added, "If you keep your head down and listen to what I tell you, there should be no problem."

Delaney hated it when someone said 'no problem,' because it usually meant a *big* problem. She was one fine looking lady, but he was beginning to regret agreeing to this trip.

Brunetta rubbed his hands together. "Okay, it's settled," he said, relieved to be getting Delaney out of the way for a day and a night. Then an image of the murder victims flashed into his mind and he was suddenly uneasy. If there was a sexual killer lurking in Crater Cove, he was sending his best friend and an inexperienced deputy on a very dangerous assignment.

An hour after Delaney left to meet JT at the boat, Dr. Bynum arrived with the autopsy report looking considerably better than he did the day before. A decent night's sleep had put some color into his cheeks, a sparkle in his eye, and an air of confidence.

Bynum slid the report across his desk. "Hear it is, Chief."

Brunetta looked at it, but he didn't pick it up. Autopsy reports were full of medical jargon and procedures that Brunetta suspected were designed to impress other doctors and confound attorneys. He found it more expedient to get a verbal summary from a pathologist. "I'll read it later, Doc. What's the bottom line? How did they die?"

"Her cause of death was the result of a severe trauma to the left front temporal area of the brain caused by a blunt instrument."

Brunetta slid a picture of the recovered tire iron across the desk. "Could this have caused it?"

Bynum studied the photo. "Yes, it could."

"What else?"

"The windpipe was severed and her abdomen was lacerated from breast to pubic bone."

"Any organs missing?"

"No."

Brunetta frowned. "You sure?"

Bynum's eyes flashed in indignation. "I think I can recognize internal organs. Nothing was missing."

"Go on."

"There were three tentative cuts around the breast area."

Brunetta's frown deepened. *Tentative*? He didn't like the sound of that. Ritual killers were anything but tentative.

Bynum continued. "I did find something curious. Two knives were used. One, a heavy, single-edged blade, possibly a hunting knife, caused seven stab wounds. The other knife had a thin, single-edge blade. Very sharp and...." Bynum paused.

Brunetta leaned forward. "What?"

"Well...I don't know if I should offer an opinion or just stick to the facts."

"The facts will speak for themselves. If you have any opinions, let me hear them."

"With the exception of those three hesitation cuts, it's apparent that the individual who wielded those knives knew how to use them."

"You mean like a doctor?"

"No, there was nothing surgical about the cuts, but they were clean...sure."

Brunetta knew what the doctor was trying to say. As a hunter he'd seen a lot of men gut and clean game. The inexperienced either pressed too lightly or cut so deeply that they damaged the organs beneath the skin. The experienced hunters were more sure and deft with the knife. Maybe the perp was a hunter? But that bit of information wasn't much help. New England was full of experienced hunters. "Doc, was there sexual intercourse?"

"Tests were negative for semen. No sign of vaginal entry."

None of what the doctor was saying made sense to Brunetta. The way the woman's legs were splayed, he'd assumed there was some sexual connotation to it. So far, Bynum's findings weren't squaring with what he knew to be the typical patterns of a sexual-ritualistic murderer. "How'd the man die?"

"A slash wound to the throat severed the carotid artery. That was the cause of death, not the other cuts on the body. All together I counted twenty knife punctures in the stomach area, none of them deep, and both thighs were slashed."

"So she died from a fractured skull and he died from a severed carotid artery. Did the other wounds come before or after death?"

"After they were both dead."

"What about the time of death?"

Bynum frowned, knowing he was getting into shaky territory. "Establishing time of death is difficult. Rigor mortis can be affected by ambient temperature, chemical ingestion, even the physical condition of the body at death and so—"

"I know all that," Brunetta said impatiently. Clearly, Bynum had spoken to Sol Grossman. Solly was the best ME in the city, but like all MEs, he liked to hedge his bets and he'd instructed Bynum well. "What's your guess, Doc?"

"As best as I can determine, they've been dead for approximately six days."

Brunetta looked at the calendar on the wall. Today was the twenty-sixth. The old man saw the boat in Crater Cove on the twenty-fourth and said it had been there for three days. So the boat must have come into the cove on the twenty-first. That means they were probably murdered sometime the night of the twenty-first or possibly the early morning of the twenty-second.

Brunetta tossed the autopsy report into his in-basket. "Thanks Doc. You did real good," he said, genuinely pleased with the job Bynum had done.

Bynum smiled for the first time. "Mr. Delaney's suggestion to call his medical examiner friend in New York was a good idea. Dr. Grossman was very helpful."

Brunetta stood up. "I'm glad. Let's hope you never have to put this new expertise to use again."

CHAPTER NINE

Delaney arrived at the marina just after four in the afternoon. He'd tried to follow JT's instructions, but all those damn rural roads looked alike and he'd gotten lost.

As he nervously made his way down a rolling dock, he caught a glimpse of her through a forest of swaying masts and he immediately noticed two things. First, she was even more stunning out of uniform. When he'd seen her in Brunetta's office, she'd had her hair pulled back in a tight bun, but now the bun was gone and in its place a long, blonde pony tail blew in the breeze. She was wearing a worn tee shirt that said: I'D RATHER BE SAILING and tight, white shorts that emphasized her long, tan legs. The second thing he noticed—with some alarm—was that the sailboat was *very small.* He distinctly remembered Tony saying it was a large sailboat.

JT was removing the sail cover when she spotted him stumbling down the dock. Her first impression of him in the chief's office had not been a good one. From Brunetta's description she'd expected a serious, hard-nosed professional detective. But he'd come across as confused and muddled. She fervently hoped his less than impressive condition was due to his hangover.

His overall appearance was quite unremarkable. He wasn't good looking in any classical sense, but he was—*interesting* was the only word she could think of. He was a little flabby and obviously out of shape, but underneath that soft exterior she sensed an understated strength. His best feature was his inquisitive blue eyes that seemed to take in everything. But she was struck by the depth of sadness she saw in them. It was as though those eyes had looked into the very bottom of hell. And then she remembered. Of course they had. Chief Brunetta had told her how his wife and son had been killed when a drunk driver T-boned them at an intersection just four blocks from their home.

There was a certain innocence and vulnerability about him. Years ago she would have been attracted to such a man, but she'd had her fill of vulnerable men. Now, watching him make his way down the dock, she hoped he was up to the job. She loved sailing and had jumped at the chief's request that she undertake this assignment. But now she was having second thoughts. She wasn't looking forward to being a decoy in Crater Cove with the chief's broken down friend.

Delaney stopped in front of the boat, a cigarette dangled from his lips. "Here I am," he said, trying to sound cheerful.

"I was expecting you sooner."

He shrugged. "I got lost. Should I get on?"

"You smoke." It was more a statement than a question.

He took the cigarette out of his mouth. "Yeah. A problem?"

"I hate the smell of cigarettes, secondary smoke causes cancer, and careless sparks burn holes in sails."

He flipped the cigarette into the water. "JT, you've got to learn to come out of your shell and just say what's on your mind." He saw her looking at his feet with a puzzled expression. He looked down at his scruffy loafers. "What? They're the same color."

"Shoes scuff up the deck and they're slippery. Why didn't you wear sneakers?"

"Because I don't own a pair of sneakers. I'm not a jock."

"I'll say," she muttered.

"What?"

"Why don't you toss me your bag and take your shoes off before you come on board."

Delaney was beginning to regret this trip even more. If he'd known he was going to spend a night with a female Captain Bligh, he'd have refused to come. "Aye, aye, Captain," he said, handing her his bag. "I suppose you know they outlawed keel-hauling years ago."

When he stepped aboard—jumped, actually—the boat rocked. He grabbed for the nearest solid object—the boom. Unexpectedly, it swung toward him and he would have fallen backward into the water had she not grabbed him.

"Just sit *down*," she said sharply.

He did as he was told. "Hey, this little boat *rocks*!"

"So does an aircraft carrier," she said, willing herself to remain calm. "You know, it's never a real good idea to jump into a boat."

"You didn't tell me."

"You're right. I should have."

Holding onto a lifeline with a death grip, he said, "How small is this thing?"

"It's a twenty-five."

"That's awfully small for the ocean."

"We're not going to sail her around the horn, Pete. We're just making a short run down the coast." She poked his pale, freckled arm. "God, I've never seen anybody as white as you."

"I work real hard at maintaining this pallor."

"Don't you ever go out in the daylight?"

"As little as possible. When the sun's up I feel more comfortable curled up in a casket packed with my native soil."

"You'd better put on a lot of sun blocker—especially the top of your head."

Delaney, who was sensitive about his thinning hair, quickly put his baseball cap back on. "I'm on vacation. I have an obligation to get sunburned."

She shrugged. "Suit yourself."

Ten minutes later, they were headed out the inlet and Delaney still hadn't moved from his spot. She'd started the engine and cast off the dock lines herself. As they got to the mouth of the inlet, incoming rollers gently hobby-horsed the boat.

"Is it always this rough?" he said.

She flashed him the same you-dopey-asshole smile *he* gave suspects when he was about to announce that they were under arrest. "These are only two feet seas. When there's a nor'easter the swells can be eight to ten feet."

"Have you ever been out in seas like that?"

"All the time. I used to crew on a fifty-six foot racer."

"Fifty-six feet," he repeated, thinking that sounded a lot safer than twenty-five feet.

Once they cleared the inlet, she said, "Okay, I'm gonna put up the main."

"OK. What should I do?"

"Nothing. I can handle it."

He was embarrassed that, so far, he hadn't done a damn thing except almost fall overboard. "JT, I'm not an invalid. Let me do something."

"OK. You want to take the tiller or do you want to raise the main?"

He opted for the tiller because it was something he could hold on to without looking like a wuss. And better yet, he didn't have to leave the safety of the cockpit.

"Keep her headed into the wind," she said, as she made her way toward the mast.

"Where's the wind?"

She pointed at a buoy off shore. "Just aim for that."

As she climbed onto the top of the cabin's roof, his eyes drifted from the buoy to her shapely legs.

"You're falling off," she said, pointing toward the buoy that had suddenly moved to the left of the bow. "Head up."

He yanked the tiller to the left. The bow shot to the right. "*What the—*"

"*The other way*," she shouted.

"What other way?" He yanked it harder to the left and the bow went harder to the right. To his amazement the boat made a complete one-eighty and now they were headed back toward the inlet. "*What the hell's going on?*"

She dove into the cockpit, wrestled the tiller from him, and got the boat turned around. He stared at the offending tiller with more anger than embarrassment. "That thing doesn't work right. Why don't I raise the main?"

"Are you sure you want to do that?" She really didn't want him to leave the safety of the cockpit. What would she tell Chief Brunetta if his best friend drowned a half mile off shore?

"Piece of cake." He stood up and promptly smacked his head on the boom. "*Jesus*—"

"You okay?"

He rubbed his head. "I'm fine. It's just a concussion. All right, what do I do?"

"There's one rule on a sailboat that you never want to forget: One hand for the boat, one hand for you."

"Why?"

"Because if you're doing something with both hands and you lose your balance, you'll go over the side."

He started forward, using *both* hands to hang on. "Good rule."

After several heart-stopping slips and grabs, he finally managed to get the main sail up. He crawled back into the cockpit breathing hard. "Not bad for a beginner, huh?"

"It's up," she said noncommittally.

Except for an anxious moment when he almost got his fingers caught in the winch, the jib was unfurled with little difficulty. JT turned the bow south, trimmed the main and the jib, and the little sloop jumped forward, gracefully cutting through the gentle swells.

The rest of the trip down the coast was uneventful except for one gust of wind that put the boat's lee rail awash. Clawing at the lifeline and looking straight down at the water with wide eyes, Delaney barely had a chance to yell, "*Jesus Christ!*" before the boat righted herself. He shot a panicked look at JT, but, to his astonishment and irritation, she was smiling radiantly. *She was actually enjoying this*!

Two hours later, she announced, "Okay, we're here. Time to drop the sails."

They were less than a mile from shore but Delaney couldn't see any openings in the solid, craggy rock-faced coastline. "Where's Crater Cove?"

JT furled the jib. "It's hard to see from out here. That's why only locals go in there."

Delaney started getting nervous again. "You know how to get in, right?"

"Sure. No problem."

After she dropped the main, she said, "Here, take the tiller."

"Oh, I don't think—"

"It's okay. The wind is down and the sails are furled. Just aim for that big pine on top of the hill." She stood up.

"Where are you going?" He asked, trying to keep the panic out of his voice.

"I have to go below to get the plow anchor," she said disappearing into the cabin. "It'll hold better than the Danforth."

When she came up carrying the anchor, he said, "I think you'd better take the handle," he said anxiously. "We're getting awfully close."

"That's a tiller." She looked over her shoulder. "We're OK. We're still a quarter of a mile off."

As she made her way forward with the heavy anchor cradled in her arms, they passed through the wake of a fishing trawler. The boat dipped. JT tried to counter-balance the effect of the roll, but it was quickly followed by another. A helpless Delaney, clutching the tiller in a death grip, witnessed what followed in agonizingly slow motion. She leaned left, precariously teetering as her elbows worked to restore balance. Then she leaned right. He was about to shout: "One hand for the boat, one hand for you..." when she disappeared over the side.

"*Jesus H. Christ!*" He jumped up and whacked his head on the boom again, but this time he didn't feel the pain. He was too busy searching the waters for her. After what seemed like an eternity, a blonde head bobbed to the surface. He flung a floatation cushion at her and it hit her on the head. Now that *she* was safe, he began to worry about himself. He was heading toward a rocky coastline and he didn't know how to stop the damn boat.

"Pull the tiller hard over," she yelled from the water.

"Which way?"

"Doesn't matter."

He yanked the tiller to the left and the boat started a slow turn to the right, away from the looming rocks that to a panicked Delaney appeared to be fifteen feet in front of him. As the boat came toward her, she yelled, "Keep it like that and put the engine in neutral."

He looked down. There were two handles. *Which one was the gear shift?*

"Just turn the engine off," she shouted.

He turned the key off and the engine died. "What'll I do now?"

"Nothing. Don't touch anything. I'll swim over."

He lowered the swim ladder and helped her climb aboard, mildly disappointed that she was wearing a bikini top under her tee shirt.

For a moment he said nothing while she caught her breath. Then, "JT?"

"What?" she said, still breathing hard.

He looked at her very seriously. "Next time remember: One hand for the boat, one for you."

She shot him a withering look and started the engine.

CHAPTER TEN

As JT steered the boat toward the rocky shore, Delaney was certain they were going to be dashed into a line of jagged rocks that looked like a giant sea serpent's teeth. But as they came closer, he was relieved to see an opening dead ahead. She guided the sloop between two menacing rocks and they glided into Crater Cove. He'd been there earlier with Tony, but the view from the boat was even more spectacular. Tree lined cliffs soared over the peaceful cove. Delaney immediately noticed two things. The rocks at the entrance acted like a jetty blocking the incoming swells. The water in the cove was bathtub calm. The other thing he noticed was Sanborne Castle off to the right. All the windows facing the cove would have a clear view of anything moving around here.

JT turned off the engine and the sudden silence startled Delaney.

"This is about where the sailboat was anchored," she said.

For a moment they both looked at each, wondering the same thing: *What the hell are we doing here?*

JT set the anchor and came back to the cockpit and pulled off her wet tee shirt. "Time for a swim," she said. "You coming?"

Under her shorts she was wearing a hot-pink bikini. Outside the cover of *Sports Illustrated* Delaney had never seen a more perfect body. He started to rip his tee shirt off and then he looked down at his pale, flabby stomach. He tried to suck in his gut, but it was hopeless. He was ten pounds of shit in a five pound bag. Reluctantly, he pulled his shirt back down.

She climbed up on the cabin roof. "Aren't you coming in?"

"Naw, I don't feel like it."

Forlornly, he watched her make a perfect 9.8 dive off the boat and with strong, rhythmic strokes swim toward the beach. He sat down, lit a cigarette, and studied the unspoiled shoreline. Except for Sanborne castle, looking vaguely malignant through the trees, there were no other signs of life in the cove.

He'd never been a great admirer of the outdoors but he had to admit Crater Cove was beautiful. Protected from the sea by the barrier beach and a tree-lined cliff, it was a tranquil sanctuary away from the world. He imagined that's what the people on the sailboat must have been thinking, until a homicidal maniac came aboard and slashed their throats.

JT reached the beach and started back. She looked so happy, so at home in the water. He shuddered, suddenly overwhelmed by a wave of unbearable sadness—a feeling of unattainable goals, of lost worlds.

He stood up to shake off the feeling. "All this goddamn nature shit is giving me the creeps," he muttered into the wind.

She swam to the boat and thumped on the hull. "Pete, there's a bucket and a clam rake under the starboard seat. Would you hand them to me?"

He lowered them over the side. "What are you gonna do?"

"Get some fresh clams for the posillipo sauce."

"Sounds good to me," he said, delighted that they were going to have real food tonight. When she'd said she would take care of the food earlier in Tony's office, he'd had visions of eating peanut butter and jelly sandwiches for dinner. Then this afternoon, after getting yelled at on the dock, he feared the menu might be hardtack and water.

Twenty minutes later, she was back, handing him a bucketful of clams. As she toweled off on deck, Delaney tried his best not to stare at her body, but he didn't know where else to look. Finally, not knowing what else to do, he stuck his head into the bucket and poked at the clams. "You're very resourceful."

She sat down and ran her fingers through her hair. "Not really. You'd have to be blind not to find clams around here."

"Or a city boy."

She pulled her hair back and tied it in a pony tail. "You're not much of an outdoorsman are you, Pete?"

"That's like saying Osama bin Laden isn't much of a humanitarian."

"Have you ever done anything outdoors?"

"I tried fishing the other day. Last time before that I was ten years old and it was a traumatic experience that left a permanent scar."

"What happened?"

"I went fishing with a few buddies off a Canarsie pier. Next thing I know I hooked a huge snake."

"A what?"

"Well, a pretty big eel. I reeled him and was starting to take the hook out of his mouth when the sonofabitch suddenly coiled around my arm and slimed me. Scared the crap out of me. I jumped back, tripped over a tackle box, landed on my ass, and the death struggle was on."

She bit the end of the towel, trying not to laugh. "Didn't anybody help you?"

"They were too busy laughing, just like you are. So there I am, rolling round and round with this monster when suddenly I feel this excruciating pain in my butt."

Her green eyes widened. "Ohmigod! He bit you?"

"Naw, I had a package of hooks in my back pocket and they stuck in my ass. The eel wiggled off the hook and slithered back into the water leaving me on the pier slimed, three hooks in my ass, and no eel. Right on the spot I sold my rod to another kid for two bucks."

"You poor boy."

He shrugged. "It wasn't a total loss. I learned my first valuable lesson in life."

"Which is?"

"Shit happens."

She wiped a tear from the corner of her eye and stood up. "It's starting to get dark. Do you think you can fire up the bar-bee without blowing us out of the water?"

Delaney stood up slowly, careful not to bang his head on the boom. "I'll do my best."

He didn't know how she did it, but within the hour they were sitting down to a magnificent meal of Caesar salad, clams posillipo, Italian bread and, to Delaney's delight, a bottle of chilled white wine. After they finished he helped her clean up. It was tight quarters in the cabin and at one point, as he squeezed past her, he put his hands on her hips. The feel of her, warm, silky skin was electrifying and he didn't want to let go.

She was wiping a pot. Without turning around she said, "Pete, don't do that."

Embarrassed, he pulled his hands back as though he'd been burned. "I'm sorry," he mumbled.

She broke the tense silence. "It's a little bit crowded down here. Why don't you go topside."

He went up on deck, feeling his cheeks burning, and muttered into the dark, moonless night, "*You are such an asshole.*"

A cool breeze blew in off the ocean gently rippling the water's surface. He studied the shapeless shoreline and saw nothing except a faint, yellowish light coming from a window in Sanborne castle. He wondered if Andrew was at the window watching him through night-vision goggles.

She came up on deck carrying two mugs of coffee and handed him one. Delaney was mildly relieved to see that she'd put on a jogging suit. Her more modest attire would make it easier to keep his mind on business. He pushed the tiller out of the way and sat down. "JT, about before. I didn't mean—"

She sat down opposite him. "Let's just forget about it."

In the darkness he couldn't see her face, but he thought he detected disappointment—or was it weariness?—in her tone. That sort of thing probably happened to her all the time. "That was a great meal," he said, trying to lighten the mood.

"Thanks."

"And healthy, too."

"You probably don't eat right, do you?"

He noticed she had a way of making questions sound like statements. "The microwave is my life support system. Without it I die."

"What do you do when you're away from home?"

"I favor Greek diners and fast food fixes."

"I don't think grease is one of the four food groups."

"It is to me. I just hope I don't go through withdrawals tonight."

He heard a fish splash and tensed. "What was that?"

"Bait fish jumping."

When it was quiet again, he said, "What does JT stand for?"

She groaned. "I don't like to talk about."

"You forget. I'm a detective. I have ways of finding out these things."

"Jiniwin."

"Jiniwin. That's an... interesting name." He was glad she couldn't see him grinning in the darkness. "Named after your mom?"

"A character in Dickens' *Old Curiosity Shop*."

"I can hardly wait to hear what the T stands for."

"Titania."

"You're kidding. You're named after a sunken ship?"

"Worse. The queen of the fairies. *A Midsummer-Night's Dream.*"

"What did your folks have against you?"

"It was my dad's fault. He taught literature at the local college and was a big fan of Shakespeare and Dickens."

"How did you end up here in Haddley Falls?"

After I graduated from college, I got a job in an accounting firm. *Bor-ing!* I left that job to crew on racing boats for a couple of seasons. Then, I decided I needed a steady job and became a flight attendant so I could travel the world."

Delaney caught a hint of disillusionment in her voice. "And you found out the world sucks?"

"Something like that. I packed it in after a year."

"How come?"

"I got tired of being groped and lied to by married businessmen."

"Were you ever married?"

"I lived with a pilot for a couple of years. It took me that long to find out he didn't need a woman, he needed a mother. I came here to Haddley Falls to chill out for a week. That was three years ago."

While she'd been talking, Delaney was mentally trying to add up the years.

"I'm thirty-five," she said, as though reading his mind.

He was astonished. He'd figured her for twenty-eight tops. "So what brought you into law enforcement?"

Her warm laughter sent a pleasant shudder through him. "The Haddley Falls Police Department is hardly law enforcement. I couldn't stand the idea of being locked up in an office all day, so I applied for a job with the police department. The work's easy, sometimes interesting, but the best part is it gives me a lot of time to do the things I like to do."

"Such as?"

"Sail, ski, run."

"Sounds exhausting." In the darkness he pictured her lean body. "You must run a lot."

"I try to do five or six miles a day. I've run the Boston and New York marathons a few times."

Delaney patted his spare tire, getting more depressed by the minute. He stood up. "I'll be right back. I have just the thing for this coffee." A moment later he appeared with a full bottle of scotch and held it out to her.

"No, I don't think so."

"Hey, I know you're on duty, but I won't tell your boss. I swear."

Recalling his hung over condition this morning, she said, "Pete, I think we should both keep clear heads tonight."

"Absolutely," he answered, not noticing the tension in her voice. He poured a generous amount into his mug. "Just something to take away the night chill."

After awhile she said, "So how long have you been a detective?"

"Twenty-one years, the last ten in homicide."

"That's a long time in that line of work."

"Yeah, way too long."

Brunetta had told her about the tragic death of Delaney's wife and son and decided not to bring it up, but she was concerned by the note of despondency in his tone and the presence of a full bottle of scotch was not a good idea.

"Maybe I will have just a drop." She picked up the bottle and splashed a little into her cup. As she was putting the bottle down, she tripped over a line and fell forward. As the bottle slipped from her grasp, Delaney lunged for it, but it plopped into the black water and disappeared in a circle of tiny bubbles.

He spun around. "Did you do that on purpose?"

Her green eyes were wide with innocence. "No, I didn't. I tripped." She picked up the offending line. "Who left this on the deck?"

"I did," he muttered.

She coiled the line. "Another rule, Pete. Never leave uncoiled lines lying on deck."

"I'll make a note of it," he said, glumly peering into the watery grave of his scotch bottle.

She looked toward the shoreline and laughed nervously. "I guess we should go below. If someone is planning to slash our throats we shouldn't keep them up all night."

"Yeah, that wouldn't be polite."

"I should have brought thumb tacks," she said, still looking out into the blackness.

"Why?"

"Joshua Slocum, probably the most famous single-handed sailor ever, used them when he was sailing the waters of Tierra Del Fuego. Every night the natives boarded his boat and stole his food and supplies. Then he hit upon the idea of laying thumb tacks on deck at night."

Delaney grunted, remembering Brunetta's vivid description of the condition of the bodies. "I think it will take more than a handful of thumb tacks to stop this guy."

JT swallowed hard. "You think so?"

Delaney sympathized with the apprehension in her tone. Using yourself as bait for a murderer wasn't in the Haddley Falls Police Department job description. "Don't worry. We won't be caught off guard like that couple."

Down below in the darkened cabin Delaney scanned the shoreline with binoculars. "I wish we had night-vision goggles," he said.

Peering through another window, JT said, "We don't have a lot of call for night-vision equipment in the Haddley Falls PD. You see anything?"

"No. What kind of fire power do you have?"

"I have my nine millimeter and the chief told me to take a pump-action shotgun."

Delaney, still looking through the binoculars, said, "I bet you're pretty good with the 'nine.' Am I right?"

"Second in my class at the Academy."

"How did I know that? I'll use the shotgun."

At his direction, she cleared away everything between the bunks and the companionway. If he had to get on deck fast, he didn't want to be tripping over coolers and flotation devices.

When he was satisfied that everything was out of the way, he said, "Okay, here's the drill. We'll alternate watches. Two hours apiece. If at any time you feel yourself getting sleepy, wake me. I don't want us both sleeping at the same time."

She shuddered slightly. "Don't worry. I don't think I'll be able to sleep at all."

"If you hear anything on your watch, wake me right away. Under no circumstances are you to go up on deck alone."

"You don't have to tell me twice."

"If someone boards the boat, *I* will be the first one up the stairs. Understood?"

She nodded, astonished at the change that had suddenly come over him. No longer the uncertain, slightly muddled man she'd seen all day, he'd morphed into the confident, business-like detective she'd expected to see in the chief's office this morning.

He picked up the shotgun. "You ever shoot at anybody in anger?"

"No."

He pumped a round into the chamber. The metallic sound was magnified in the confined cabin. "It's a whole lot different from shooting at a silhouette. Your heart pounds, the adrenaline flows, the hand shakes. And if that's not bad enough, the person you're shooting at is usually trying to kill you. Forget all the bullshit about proper sight alignment and trigger squeeze. Fire power is what counts. Squeeze off as many rounds as you can as fast as you can. Even if you don't hit him, you'll scare the crap out of him." He climbed into his bunk and propped a pillow behind his head. "One more thing. Try not to shoot me."

She was going to ask him if he'd ever shot anyone, but the intense expression in his eyes answered that question.

She took the first watch. She propped herself up in the starboard bunk and rested the nine millimeter in her lap. She thought he was sleeping, but ten minutes later he said, "What the *hell* is that banging?"

"The halyards hitting the mast."

"They weren't making that much noise before."

"The sound is magnified down here and things sound louder in the dark."

The only good thing about a small boat was that he assumed that it would be impossible to board without making it rock. But now, as he lay in his bunk, the boat was rocking all by itself, sometimes gently, sometimes with a jerk. "*Why* is this thing rocking like this?"

"Wind action, wave action, skating on the anchor rode. A boat's always moving."

Now he understood how someone could board a boat in the middle of the night undetected. A sailboat at anchor was a noisy, bumpy place. The Rockettes could do a number on deck and you wouldn't hear them.

It was almost three-thirty and JT was on her second watch. Now that she'd become accustomed to the boat's peculiar noises, she was less jumpy. She was listening to the rhythmic sound of Pete's breathing when she felt, more than heard, a slight bump against the hull. She sat up, wondering if it was her imagination. Then there was another bump. This time distinct. The hair on the back of her neck rose. Before she could react, Delaney was out of his bunk and, to her astonishment, up on deck in two hops. She didn't think he was capable of moving that fast.

By the time she got on deck he had the shotgun to his shoulder and was pointing it into the water. "Driftwood," he said, nudging the log away from the hull with the tip of the shotgun barrel.

She holstered her automatic and realized that her hand was shaking. If he noticed, he didn't say anything.

"Why don't you get some sleep, JT. I'm done for the night."

She was suddenly very tired, too tired to argue. Down below, she curled up in her bunk and, confident in Delaney's ability to protect her, promptly felt asleep.

She awoke at dawn and saw Delaney framed in the open companionway, bathed in the soft orange glow of the rising sun. He was smoking a cigarette, deep in thought. As she watched him, she was struck by the serenity in his face. The sadness and guarded suspicion was gone from his eyes, replaced by a peaceful acceptance of the world, as though he'd suddenly come to terms with some great eternal truth.

She came up the steps. "Hi."

Furtively, like a high school kid caught by a teacher, he flipped the cigarette over the side and his tranquil expression became guarded again. "Hi, yourself. Well, I see we're still alive."

"You sound disappointed."

He looked toward the beach. "I was kind of hoping we'd catch our man."

She was startled by the disappointed expression on his face. He expected, no—*wanted*—to come face to face with the murderer. She felt a mixture of fear and awe.

"That was one hellava sunrise," he said.

"Aren't there sunrises in New York?"

"So they tell me, but I've never seen one. Usually I'm on my way home from the precinct or a gin mill when the sun is coming up. But with all those tall buildings, you really can't see a sunrise. The only way I can tell the sun has come is the street lights go out."

She suddenly felt a profound compassion for Pete Delaney. He was the big city detective, tough and sophisticated, but there was something incomplete in him. He'd seen the world, but only the worst part. She wished with all her heart that one day he could see the world that she knew—a world of beauty, a world of awe, a world of grace. She turned away. "I guess we should get ready to go."

"Yeah. Hey, maybe you can teach me how to sail on the way back."

She studied his boyish, enthusiastic smile with dismay. "You *want* to sail back?"

"Why not? I think I could get to like this."

"There's no wind, Pete," she said, surprised at how disappointed she felt. She would have enjoyed teaching him to sail. "We'll have to motor back."

He looked out at the sea, crestfallen. "Oh, okay."

She fired up the engine. "I'll go forward and pull up the anchor."

"No," he gently pushed her out of the way. "*I'll* do it. You're a bit clumsy. I don't want you falling overboard again."

CHAPTER ELEVEN

The chair groaned every time Major Chad Perrault shifted his bulky, two-hundred plus pound body. Tony Brunetta had met the Major at a law enforcement seminar a few months earlier and had taken an immediate dislike to the arrogant commanding officer of the State Police Homicide Squad. He'd only agreed to this meeting so he could tell Perrault in person that his services wouldn't be needed.

When the major smiled, which wasn't often, his little pig-eyes disappeared behind twin mountains of cheek fat. Perrault was smiling now.

"So, Chief, as we country bumpkins say, you're in a whole heap 'a trouble."

Tony Brunetta crossed his feet on the desk. "It's not the first time and it won't be the last."

"I'm here to help you out. What you need to do is have the mayor send a memo to the governor asking for our assistance and we'll relieve you of this messy investigation."

"Thanks, but no thanks."

Perrault's expansive smile faded and the pig-eyes re-emerged, puzzled and uncertain. "Well, you can't do this investigation all by yourself."

"Why not? I have access to the state's lab facilities. That's all I need."

Perrault ran his hand through his close-cropped crew cut. He'd been sent here to make sure the state police got this investigation and by God he wasn't going to take "no" for an answer. "How you gonna do it yourself?"

Brunetta was enjoying Perrault's discomfort. "I have help."

Perrault sneered. "Your deputies?"

"An NYPD homicide detective."

"He working for you?"

"Volunteering."

The befuddled major didn't know what to make of this. No small town police chief had ever refused the assistance of the state homicide squad before. Not knowing what else to do, he tried a bluff. "You know I can come in here and take over this investigation."

"No, you can't."

Unsure of the procedural law, Perrault said, "Says who?"

"The Haddley Falls charter of incorporation."

Perrault heaved himself out of the chair and tucked his big belly back into his sagging trousers. "Well, I think you're wrong about that and I'm gonna find out what's what."

At the door a red-faced Perrault said, "I'll tell you one thing, *Chief.* "You just might find the technical services in this state are not as quick as the ones in New York City. Sometimes we get backed up real bad."

After Perrault left, Brunetta thought about the ramifications of Perrault's not so veiled threat. The major was a political hack, but he did have enough weight to see to it that the State Police lab could delay much needed information, even lose or sabotage evidence. And, he, Tony Brunetta would suffer the consequences of a botched homicide investigation. He didn't like being in the middle of a political skirmish between the governor and the Mayor. Perrault was an asshole, but he'd worked with assholes before. If it were up to him, he'd gladly put up with that moron in exchange for a squad of trained investigators.

The door opened and a badly sunburned Delaney came in. "Pete, you really oughta use sun block. You Micks get sunburned standing under a forty watt light bulb."

"Yeah, yeah." Delaney went straight for the coffee and poured two cups.

"So how'd it go?" Brunetta asked.

"Nobody tried to cut our throats," Delaney said, handing Tony his cup and falling into a chair. "Is that good or bad?"

"Bad."

"Up yours, pal."

Brunetta looked at Delaney over his cup. "So how did you two get along?" he asked casually.

"Good."

Brunetta hated himself for playing matchmaker, but he couldn't help harboring the hope that Delaney and JT would hit it off. JT was a fine woman who deserved a good man and Delaney needed someone like JT who could help him get his life back in order.

"You like her?"

"She's a hellava sailor."

"Good looking, too."

"Yeah."

"Great body."

"Brunetta, will you knock it off? You sound like a talking email from *Match.com* for chrissake."

Brunetta slid the autopsy report across the desk. "Read that."

Delaney read the report in silence. When he was finished, he tossed it on the desk. "Why isn't anything ever easy?"

Brunetta tapped the report with his finger. "What's wrong with this picture?"

"No missing organs, tentative cuts, no sexual mutilation. What the hell kind of ritualistic murderer is this guy?"

"Maybe he's not."

Delaney cocked his head. "You think he did it to muddy up the waters? No pun intended."

"It's a possibility."

"If he's not a perv, why would he do that?"

Brunetta smiled ruefully. "I was hoping you could answer that question since you're the best goddamned detective in the country."

Delaney grunted at the jibe. "For the time being, I'm sticking with the ritualistic murderer."

"The facts don't support it."

Delaney gingerly touched the tip of his sunburned nose. "Maybe the guy's new at this. Give him a little time to work out the kinks."

"That's not funny."

"Speaking of funny, who was that fat clown I saw leaving your office?"

By the time Brunetta finished telling Delaney about his visit from Major Perrault, it was almost six o'clock. He stood up. "Come on, Pete. Let's call it a day."

Delaney got up and stretched. "Sounds good to me. What's the best restaurant in town? I'm taking you and Rosemary to dinner."

"Can't. We're going to the country club tonight."

"What's the occasion?"

"The annual Haddley Falls summer ball."

"Jeez, you sound all choked up."

"It sucks. Not counting waiters, I'll be the poorest sonofabitch in the joint."

"So why go?"

"I'm the token peasant. The mayor insists that Rosemary and I attend these functions. It gives the wealthy taxpayers a chance to talk to their tax dollars."

"You poor bastard. You can tell me all about it tomorrow."

"You're going, too."

"Like hell I am. You just described the country club from hell and you want *me* to go? Nothing doing. Point me toward the nearest Mickey D."

"Pete, you have to go. The mayor specifically invited you. He knows you're volunteering your time and he wants to show his appreciation."

That wasn't exactly the truth. He'd *told* Gardiner he was bringing Delaney. He was uneasy about turning Pete loose on the country club set, but the alternative—leaving him home alone with a bottle of scotch—was worse.

Delaney was unimpressed. "If they really want to show their appreciation," he said, "tell them to give me a hundred dollars worth of gift certificates to the Golden Arches. That'll take care of two weeks' worth of dinners back home."

CHAPTER TWELVE

In keeping with the formality of the occasion, Tony Brunetta left the department Toyota home and took his respectable three year-old Buick to the Haddley Falls Country Club.

Delaney, taking note of the long line of gleaming luxury cars in front of them, said, "Hey, Tony, next time your contract comes up for renewal, hold out for a Beemer to go with the free house."

From the back seat Rosemary said, "Remember, Pete. You promised to behave." She exchanged an uneasy glance with Tony through the rearview mirror. Earlier, she'd told her husband in no uncertain terms that it was not a good idea to bring Pete along. She'd even offered to stay home with him, but her husband had vetoed the idea, pointing out that it wasn't fair for *her* to stay home while *he* had to go to the country club alone.

While they were waiting in line for the club's parking attendants to extract the elite of Haddley Falls from their cars, Brunetta pointed out the movers and shakers to Delaney. The mayor and his wife got out of a Mercedes.

"That's the town mayor, Royce Gardiner. He runs the top law firm in the county. And that's his wife, Helen."

Delaney studied the skittish woman with the emaciated body of an anorexic. "She's looks like she's wound way too tight."

"She is."

Another Mercedes pulled up and a man and woman got out. "That's Jonathan Talbot and his wife, Irene," Brunetta continued. "He owns most of the land and the money around here. He's also our local celebrity. He's going to be tapped for the Secretary of Commerce job."

Delaney remembered the old factory he'd seen his first day in Haddley Falls. "Is he the Talbot of Talbot Meatpacking Inc.?"

"The same."

"How does a guy from little Haddley Falls get offered the job of Secretary of Commerce?"

"Money. He was a real rainmaker for the president during the last election. He brought in millions for the presidential campaign. I heard a rumor he was offered the ambassadorship to France, but he turned it down."

"Secretary of Commerce isn't a bad consolation prize," Delaney said, watching a lanky octogenarian with snow white hair cut like a man's leap out of a fire engine-red Land Rover. She whispered something in the attendant's ear and roared with laughter. "Who's the feisty old broad?" Delaney asked.

"That would be Eleanor Haddley. The town is named after her great, great, something or other. She probably just told him a dirty joke. She's a tad eccentric."

Delaney grunted in satisfaction. "Sounds like my kind of broad."

As they entered the ballroom, a fifteen piece band was playing *Time on My Hands*. Recognizing the tune, Delaney whispered to Rosemary, "Very appropriate for this crowd."

At their table Tony Brunetta introduced Delaney to Royce, his wife, and Eleanor Haddley.

The mayor gave Delaney his best grandfatherly smile. "Mr. Delaney, thank you for helping the chief with this most unfortunate occurrence."

Unfortunate occurrence? A double homicide? The man is in serious denial. "Glad to help."

Eleanor Haddley, who had the grip of a truck driver, pumped Delaney's hand. "Mr. Delaney," she gushed, "I'm absolutely thrilled to meet a real detective."

"Please, call me Pete. Are you interested in law enforcement, Mrs. Haddley?"

"Call me Eleanor. Dear me, yes. I'm an avid fan of Hercule Poirot and Sherlock Holmes. I've read all their books."

The only thing Delaney detested more than cop TV shows were fiction detective stories. "Well, I'm afraid I'm not in their league."

"Nonsense. They're just paper detectives. *You* are the real thing." She elbowed him in the side. "At dinner you'll have to tell be about some of your big capers."

All through the soup, the appetizer, and the start of dinner, Delaney, much to the dismay of Hillary Gardiner, the exasperation of Tony Brunetta, and the delight of Eleanor Haddley, recounted in gory detail the highlights of several murder cases he'd worked on.

At one point, in an attempt to change the subject, Royce Gardiner said, "Eleanor, I understand you shot a forty on the back nine yesterday."

"I'd have done better if my damn arthritis hadn't been acting up," the spirited woman replied. Then, without missing a beat, she turned to Delaney. "So tell me, Pete, what did you do after you found the severed head in the toilet bowl? Did you just pull it out of the crapper or wait for forensics?"

Hillary Gardiner, who was cutting into her rare prime rib, gagged and bolted from the table.

"Oh, dear," Eleanor said. "I guess this isn't a suitable topic of conversation for dinner."

"No, Eleanor," Royce Gardiner said firmly. "It certainly is not."

"I'm so sorry. It's just that I don't often get the chance to talk to a real detective." She patted Delaney's arm and whispered, "We'll resume our conversation over dessert."

Delaney nodded, grateful for the break. While he'd been regaling Miss Haddley with stories of murder and mayhem in the Big Apple, he'd been studying the elite of Haddley Falls. He'd also been hoping that JT Bryce might appear but, looking at the sea of expensive gowns and pounds of diamonds hanging from a hundred scrawny necks, he realized she wouldn't come here, even if she'd been invited.

Delaney, an inveterate people watcher, studied Talbot sitting at a table on the other side of the room. His wife, a bored, jewel-bedecked woman who was making the best of the fact that she'd married well, sat ignored while a constant stream of men, looking important in their own right, stopped by the table to chat with her husband. Now *that* was real power, Delaney thought. When you're in a roomful of rich people and they all come to genuflect at *your* table, you gotta be holding all the aces.

As the waiters were clearing away the dinner plates, Talbot began working the tables with the enthusiasm of the Energizer Bunny. He roamed the room chatting, slapping backs, and laughing at jokes he'd probably heard a thousand times. Finally, he stopped at their table. "Hello all," he said cheerfully.

Delaney, who read people well, took an immediate dislike to the would-be Secretary of Commerce, whose teeth were too white and his tan too dark. But he had to admit he had the unique charisma all successful politicians possessed; that certain something that made heads turn within a fifty foot radius and strain to hear what he had to say.

Talbot shook Delaney's hand. "I understand you've been helping Chief Brunetta and I just want to thank you on behalf of everyone in our little hamlet of Haddley Falls. We are eternally grateful for your help in our hour of need."

"Glad to help," Delaney said, thinking that if Talbot's political career stalled, he had a great future in TV evangelism.

After a little small talk—"Rosemary, I love your hair," "Hillary, you look striking in that dress," "Eleanor, you look younger everyday"—he put his arm around Brunetta and led him away from the table.

"I heard you found a tire-iron, Chief."

Brunetta nodded, not surprised that Talbot knew about the find in the cove. This was a small town and it was impossible to keep a secret, especially from Jonathan Talbot.

"I also understand you had a visit from Major Perrault today. How did that go?"

While Brunetta was telling him about his conversation with Perrault, Talbot nodded, winked, and waved to clusters of people in all the far-flung corners of the room. Brunetta found the habit irritating, but he had to admire Talbot's ability to listen to a conversation and respond to other people at the same time.

When Brunetta finished, Talbot said, "You handled it well. If you get any flack from the governor's office, just let me know." He started to walk away, but turned and came back. "By the way, that man at your table—Pete Delaney? He seems like a nice chap."

"He's my old partner and my best friend. We worked together for almost twenty years in the NYPD. We're like brothers. Actually, more than that. We were godfathers to each other's children. Truth is, we'd give our lives for each other, and there were times when we almost did just that."

"Very commendable. There is nothing more valuable than a good friend who will do anything for you. I must confess I'm jealous, Tony. I have no one like that. Chief, let me ask you a question. Please be frank with me. Can you solve this case alone?"

"Absolutely, Jonathan," Brunetta said with conviction. "I've never had an unsolved homicide and I'm not about to start now."

Talbot's eyebrows went up. "My, you seem very confident."

"I've been in this business for a long time. Murderers always make mistakes. I just have to wait for that mistake and then I've got him."

Talbot studied the ex-homicide detective with deadly serious gray eyes. "I believe you just might do that." He slapped Brunetta on the back, turned on his politician's bogus smile, and moved off to charm the next table.

During coffee and dessert, Delaney and Eleanor—at her instigation— began a macabre, Q&A.

She went first. "Does hair grow after death?"

"No."

Then, in rapid succession, they fired questions and answers back and forth, trying to stump each other.

"How about fingernails?"

"No." His turn. "Tiny pinpoint hemorrhages in the whites of the eyes."

"Strangulation. Smell of almonds."

"Cyanide poisoning. Tattooing."

"Powder burn marks from firing a gun at close range. Lividity."

"Caused by blood settling after a body is dead…"

"Hey," Delaney said, genuinely impressed. "You really know your stuff."

Rolling his eyes, Brunetta took Rosemary's hand and led her to the dance floor.

"Tony, can't you stop him?" she asked.

"It's not him. Eleanor's a morbid old broad and she's egging him on."

"Why can't she talk about flowers like other old women?" Rosemary muttered into his chest.

"It's not all bad. At least she's keeping Pete's mind off booze."

"Thank God. He came here with a buzz."

"I know, but he's behaving himself. If only— Oh, oh."

She pulled away. "What?"

"Don't look now, but Blair Lowell spotted Pete and is making a bee-line for our table and she'd got that predatory gleam in her eye. What is it about Delaney? He's an ordinary looking guy, a little overweight, starting to lose his hair, but he still attracts broads like a bug zapper."

"Something you men wouldn't understand."

"His ass. Right? You women have a thing about men's asses."

"How do you know that?"

"I read it in a magazine once when I was standing in a checkout line."

"It's not that. He has that... little-boy-lost quality. That and his eyes."

"What about his eyes?"

"A woman looks in those big blue eyes and sees sadness, wisdom, seductiveness."

"In Pete's eyes? Usually all I see is bloodshot."

"I told you you wouldn't understand."

While Delaney had been studying the quaint social habits of the rich, he'd also noticed Blair Lowell. She was hard to miss. Tall, blonde, and attractive in a decadent sort of way. Mid-forties he guessed. Great body—probably the result of long hours in the gym and the magic knife of a plastic surgeon. And she knew how to use it. She was the center of attention of half the men in the room. Either she was very influential or a nympho. Maybe *both*! He also noted that she liked her booze. She hadn't been without a drink since she'd come in. *Now that was his kind of woman.*

He watched her walk across the dance floor in a tight red dress that emphasized her drop-dead figure and wondered why someone like her would waste her time in a burg like Haddley Falls.

Blair Lowell slid into Hillary Gardiner's vacant seat and sloshed some of her martini on the table cloth. "Hello, Eleanor."

The old woman, displeased at having her Q&A game interrupted, especially by Blair Lowell, said, "Oh, hello, Blair." When she saw the tiresome woman wasn't going to leave, she said, "Have you met Mr. Delaney?"

Blair shook his hand, holding it a beat longer than necessary. "I just got back from Europe yesterday, but I've been hearing a lot about you."

"I deny everything."

She fixed him with alcohol-induced bright eyes that promised everything and nothing. "Would you like to dance, Mr. Delaney?"

"I don't dance."

She took his hand and yanked him to his feet. On the dance floor she pressed her body to his and he caught the subtle scent of expensive perfume. Up close, her true mileage was evident in the tiny lines around the eyes that even cosmetics and the skill of a surgeon's knife couldn't hide.

"Well," she said, flashing even white-capped teeth, "have you cracked the case yet?"

Her jocular tone irritated him. He didn't like civilians making fun of murder. "It's been difficult fitting it into my vacation schedule."

"You poor man. A regular busman's holiday. How long will you be staying?"

"I go back tomorrow night."

"Oh, that's too bad. I was going to invite you out to the house. I have a very large swimming pool and a very well-stocked bar."

"One out of two ain't bad, but I'll have to pass."

She pressed her body closer. There is no Mr. Lowell," she whispered in his ear.

"It's not that. I'm helping Tony with these homicides."

She pulled away, unaccustomed to being rebuffed. "It's *so* terrible," she said, coldly. "We're just not used to this sort of thing in Haddley Falls."

He wanted to tell her that most respectable people weren't used to murder in their communities either, but instead he said, "Have you lived here long?"

"Five years. I'm from Connecticut originally, but this is—*was*—my third husband's hometown. Since his death I just stay for the season. I can't take too much of these yahoos. It's a wonderful place in the summer and the beach house was part of a very substantial settlement."

He found her honesty refreshing. "He didn't insist on a prenuptial agreement?"

"*Please*. I refuse to marry any man who wants to start a relationship on the premise that it won't last. That's what I told all my husbands."

"Isn't a prenup usually the lawyer's idea?"

"No, that's a fiction perpetrated by wealthy men. It's always the man's idea. He just blames it on the lawyers. In my experience I've found that most rich men are stingy bastards."

"Being a peasant I don't have that problem."

"Let me guess. You don't make much money, but you are fulfilled in your work."

"Actually, police work sucks."

She threw her head back and laughed. The movement thrust her pelvis into his and he felt primal stirrings. "How'd he die?" he asked.

"Who?"

"Your husband."

"Heart attack."

"I guess you have to work really hard to make all those millions."

"He died taking his slippers off. He was eighty-one."

He pulled away to see if she was kidding.

"What? It's not easy finding a rich *young* man."

"I guess not. But now you can afford a younger guy."

"I'm not into boy toys. I like real men."

Delaney felt as though he were being interviewed for a job.

"It's time for a drink," she said. "What do you think?"

"You're absolutely right." Delaney took her hand and led her toward the bar on the patio.

Without asking, the bartender made her a double martini with two olives. Delaney ordered a scotch on the rocks. While they were having their second drink, Talbot hurried by. He acknowledged Delaney, but barely looked in Blair's direction.

Delaney watched him go. "An important man in a hurry."

Blair speared an olive. "So he thinks."

"What's his money source?"

"The Talbot Meatpacking fortune."

"Oh, yeah, I saw the plant the day I came into town. Must be boring cutting up meat all day."

Blair laughed. "The only meat Jonathan cuts is his sixteen ounce Porterhouse steak."

Delaney watched Talbot work another table. "I hear he's up for the secretary of commerce job. Think he'll get confirmed?"

"Jonathan Talbot always gets what he wants."

Delaney heard the caustic tone in her voice but decided not to pursue it.

After the fourth drink he stopped counting, but he was impressed with her ability to keep up with him. Rosemary and Tony took turns coming out to give him dirty looks and mutter thinly veiled threats about what would happen if he didn't rejoin the party inside. But he didn't want to go back inside. He was having a lot more fun out here.

Blair popped an olive in her mouth. "What do you think of that crappy band?" She was beginning to slur her words.

"Pretty crappy," he answered. "Who are those guys?"

"Some society band. A Miles Davis clone band?"

"*Myer* Davis. Miles was a jazz trumpeter."

"Whatever."

Delaney drained his scotch. "You know, I'll bet those guys could play some real music if we asked them."

She slammed her empty martini glass on the bar. "Lez go ask 'em."

As Blair and Delaney weaved their way toward the bandstand, the leader, a young tenor sax player, whose long hair was plastered down and tied it in a tight ponytail, watched them approach. To combat terminal boredom at these society gigs, he made a game of trying to anticipate what people were going to request. His fellow musicians didn't believe him, but he could always tell who was going to ask for *Stardust* and who was going to request *Memories*. Watching these two stumble toward him he decided the guy was a *Melancholy Baby* and she was definitely *The Stripper*.

As he leaned forward to hear their request, Blair grabbed his tuxedo lapel and almost yanked him off the stage. "Hey, Miles, can you guys play anything written after 1940?" She slipped a hundred dollar bill into his hand.

"Sure, Ma'am. What would you like to hear?"

"Elvis, Tina Turner, James Brown, anything. If I hear *You Light Up My Life* one more time, I'll puke."

You and me both, the bandleader thought as he disengaged himself from her grasp. He scanned the crowd, trying to judge their mood. He was getting ready to move into his wrap-up-the-evening up-tempo set. But he didn't think the *Bunny-hop* and the *Mexican Hat Dance* was what she had in mind.

He said something to the other musicians—all closet heavy metal rock musicians disguised in staid tuxedos—and a second later, they launched into aa ear shattering "Trashed" by Black Sabbath with the drummer providing the appropriate shrieks.

Blair, gyrating her hips to the throbbing rhythm, dragged Delaney to the middle of the dance floor. Even though he was drunk, he couldn't help noticing the stunned expressions on the faces of dancers who'd been interrupted in the middle of *Moon River*. Maybe this wasn't such a hot idea after all, he thought.

An old couple started to back off the dance floor, but Blair grabbed them. "Milly, where are you going?"

"Oh, Blair, I can't do this..."

"Sure you can. Just stand still and shake your ass."

The woman shrugged shyly and started to dance. She shuddered more than she shook, but judging from the smile on her face, she seemed to be enjoying herself. Encouraged by her willingness to give it a shot, a few more geriatric couples decided to brave Black Sabbath and soon the dance floor was packed. Watching the old geezers jerk and lurch around the floor, Delaney shimmied up to Blair and whispered in her ear, "If I had the Ben-Gaye concession at the local drug store, I could retire tomorrow."

Hillary Gardiner, the chairwoman of the ball, almost swallowed her lime wedge when the band broke into heavy metal. She'd distinctly told that fool of a band leader what type of music she wanted to hear, even going so far as to write out a list of her favorite fifty songs, which she'd compiled from her extensive collection of Lawrence Welk records.

Furious, she made her way through the tables toward the bandstand with every intention of threatening a lawsuit. But she was stunned to see that the dance floor was jammed. She saw people up there that's she'd never seen dance before. The club president's wife, a sour-faced octogenarian, came off the floor wiping her brow with a napkin. "Hillary, what a *wonderful* orchestra! Aren't you the clever one to think of such lively music."

With a stupid smile plastered on her face, Hillary continued past the bandstand and on into the ladies room, where in the privacy of a stall she popped a fistful of Valium.

Meanwhile, the band, inspired by the enthusiastic reception, segued into Metallica's "It's Electric" and Megadeath's "Psychotron", albeit at a greatly reduced decibel level.

Delaney—fortified with several more scotches—was thoroughly sloshed and having the time of his life. *He had no idea he was this good a dancer*! In his drunken stupor he thought his stumbles and staggers were clever Fred Astaire-like dips and spins. During an especially hot Dave Mustaine guitar rip, he attempted a double pirouette, but at that critical moment his internal gyroscope, sloshing around in a sea of scotch, experienced power failure.

He came out of the spin thinking he was moving forward, but realized, too late, he was stumbling *backward*. With arms flailing, he landed flat on his back on Talbot's table, crushing a floral center piece and scattering assorted crystal and silver. For a moment he was suspended in time. Then, as a squad of waiters rushed forward to help him, two table legs buckled and, like a slow motion version of a newly christened ship sliding down the ways, he skidded off the table head first and came to rest between the feet of a smiling Jonathan Talbot.

CHAPTER THIRTEEN

Back at the house, Rosemary helped her husband put Delaney to bed. "Aren't you going to take his clothes off?"

Brunetta stripped the tie from around his neck. "Just this. I don't want the dopey bastard strangling himself during the night. *I* want to do that in the morning."

Rosemary spread a blanket on him. "My God. How embarrassing."

"He was doing fine until he did the back flip onto the table." Brunetta stared down at the sleeping figure of his friend. "He's out of control, Rosemary. I don't know what I'm gonna do with him."

"Are you going to be in trouble with Gardiner?"

He put his arm around his wife and led her out of the room. "What's he gonna do? Ban me from the country club? I should live so long."

While Rosemary was in the bathroom getting ready for bed, the phone rang. Brunetta, expecting it was Gardiner, picked it up. "Royce, I'm sorry about tonight. I take full—"

A muffled man's voice on the other end of the line interrupted him. "I know who killed those two people on the sailboat."

Brunetta reached for a pad. "Who is this?"

"Never mind who I am. Meet me behind the Sunrise diner off the interstate. If you're not there in thirty minutes, I'm gone."

Rosemary came out of the bathroom and saw the concerned look on his face. "You are in trouble aren't you? Was that Gardiner?"

"No." He went to his bureau drawer, took out his holstered automatic, and slipped it inside his waist band.

Rosemary stiffened. "Tony, what's going on?"

"Some guy just called and said he knows who killed that couple. I've got to go meet him."

"Some guy? What's his name? Where are you going to meet him?"

"He wouldn't give me his name. He wants to meet me at an all-night diner off the Interstate."

Rosemary felt a lump forming in the pit of her stomach. "It's after one, Tony. Can't it wait till the morning?"

"No, it can't, babe. When someone gets an attack of good citizenship, you talk to him before he changes his mind."

"Tony, please... I don't like this. Why don't you—"

"Rosemary, for God's sake, I'm a cop. I know how to take care of myself."

"At least take Pete with you."

He shot her an exasperated smile. "Even if I could wake him, which is doubtful, what good would he be? He's smashed out of his gourd." He kissed her on the cheek. "Go to bed, I'll be back soon."

The Sunrise diner, a few hundred yards off the interstate exit, was usually crowded with truckers this time of night, but tonight there were only a few rigs parked in front. Brunetta drove around to the back. A dark Taurus parked at the far end of the parking lot flashed its lights. He pulled up alongside. The interior of the car was dark and he couldn't see who was behind the wheel.

None of this looked right to him, but he ignored the warning bells because he just wanted to solve these murders and put his life back on track. He got out of his car and warily approached the other car. The front passenger door swung open and Brunetta's eyes widened in surprise when he saw who was behind the wheel. "*You called me?*"

"Yes. Get in, Chief."

Brunetta slid into the front seat. "Do you really know who killed that couple?"

"Yes, I do."

Before Brunetta could ask his next question, a figure, who'd been hiding on the floor in the back seat, rose up and pumped three bullets into the back of Tony Brunetta's head.

A panicked Pete Delaney clutched the lifeline of the sailboat and watched the wind-whipped white caps with mounting apprehension. "It's getting kinda rough out here. Don't you think we should go in?"

There was a woman at the tiller, but it was nighttime and he couldn't make out her face. Her high-pitched laughter blended with the shrieking wind. "No, no. It's just getting good," she said.

Suddenly, a gust of wind howled through the rigging and the boat heeled hard to starboard. Delaney felt a splash of icy, green water trickle down his back and foamy green water spilled over the gunwale and into the cockpit. Terrified, he tried to claw his way up to the high side, but there was nothing to grab onto. The woman stood up and he was astonished to see how well she kept her balance on the pitching deck. Only it wasn't a *she* anymore. It was a *man* and he inexplicably began to push Delaney backward toward foaming sea. The boat heeled more and cold ocean water rushed inside the neck of his shirt. "*No!*" he gasped. "*What are you doing?*"

He tried to grab at the man, but the man eluded his grasp. Suddenly there was a large hunting knife in his hand. He slashed down at Delaney. The detective instinctively pulled back, lost his balance, and tumbled out of the boat into the black-green water. The suddenness of the cold water took his breath away and with every gasp he swallowed more water. He flailed his arms and kicked his feet to stay afloat, but it did no good. Slowly, he felt himself sinking into the cold blackness as the boat sailed away into the storm-tossed sea. "*No! No! No...!*"

"Pete, wake up..."

He felt pressure on his chest. He struggled against it, but it did no good. *He was drowning.* His eyes snapped open. He wasn't drowning. Rosemary was holding him down.

"Pete, wake up."

He bolted upright. Caught for a moment between the twilight world of sleep and intoxication, he was totally disoriented. Then he remembered the country club... dancing... Everything else was a blank. He saw the distressed look on her face and his stomach churned. *Jesus, what'd I do this time?*

"Pete, it's after four and Tony's not home."

Delaney swung his legs over the side of the bed and sat up. The room swayed sickeningly and he closed his eyes. The sour after-taste of scotch coated his tongue. "Where did he go?"

"Just after we got home, he got a call from someone who said he knows who committed those murders. He went to meet him and now it's after four and he still isn't home."

Delaney stood up unsteadily and grabbed the bed post for support.

"Rosemary, make some coffee. I'll be right out."

He went into the bathroom and splashed cold water on his face, hoping to shock his system back to sobriety. He lifted his head and froze, stunned at the apparition staring back at him in the mirror. Unable to look at himself any longer, he snapped off the light and stumbled out of the bathroom.

When he came into the kitchen, Rosemary had already poured the coffee. Delaney sat down gingerly and gratefully reached for the hot coffee mug. "Tell me everything. From the beginning."

By the time she finished, Delaney was worried, too, but for her sake he showed no emotion. He was having a hard time thinking clearly and he cursed himself for being drunk. "Rosemary, who's working at the station house now?"

"A dispatcher and two road deputies. I called earlier. Tony's not there and they haven't heard from him."

He picked up the phone and dialed the number.

"Haddley Falls Police Department," a sleepy female voice said on the other end of the line. "What's your emergency?"

"This is Pete Delaney, Chief Brunetta's friend."

"Yes, Mr. Delaney, what can I do for you?"

"Has Chief Brunetta been there any time tonight?"

"No, sir. I haven't seen him."

"What's your name?"

"Sally Dorn."

"Sally, I want you to do me a favor. The chief went to the Sunrise diner to interview someone and he hasn't come home. I'd like you to send a deputy out there to track him down."

"Yes, sir. I can do that."

"Good. And, Sally, call me back as soon as you find him."

Delaney hung up and sat across the table from Rosemary not knowing what to say. There was no point in trying to humor a woman who'd been a police officer's wife for over twenty years, but he tried anyway. "Rosemary, you know Tony's an experienced cop. He can take care of himself."

Rosemary silently stared into her coffee cup.

Fifteen minutes later the phone rang, startling the both of them. Delaney grabbed it, hoping to here Tony Brunetta's voice on the other end of the line and prepared to chew out his friend for scaring the crap out of his wife. "Delaney."

"It was the dispatcher. "Mr. Delaney, the deputy found the chief's car in the lot behind the diner. The deputy talked to the cook and the counterman. Neither one of them saw the chief."

Delaney turned away from Rosemary's intense gaze. "OK, Sally, I want you to do me another favor. Call Lieutenant Tucker and every off-duty deputy. Tell them to report to the station house immediately."

The dispatcher paused. "Sir, I don't have the authority to—"

"This is on the mayor's authority," Delaney lied. "Start making the calls."

"Gee, I don't know. Maybe I should call the mayor myself. Just to be sure..."

"Good idea, Sally. I'm sure he won't mind being awakened again."

"Oh.... well, then..."

"Just make the calls to the deputies. I'll be right in."

When he hung up, Rosemary grabbed his arm. "Pete, what's going on?"

"He wasn't there," he said, trying to sound unconcerned. "You know how he can lose track of time when he's on an investigation. We'll form a posse and round him up."

Rosemary chewed on her lower lip. "Where do you think he is?"

"If this informant has good information, Tony's probably driving around with him checking his story out."

"But why didn't he call?"

He pushed an errant strand of hair away from her eyes. "Because your husband is a good detective and he doesn't have time to call a worried wife."

He downed the rest of the coffee and headed for the door. "I'm going to the station house. When the deputies show up, I'll send them out to beat the bushes. When we find him, I'll sent him home and you can chew his ass out." He knew there was no point in telling her to go to bed. "I'll keep in touch, Rosemary."

By the time Delaney got to the station house, a handful of sleepy and puzzled deputies were milling around the muster room. A few minutes later, an angry Lieutenant Tucker arrived and went straight for Delaney. "What the *hell* do you think you're doing?"

Delaney motioned him into Brunetta's office. As soon as the door was closed, Tucker jabbed a finger in his face. "You don't work here, Delaney. You don't have the authority to call in the entire damn department."

"Keep your voice down." Delaney didn't want the others to hear them arguing. Besides, the lieutenant's loud voice was playing havoc with his thundering headache. "Listen," he said quietly, "Chief Brunetta is missing. We need every available man out there looking for him."

The big lieutenant, who hadn't forgotten the needling at the cove, screwed his face up in anger. "I don't have to do anything you—"

Delaney put his hands up in supplication. "Lou, let's not argue. This is important and—"

"Hey, big city detective, I don't give a good goddamn what you consider important—"

With a primal grunt Delaney grabbed the much larger man by the lapels and slammed him against the wall. "Listen to me, you stupid sonofabitch," he said through clenched teeth. "Tony Brunetta is missing and we're going to find him. What part of that don't you understand?"

The lieutenant didn't know what he was more afraid of—Delaney's strength that had him standing on his tiptoes or the hard, almost inhuman gleam in his eyes. "All right," he muttered.

Delaney shoved him away. "I want you to go outside and assign each deputy to a specific sector. Make sure someone checks out Crater Cove. He may have gone there."

Delaney stayed in Brunetta's office. He knew JT was out there and he didn't want her to see him in this condition. When the sullen lieutenant came back he said, "They're all out on the road."

"Good." Delaney rubbed his temples. The headache was making him nauseous. He looked up at Tucker with blood-shot eyes and exhaled slowly. "All we can do is wait."

The lieutenant folded his arms and silently glared at Delaney.

During the next hour the phone rang constantly as the deputies reported in. All the reports were the same: No sign of the chief.

Delaney went to the window and opened the blinds. In a few hours Main Street would be teeming with tourists haggling over clamshell collages, phony diving helmets, and genuine New England woodcarvings imported from Taiwan. But now, with the newly risen sun casting an orange glow on the row of empty stores across the street, it looked like a serene Edward Hopper painting.

    The phone rang and Lieutenant Tucker picked it up. Delaney turned away from the window and saw the color drain from the lieutenant's face. Slowly, he put the receiver down and looked up at Delaney. "That was Deputy Avery," he said, his voice cracking. "He found Chief Brunetta."

CHAPTER FOURTEEN

Delaney was out of the police cruiser and running before the vehicle came to a stop. As he neared the assembled deputies clustered at the far end of the beach, Clint Avery—confusion and horror etched in his face—emerged from the group.

"Mr. Delaney... I found him... there." He pointed toward a high dune not far from where Delaney and Brunetta had argued just three days earlier about interviewing the people in Sanborne castle.

Delaney climbed to the top of the dune and numbly stared down at the sheet-covered body. How many times had he seen that familiar sight? But this time the body lying under the sheet wasn't just another case number, another faceless victim. It was Tony Brunetta, his friend.

He slid down the side of the dune, remembering Tony's description of the mutilated bodies in the boat. Not knowing what to expect, he held his breath and gently pulled the sheet back. Tony was lying on his stomach. The sand encrusted face was turned to the left and his eyes, that had been so expressive in life, fixed vacantly on some invisible object.

Delaney exhaled sharply, grateful that at least there was no mutilation.

He observed caked blood in the hair at the back of his head and blood stains on the white collar of the shirt he'd worn to the country club dance. Forcing himself to forget for the moment who it was, he examined the area with his fingers and felt three small holes. He reached under the body and tugged Tony's Browning 9mm automatic out of its holster. He sniffed the barrel. No gunpowder smell. Then he popped the clip and counted the bullets. All the bullets were in the clip. The gun hadn't been fired.

He rested his hand on the body, intending to say a prayer, but he couldn't think of one. Instead, his mind flooded with a kaleidoscope of images: Tony laughing at one of Delaney's bad jokes, frowning the way he did when he read a witness statement, pensive as they discussed potential suspects, happily carrying a three-year-old Betty on his shoulders. The twenty year reprise—lasting just seconds—ended, jolting him back to reality.

He stood up slowly and turned to face the group of deputies standing on top of the dune looking down at him with expressions of sorrow and bewilderment.

"Clint, did you move him or touch him?"

"I... I felt for a pulse. Once I was sure he was..." His mouth worked awkwardly, unable to mouth the word "dead." "I put the sheet over him and called the station house."

Delaney nodded. "You did good."

Avery, uncertain about so many things in the past few days, exhaled in relief, grateful that he'd done the right thing.

Delaney turned to Lt. Tucker. "Lou, get some evidence tape. I want a fifty foot radius around the body cordoned off. No one is to come into this area except the coroner and a photographer. Line up your deputies and start a detailed search of the area, starting from the road on out to the end of the beach."

"What are they looking for?" Tucker asked hesitantly.

"Shell casings, blood stains, footprints. Anything nature didn't put here."

"Yes, sir." Still stunned by the sudden turn of events, it never occurred to Tucker to dispute Delaney's instructions.

"And send a car for Dr. Bynum. Bring him out here in handcuffs if you have to, but I want him here *now*." Delaney didn't want Tony laying on the cold damp sand anymore than was necessary.

Tucker nodded to a deputy, who hurried away.

Emotionally drained and blinded by a thundering headache, Delaney stared out at the water where just two nights ago he and JT had spent the night. More than anything, he wished he could go back to that night. In spite of the reason they were there, it had been the most peaceful night he'd spent in a very long time.

He rubbed his temples and the wishful thought passed. Tucker was still standing there, watching him tentatively.

"You got someone who can take pictures?" Delaney asked.

"Thompson, our accident investigator."

"As soon as Bynum is finished, have Thompson take pictures."

"He's never done a... a..."

"A homicide scene? I suspected as much. It's not much different from an accident scene. Just tell him to give us the works—establishing long shots, close-up of wounds, everything. Don't spare the film. Understand?"

Again, Tucker nodded. Delaney's manner was so authoritative that no one, including the lieutenant, thought to question his authority.

Delaney climbed slowly up the side of the dune. "Oh, one more thing. I'll need a ride."

"Where to?"

Delaney gazed out at the peaceful waters of the cove. "To Tony's house. I have to tell Rosemary."

Grateful that he wouldn't be stuck with that thankless job, the lieutenant turned to JT. "Bryce, take Mr. Delaney wherever he wants to go."

As Delaney and JT made their way back down the beach toward the parked cars, they were both silent. Finally, JT said, "Pete, I'm so sorry."

He looked into her green eyes now red-rimmed from crying. "Yeah, me, too"

"What are you going to do now?" she asked.

Delaney shrugged. Since getting the telephone call, he hadn't allowed his mind to wander that far into the future. "Help Rosemary with the arrangements. Then get the hell out of this godforsaken place."

"Who's going to handle the investigation?"

"The State Police."

"The mayor won't want them involved."

Delaney whirled on her. "Fuck the mayor," he snarled. "The only man who could have investigated these homicides is dead. Gardiner doesn't have a choice."

"What about you?"

Delaney heard the challenge in her tone and kept walking. For a brief moment, as he knelt beside Tony, that thought had occurred to him as well. But there were too many obstacles, not the least of which was that he was an outsider and there was no investigative support in the Haddley Falls Police Department. But there was another, much more important reason why he could not allow himself to conduct this investigation. He knew if he caught Tony's murderer he would kill him.

JT pulled the police cruiser into the driveway of Brunetta's saltbox house and Delaney got out. As he walked toward the front door, Rosemary opened it. On the short ride from the cove he'd been trying to think of the proper words. But how do you tell a woman that her husband is dead? Then he saw the desolate expression on her face and he knew he wouldn't have to. She was, after all, a cop's wife and had been preparing for this moment all her married life.

It took all of his courage to look her in the eye. "Rosemary, I'm... sorry."

She nodded imperceptibly, stiffly, as though any abrupt movement might shatter her fragile composure. He led her inside and they sat on the living room couch.

"How did he die?" she asked in a small voice.

"Rosemary, you don't want to—"

"Pete, I want to know."

"He was shot."

Her eyes bored into his as though she were trying to understand an extremely difficult concept. "Is he ... mutilated?"

"No, Rosemary. Nothing like that."

"Thank God." She twisted a handkerchief in her hand. "I have a lot to do. I'll have to call Betty... make arrangements…"

"Deputy Bryce is taking care of arrangements."

"Thank you." She took a deep breath. "Pete, I don't want to drag this out. I want the wake tonight and the burial tomorrow."

"Isn't that a little... fast?" He was thinking about the autopsy that would have to be performed first.

"No. I've always thought that long wakes were cruel to the survivors. Tony and I talked about it and we agreed. One night, no more."

"You'll bury him here?" He'd assumed she'd want to bring Tony back to New York.

"Yes. Tony loved the mountains and the ocean. He'll be happy here."

"Rosemary, there are an awful lot of cops back in the city who will want to come to the funeral. There won't be time to—"

"Pete, this is hard enough on me. I don't think I could handle seeing all his friends here. Not now." Her voice cracked. "They'll understand. Maybe when we get back to the city... later, they can have some kind of memorial service."

"The guys would like that."

She stood up and crossed her arms rigidly across her chest as though she were physically trying to hold herself together. "Pete, I'm glad you're here." She blinked rapidly. "It's good to have a friend..."

Delaney stood up and wrapped his arms around her. "Rosemary," he whispered into her ear, "it's okay to cry."

She buried her head in his chest and her grief-stricken sobs racked her thin body. He held her tightly, wishing he could absorb her sorrow into his own body.

Later, when several neighbors arrived to comfort her, he took the opportunity to call Lt. Tucker.

"Has the coroner been there?" he asked.

"Yeah. The chief's body is on the way to the morgue."

"Where's Bynum now?"

"Back at his office."

Delaney watched Bynum pour the coffee, relieved to see the doctor's hand sure and steady. There was no time to sober him up this time.

The doctor, studying Delaney with a practiced eye, handed him a cup. "I think you can use this."

"You're right. I'm hung over."

"You won't get a lecture from me." Bynum sat down behind a desk cluttered with folders. "I'm truly sorry about Chief Brunetta. He was a good man. I liked him."

"What do you know so far?"

The doctor took off his wire-rimmed glasses and rubbed the bridge of his nose. "It's only preliminary of course, but it appears that Chief Brunetta died of three gunshot wounds to the back of the head."

Delaney had figured as much. "Okay, Doc, let's go."

"Where?"

"To the morgue."

"Why?"

"So you can do the autopsy."

"Now? I'm just writing up the preliminary report. I—"

"Rosemary wants to hold the wake tonight and the burial tomorrow. You don't have a whole lot of time to do a thorough autopsy."

Arthur Bynum saw the cold, determination in Delaney's eyes and knew there was no point in arguing. "All right, let me get my bag."

At the hospital, Delaney went to wait in the autopsy room while Bynum went to prepare himself. He lit a cigarette to mask the odor of formaldehyde. In spite of the hundreds of autopsies he'd been to, the smell still made him queasy.

The windowless room was smaller than the ones he was used to, but it contained all the necessities. An austere stainless steel table equipped with water hose, drainage system, and a sink. A suspended scale, used to weigh body parts, hung from the ceiling. A tape recorder which Bynum would use to dictate his observations and a set of gleaming knives, saws and probes, were laid out on a rolling cart table.

Delaney wiped his perspiration-soaked palms on his pants legs. Against his better judgment—and Bynum's strenuous objection—he'd decided to witness the autopsy. The coroner had done a credible job on the other two victims, but Delaney wanted to make certain that Bynum didn't miss anything.

The door opened and the doctor, dressed in green scrubs, glanced at Delaney with disapproval. "I really don't think you should stay."

Delaney's eyes flicked to the cold stainless steel table. In a minute they would wheel in Tony Brunetta's sheet-shrouded body and place it on that table. He knew what would follow. After a careful physical examination of the body, Bynum would make the usual Y-incision from each armpit to the center of the sternum and then straight down to the pubic bone. Then would come the removal, examination, and weighing of each body organ.

Delaney felt a rushing in his ears and black spots floated before his eyes. He stood up abruptly, brushing against the hanging scale. "Maybe I'll wait outside," he muttered. At the door he turned, "Doc, I have to find out who murdered him. I'm counting on you to give me all the help you can."

Bynum nodded grimly and picked up the telephone. As Delaney closed the door behind him he heard Bynum ask the attendant to bring in the body.

While Bynum went about his task, Delaney kept vigil on a wooden bench out in the corridor. From time to time a doctor or a nurse passed, but Delaney, intently studying the highly polished tile floor, never looked up.

As he was crumpling an empty pack of cigarettes, a drawn Dr. Bynum came out. Delaney jumped up. "Well?"

The doctor slowly lowered himself onto the wooden bench. He'd been standing for over two hours and his back was giving him trouble. "As I suspected from my preliminary examination, Chief Brunetta died of three bullet wounds to the back of the head. They appear to be nine-millimeter, but I'll have to wait for—"

"Were there defense marks or bruises indicating a struggle before he was shot?"

"No. I looked very carefully."

Delaney sat down, puzzled. "Tony was too good a cop to let himself get shot without putting up a struggle."

"There were powder burns on his scalp. The gun was fired at very close range."

Delaney wearily pushed himself off the bench. "Okay, Doc. Thanks."

Bynum peered into Delaney's blood-shot eyes, distressed by the detective's unfocused look. "Are you all right, Mr. Delaney?"

"Yeah, I'm fine."

Bynum wasn't convinced. "I've been a doctor a lot longer than I've been a coroner. I suggest you get some rest."

"No time," Delaney said over his shoulder as he hurried down the hall.

CHAPTER FIFTEEN

Awakened before dawn by the soft hum of rain beating down on the trees, Pete Delaney had been sitting on the side porch, smoking cigarette after cigarette. He gazed out into the murky green forest of droopy limbed trees and tried not to think about Tony Brunetta.

He'd given up his bedroom to Betty and her husband Tom, who'd arrived last night. They'd all agreed that the children were too young to experience their grandfather's funeral and they'd remained behind with Tom's parents. Delaney was grateful that Betty had been such a tower of strength for her mother through the long vigil of the wake in which it seemed the entire town had come to pay its last respects. He was no good at this sort of thing. It had taken all of his courage just to stay in the chapel for the whole evening.

He'd always hated wakes. He considered it a barbaric custom and unnecessarily painful for the survivors. As a teenager he'd refused to attend them. But then he'd become a cop and discovered that wakes were an integral part of the police culture. In time he learned to tolerate the wakes of old retired cops because they followed a safe, predictable pattern. A group of cops would huddle in the back of the chapel, convincing each other that the deceased had been a great guy who had led a full life. Then, after a minimum, but respectable amount of time, they'd retreat to the nearest gin mill and use the man's death as an occasion to get drunk.

It was the wakes of young cops who had died in the line of duty that were the hardest. What did one say to young grieving widows? To dazed, bewildered children? Their husband and father had not had a full life. More often than not it had been taken away from him violently and unexpectedly by some brain-dead sonofabitch who would be out of prison before the cop's fatherless kids were out of high school.

Last night, after they'd come back from the wake, Rosemary had asked him if he would do the eulogy. He'd declined at first. What would he say? But she'd persisted and, against his better judgment, he finally agreed. Since then he'd been trying desperately to think of what he should say and he still hadn't come up with anything suitable. He didn't know how long he'd been staring out at the rain-soaked trees, but soon the clattering of dishes in the kitchen and the smell of fresh brewed coffee told him that the family was up and getting ready to face the second hardest day of their lives.

Delaney left right after breakfast, telling Rosemary he had something to do in town. By the time he got to the picture-postcard clapboard church, the steady rain had turned to a light drizzle. Huddled in the church doorway, Delaney watched police contingents from surrounding communities form up as part of the honor guard. Rosemary had been adamant about not notifying people back in the city about Tony's death, but he had managed to get one concession out of her. Now that concession pulled up in front of the church and lowered the window.

    Delaney dropped his cigarette in a puddle and leaned in the window. "Hi, Matty."

    Matthew Coyne, a beefy, red-headed detective climbed out of his car and pulled his trench coat collar up against the downpour. "Jesus, Pete, I can't believe Tony's gone."

    "I know. Thanks for coming on such short notice. You must have been on the road half the night."

    "I'm glad to do it. We all wanted to come."

    "I know, but Rosemary is taking it hard and she didn't want a big fuss. I had a hell of a time talking her into letting you come." He squinted up at the dark clouds scudding across the sky. "Is the rain gonna be a problem, Matty?"

    "No. It always rains at funerals." He glanced at his watch. "I'd better get ready."

    Ten minutes later, it was still drizzling as Delaney stood by the curb and watched the hearse and limo slowly approaching. The church was several blocks from the tourist section, but a few tourists, with cameras slung around their necks, had wandered into this part of town. A man, wearing a green plastic garbage bag as a makeshift raincoat, stopped to snap a photo of the three ranks of somber uniformed police officers standing in front of the church.

    That'll make a hell of a vacation photo for the old family album, Delaney thought as he stepped out into the rain to meet the limo.

    With Rosemary on one arm and Betty on the other, they climbed the steps and entered a church smelling of incense and candles. The priest, accompanied by two altar boys came out of the sacristy, signifying the beginning of the funeral mass.

Delaney turned away. He had no interest in the mass. He had long since given up the inane superstitions of the Catholic church and had become a confirmed atheist. To keep his mind off the reason for being there, he studied the stained glass windows behind the altar, the ceiling lighting fixtures, and the pious faces on statutes of saints he didn't recognize. He'd just turned his attention to a ceiling painting when he heard the priest mention his name.

"Mr. Delaney, a co-worker and personal friend of Chief Tony Brunetta, will now offer the eulogy."

As Delaney made his way to the pulpit, he still didn't know what he was going to say. He gazed out at the closely packed mosaic of faces and recognized a few people. The mayor and his wife were seated in the front row next to Jonathan Talbot and his wife. Even the sour-faced Whittier Sanborne III was there. Toward the back of the church, among a sea of uniforms, he spotted JT and Deputy Clint Avery.

He gripped the sides of the smooth wooden pulpit, overwhelmed by the futility of his task. How could he explain Tony Brunetta to these strangers? He swallowed hard, fighting back a lump in his throat.

"You knew Tony Brunetta as the Chief of the Haddley Falls Police Department," he began. "A man who kept the peace and saw to it that traffic flowed easily on Main Street. He responded to your concerns and allayed your fears. But you didn't... *know* him. Tony and I were sworn into the New York City Police Department on the same day almost twenty-one years ago. We were best men at each other's weddings. I'm Betty's godfather and he was godfather to my son..." He stopped. He was veering into his own personal life and he didn't want to go there.

He cleared his throat and continued. "We worked together for ten years, first as partners, later, as superior and subordinate. He was only ten years older than me, but in many ways he was the father and I was the son. Tony was a lot smarter than me, but he had a way of teaching me so I thought I'd figured it out for myself. Later, when he became my boss, it really tried our friendship." Delaney smiled sheepishly. "I shoot from the lip. Tony was a thinker, always looking for a way to finesse things. Most friendships would have fallen apart under that kind of pressure, but Tony wouldn't allow it. In the four years he was my boss, I don't recall him ever yelling at me or giving me a direct order. His style was much more subtle. He'd make a suggestion and explain why that suggestion should be acted upon. It was always so logical that I had no choice but to do as he suggested."

Consciously avoiding the flag-draped casket, Delaney's gaze focused on the large rosette-patterned stained-glass window at the back of the church while he collected his thoughts. He was about to get into something painful and he wasn't sure he wanted to go there. Then his eyes dropped to the coffin and he decided he owed it to his friend. "Tony invited me up here to take it easy and enjoy the sunshine. At least that's what he said. But that was just an excuse. He knew I was having a... a personal problem and he wanted me up here so we could talk about it. Over the years we've had a lot of such talks."

A recollection of the endless, late-night discussions in which Tony did his best to offer some explanation to help him reconcile his wife and son's untimely death flashed into his mind.

"But this time, things got in the way and... and well, we never did get around to having that talk."

The faces in front of him had become a blur. He wanted so much for them to know Tony the way that he did, but he couldn't find the proper words. He gripped the pulpit until his knuckles were white.

"I have a lot of regrets about Tony's death, but the biggest regret is that I never told him I loved him." He cleared his throat. "Men don't say things like that to each other. God knows, especially not homicide cops. But I did love him and I count myself fortunate that he was my friend."

As Delaney returned to his seat, Rosemary squeezed his hand and mouthed a thank you.

Outside, the rain had stopped, but a swirling mist drifted in the air. When the coffin, carried by six uniformed deputies reached the church door, Lt. Tucker called the honor guard to attention. As the coffin was carried down the steps, the colors dipped and the three ranks saluted smartly.

Suddenly, there was the muffled whirl of a lone bagpipe and Matthew Coyne, dressed in the full regalia of an Emerald Society Piper, appeared out of the mist, marching in solemn half-step.

By the time the last strains of *Amazing Grace* faded, the hearse, followed by a long line of cars, had vanished into the fog.

When they got back from the cemetery the rain had stopped and the sun had burned off the fog. In spite of the mayor's offer to let her stay on in the house for as long as she wanted, Rosemary had decided to go back to the city right away. The furniture would follow later. While Betty and Tom loaded the station wagon, Delaney and Rosemary sat on the porch talking about old times. The formal ritual of the wake and funeral had given her the time to accept the fact that Tony was gone, although she still couldn't mention his name without tears welling up in her eyes. They both knew that there would be difficult days ahead. But they left that unsaid. It would take time getting used to sleeping alone, celebrating holidays without him, and no longer sharing the hundreds of other little things that husbands and wives took for granted. And it wouldn't be any easier knowing that the cause of her unhappiness was an unknown murderer.

A half hour later, Betty, a younger version of her mother, came out on the porch. "Mom, we're ready anytime you are."

Rosemary stood up and took both Delaney's hands in hers. "Pete, that was a beautiful eulogy."

"It didn't say enough."

She squeezed his hands. "It was just fine." Her smile turned to concern. "Pete, come back to the city with us."

"I can't. There's a few things I have to wrap up first."

"What about your boss?"

"I told Weber I needed another day. Personally, I think he's relieved I'm staying up here." That was a lie.

When Weber told him he couldn't have another day, Delaney had hung up on him. "How about you? Are you sure you want to go back so soon?"

"Yes. Tony loved this place, but I never did. To tell you the truth, I could never understand why he loved the country and the outdoors so much. He grew up in the Bronx for goodness sake. Besides, I miss Betty and the kids. Now that he's gone, there's no reason for me to stay."

CHAPTER SIXTEEN

Pete Delaney stood in the driveway long after the station wagon, weighed down with both physical and emotional baggage, had departed. With so much to do he had not allowed himself to think of the full implications of Tony's death. But now, those threatening, accusing thoughts, which he'd willed out of his consciousness, began to gnaw at his troubled mind. "Not yet," he muttered, yanking the car door open. "I'm not ready for you bastards yet."

He drove back to the station house to find out how the investigation was progressing. Tucker told him that the search at the cove had uncovered nothing, not even a discarded beer can. He also told him that Gardiner, Talbot, and some others had been huddling in the mayor's office since the funeral, but he had no idea what the deliberations were about. To Delaney's surprise—considering how he'd treated the lieutenant—Tucker was courteous and deferential, but, still, it was awkward. Clearly, Delaney was an outsider and didn't belong there.

Unwilling to go back to the house, he killed time driving aimlessly around town. He parked by the pier for awhile and watched the fishermen. He looked for the old guy who wouldn't give him a beer, but he didn't see him. Then the ferry came in and a stream of cars and vacationers disembarked. When he saw their happy faces he felt an unreasonable anger welling up in him. He started the car and pulled away. He didn't want to be around cheerful people.

    A few minutes later, he found himself driving up the same hill he'd discovered the first day he'd arrived. He sat on the same rock wall, lit a cigarette, and thought of all that happened in the past five days. When the cigarette was finished, he ground it out with his shoe. The sun was sinking behind the mountains to the west and Delaney got back into his Honda. He'd put it off long enough. It was time to face the demons.

    The interior of Tony Brunetta's house was filled with an oppressive silent, as though it, too, were mourning the loss of its' occupants. He took the brand new bottle of scotch out of the bag and held it up to the light to study the amber liquid. Would it be enough to fortify him from what lay ahead? He prayed it would. He didn't want to face the demons alone.

    As he cracked the cap, he heard the haunting call of a whippoorwill—the same bird he'd heard the first night he'd been out on the porch with Tony. It sounded close. Curious to see what it looked like, he put the bottle down on the kitchen table and went out to the porch to investigate. The rain had churned up a pleasant, musty smell of fresh earth and grass. He peered out into the wet green canopy, but saw nothing. Then he sat down, lit a cigarette, and waited for the bird to sing again. To the soul-weary Delaney, the porch and the sounds of chirping crickets and frogs, was an oasis of tranquility and peace.

This was going to be a good place to end it all. He propped his feet up on the couch, put his head back, and soon the tension and anger of the last twenty-four hours was drained away by the anesthetizing power of sleep.

JT Bryce had been sitting in her parked cruiser across the street from the station house when Delaney had pulled up earlier in the day. Even from a distance she could see that he looked worse than he did at the funeral. She'd called out to him, but he was preoccupied and didn't hear her as he hurried into the building.

Her heart went out to this strange man. From the way he'd struggled through the eulogy, it was clear he was a man who did his best to conceal his emotions. But it was also clear that the last two days had been a strain on him. She'd planned to wait around and speak to him when he came out, but the dispatcher gave her an assignment and she had to leave. By the time she returned to the station house, he was gone.

After her shift she drove past Brunetta's house, but it was locked up and Delaney's car wasn't in the driveway. Against her better judgment she made a tour of the bars in town, dreading that she would find him drunk and disorderly. But he wasn't in any of them and no one had seen him. She was relieved that he hadn't chosen to drown his sorrows, but, still, she was concerned. *Where was he?* In his state of mind, she knew he shouldn't be alone. Then she became angry with herself. *He's a grown man,* she told herself, *and certainly no concern of yours.*

Deciding that he'd probably driven back to the city, she went home, disappointed that he hadn't said goodbye. After a dinner of leftover pasta with broccoli, she tried to watch a movie on cable, but she was too distracted to follow the clichéd plot. She turned off the TV and made herself a cup of tea. As she idly dunked the tea bag, she tried to sort out her impressions of the enigmatic Pete Delaney.

Unlike most men she'd met, he wasn't conceited. If anything, he was too self-effacing. He had a good sense of humor, even if it was a bit too macabre for her tastes. He was sensitive, but he did his best to hide that trait. He was a little overweight, losing his hair, and he drank too much. Yet, there was something about him that she found intriguing.

She struggled to find the one word that would describe him and came up with the word *adrift*. Then, she remembered a morning a long time ago. She was motoring though the harbor and had come across a classic Hinkley sloop that had run aground after slipping her moorings. Seeing the graceful boat, designed for wind and speed, helplessly impaled on those rocks, she'd been seized with a profound sadness. And that, she decided, was what Pete Delaney was: A fine vessel adrift, heading for a rocky shoreline. So unlike Tony Brunetta.

Fondly, she recalled her job interview with Tony. She'd been nervous because she'd heard grumblings about the new chief. They were saying he was a tough New York City detective bent on turning a sleepy small town police department into a real police force. They also said there had never been a female police officer in the history of the Haddley Falls Police Department.

When she went into his office for the interview she didn't know what to expect, but she was pleasantly surprised by a gentle and courteous Tony Brunetta. After a half-hour of answering off-hand, friendly questions, which she didn't realize had been carefully orchestrated to establish her background and beliefs, she stammered," Chief, you might not think a woman can do the job... but I just want you to know I can."

Brunetta's expressive eyes twinkled. "Ms. Bryce, I have no trouble hiring you because you're a woman. I know you're in better physical condition than most of my deputies, and you're probably a hell of a lot smarter, too." He stood up and offered his hand. "Welcome to the Haddley Falls Police Department."

Sitting in the kitchen, JT blinked away tears. "Goddamn it," she said to the cold cup of tea, "Chief Brunetta deserves better than Chad Perrault."

The kitchen clock said eleven-fifteen. She was sure he was halfway back to the city, but she decided to make one more pass by Brunetta's house anyway.

Delaney heard a voice. He sat up and rubbed his stiff neck. He didn't know how long he'd been dozing, but it was completely dark and the trees had fused into an impenetrable black mass.

"*Hello.* Anybody home?"

He went into the living room and saw JT peering through the screen door. He switched on a lamp. "Yeah. Come in."

Her eyes flicked to the bottle on the table and then to him. He looked sleepy, but she was relieved to see that he didn't appear to be drunk. "I saw your car in the driveway. You staying the night?"

"Yeah. You want a drink?"

"Is there coffee?"

Delaney scratched his chin. "That's not what I had in mind. There's some left in the pot, but it's been there all day."

"That's okay. That's the way mine tastes all the time."

He sat at the table and watched her move about the kitchen. She was wearing tan slacks, a white silk blouse, and her long blonde hair was done up in a French twist. The overall impression was one of casual elegance. Even so, she looked perfectly at home in the kitchen.

She poured him a cup and placed it in front of him. "Major Perrault was in the station house this afternoon snooping around."

Delaney had only gotten a glimpse of Perrault when he'd left Tony's office that day, but even from a distance, he didn't like his looks. He wasn't happy at the thought of that fat clown investigating his friend's murder. But he pushed the thought to the back of his mind. "Does he have the case officially?"

"No. The town is in chaos. Gardiner, Talbot, Eleanor Haddley and some others have been huddling all day. I guess they can't decide what to do."

"What's to decide? They gotta call in the State Police."

JT slammed her cup down, splashing coffee on the table. "Tony Brunetta deserves better than that. You and I both know that Perrault isn't coming here to investigate the Chief's murder. His real job is to dig up as much dirt as he can to embarrass Talbot and the town. He doesn't give a good goddamn about Tony Brunetta or those two victims."

Delaney wiped up the spill with a napkin, surprised at the vehemence in her tone. "You're probably right, but that's the way it is."

"Pete, why are you running away from this?"

"Because I can't deal with it anymore," he snapped. Unable to face her accusing stare, he got up and stood at the back door. A puff of air came through the screen door and he took a deep breath: *fresh air*. He thought of Tony and exhaled slowly. "I want out of homicide work."

"I thought you loved it."

"Not anymore. I should have realized it a couple of months ago, after that... after my last case. But I tend to drown my doubts in booze. That's what Tony brought me up here to tell me. I finally figured it out last night."

Delaney stood facing the screen door and she couldn't see his face. She wasn't sure she should continue to probe, but she had to know. "Pete," she said gently. "Tell me about your last case."

Delaney turned around and the grief and pain in his eyes startled her. He leaned up against the door jamb and, in an unemotional, monotone voice said, "Shantelle McPherson, a sixteen-year-old kid, gave birth to a five pound four-ounce boy. There was some question as to who the father was, although the mother's live-in boyfriend topped the list of usual suspects. Shantelle was home alone when she went into labor and gave birth in the bathroom. She didn't want the kid, but she didn't know what to do with him. She tried flushing him down the toilet, but his head was too big and he got stuck. Then Shantelle hit upon a novel idea. She put the kid in the microwave and turned it on high." Delaney exhaled slowly. "Do you know what a microwave does to a human skull?"

"Yes," she said softly. Once she'd microwaved an egg and had forgotten to put pin holes in it. When the internal pressure built up, the egg exploded.

Delaney turned away to look out the door. "So I'm interviewing this dimwitted bitch and she can't understand what all the fuss is about. Suddenly, I find myself plotting ways to kill her. I figure I'll throw her out the window and say she jumped, but there's another detective with me. While I'm thinking of a way to get him out of the room, the squad commander and a couple of other detectives come in and the moment passed."

He went to the stove, refilled his cup, and continued in the same monotone. Now that he'd started, he couldn't stop. "Later, one of the guys in the squad made a sick joke about cooking time for infants and I went ballistic. It took three men, including my boss, to pull me off." Delaney sat down heavily. "And so that's why I can't investigate Tony's murder."

"Why not?"

"Because if I find the guy who killed Tony, I will kill him."

JT was taken aback by the utter calmness in his tone. But she had no doubt that he would do just that. She'd come here to talk him into taking over the investigation, but now that was clearly out of the question. "I'm...sorry." It was inadequate, she knew, but she didn't know what else to say. "I guess I'll be going."

At the door, she said, "Are you going to be OK tonight?" They both knew she was talking about the bottle of scotch.

"Yeah, I'll be fine."

She put her hand out. "Well, I guess I won't be seeing you anymore, so I'll say goodbye now."

He took her hand and looked into her soft emerald eyes. Since Kitty's death, he'd avoided emotional involvement with women. In his relationships with women it was nothing more than slam, bam, thank you ma'am. But from the first moment he'd laid eyes on JT, he'd felt stirrings that he'd thought were gone forever. Maybe it was her passion for life—something he'd lost along the way. Or maybe it was because she possessed a secret about life and he wanted to know what it was so he, too, could be part of her free, open world. He wanted to tell her all these things, but he didn't know how. "It's too bad you never got a chance to teach me how to sail," he said.

"Yeah, too bad. Goodnight, Pete."

"Goodnight, JT."

After she left he poured a tumbler of scotch and went back to the porch. The first drink burned going down, but by the time he was on his fifth drink, he could have been drinking water. The demons that had been patiently lurking in the dark recesses of his mind awaiting their chance, crawled into his consciousness and the accusations began. *"You are responsible for Tony's death,"* one reproving voice whispered. *"If you hadn't been drunk"*—another added—*"you'd have gone with him and he'd be alive today."*

"No!" Delaney jumped up and hurled the glass of scotch into the darkness. "No," he said again, his voice cracking. He slumped against a porch pillar. "Tony... I'm sorry, buddy. I let you down." With eyes blinded by tears he peered out into the darkness, barely breathing, but intently listening, as though he might

receive a benediction from the grave. But the only sound he heard was the incessant cacophony of crickets and tree frogs.

He turned abruptly and walked into the house. Moments later, he reappeared with a fresh glass, the bottle of scotch, and his Glock 20. He sat down and placed everything carefully on the table next to him.

For the next hour he drank, eyeing the gun, waiting for the alcohol to give him the courage to pick it up

"*What are you waiting for?*" a chorus of rebuking voices whispered out of the darkness. "*Just do it.*"

Delaney had long ago stopped being a religious man. In his teenage years his faith had begun to falter and by the time he became a homicide detective, what little faith he had left withered in the face of man's inhumanity to man. For a long time he'd tried to make some sense of murder, but he found no answers. Eventually, to protect his own sanity, he developed his own cynical philosophy: *Life is a pinball machine and man is nothing more than a pinball, randomly bouncing from cushion to cushion until he finally disappears down a hole.*

Sometime around three in the morning, he tried to decide which would be the most efficient way to blow his brains out. He could put the gun in his mouth, but he'd have to be careful about the angle of the barrel. He'd seen men who had tried to die that way, but aimed too low and succeeded only in blowing out the back of their throats. He discarded the idea of shooting himself in the temple because he'd seen too many brain-dead survivors of that technique. *And they say suicide is the easy way out.*

He picked up the automatic and tested the weight in his hand, marveling that such a small piece of metal had the power to end the world. He stared at the automatic for a long time, then, suddenly and inexplicably, he began to weep. As the tears coursed down his cheeks, another voice whispered in his ear. But it wasn't the accusing, tormenting voices that had been denouncing him all night, goading him to pull the trigger. This was a gentle voice, a voice of redemption, and it said: *You can't die yet. You have work to do.* And as soon as he heard that voice he knew what it was that he had to do. *He had to find Tony's murderer.*

It was just after dawn by the time he concluded his long, painful journey back from despair. The dawn had silenced the crickets and frogs. In their place, chirping birds darted through the tree limbs in search of breakfast. Above the tree line a soft pink sky promised another beautiful day.

He picked up the Glock and stuffed it in his pocket. In the light of day, the thought of taking his own life seemed like an obscene nightmare that had happened a long, long time ago. He went into the kitchen and dialed JT's number. While the phone rang, he unscrewed the top of the bottle and watched what was left of the scotch whirlpool down the drain.

"Hello," a sleepy voice said.

"I wake you? I thought you'd be up hours ago running or pumping iron."

The voice came awake. "I don't do that *every* morning."

"I'm staying."

There was a long pause on the line. "Are you sure?"

He heard the uncertainty in her voice. "Last night you were practically begging me to stay."

"I know, but—"

"Don't pay any attention to what I said last night. The bottom line is I'm the only one who can find Tony's murderer."

She was encouraged by the note of purpose in his voice. But there were obstacles yet to be overcome. "Have you spoken to the mayor?"

"No. You're the first to know."

"How are you going to get him to agree?"

"I'll think of something."

"You'd better think of something good. Gardiner doesn't like you."

"Hey, Bryce, how come you didn't bring up these problems last night?"

"I guess I didn't want to discourage you."

"Thanks a lot. Go back to sleep. I'll keep you posted."

CHAPTER SEVENTEEN

The next call Delaney made was to Lt. Harlan Weber. "Lou, Pete Delaney."

"Where are you, Pete?"

Delaney heard the edge of hostility in the lieutenant's voice. "I'm still in Haddley Falls."

"You'd better get going. I told you I wanted to talk to you this afternoon."

"I need more time, Lou."

"No."

"I have plenty of vacation left. I just want to stay up here a couple more days so I can help the cops get Tony's investigation rolling."

"You work for the NYPD, not the Mayberry PD. They can handle it without your help."

"It's not that simple. There's a lot of political bullshit going on and—"

"That's not your concern. Get your ass back here forthwith."

Delaney squeezed the phone, wishing it was Weber's neck. "Lou, I need five days—"

"Look, I told Brunetta I'd give him five days to straighten you out. I'm sorry the way things turned out, but I want you back here. End of discussion."

"I can't leave now," Delaney said through clenched teeth.

Weber exhaled sharply. "I'm giving you a direct order. You be in my office at oh-eight hundred hours tomorrow morning or you're suspended."

Delaney slammed the telephone down. It was time for Plan B.

He rummaged through Brunetta's desk and found an old NYPD telephone directory. He dialed the number for the Pension Section and asked to speak to a supervisor.

"Sgt. Taylor here. What can I do for you, detective?"

"I want to retire, Sarge."

"OK. Come on down and start the paperwork."

"No, I mean I want to retire right now."

"You mean right now this minute?"

"Yep."

There was a moment of silence on the line, then the sergeant said, "I don't think you can do that."

"It's a long story. I'm up in New England and I can't come back to the city. Tell you what I'll do. I'll fax my resignation letter to you."

"I think you're making a big mistake."

"Let me worry about that."

He hung up without telling the sergeant that he had no intention of retiring. This was just an end-run around Weber. With his accumulated vacation and leave time, he had seventy days before his retirement would become official, more than enough time to close out this investigation.

His next call was to Mayor Royce Gardiner.

At exactly eleven o'clock Pete Delaney walked into the conference room of Gardiner, Rice & Mayhew, Attorneys at law. As he'd requested, Whittier Sanborne, Jonathan Talbot, and Eleanor Haddley were there.

Gardiner, seated at the head of the conference table, motioned Delaney into a seat. "Mr. Delaney, on behalf of the town may I once again convey our deepest sympathies and thanks to you for your generous time and efforts on our behalf."

"I didn't come for your thanks."

Whittier Sanborne, still smarting from Delaney's invasion of his home, said, "Exactly why *are* you here?"

"I want Tony's job."

For an instant there was a stunned silence, then Eleanor clapped her hands. "I think that's a splendid idea."

Gardiner, regaining his composure, sputtered, "Eleanor, it certainly is not."

"You have no choice," Delaney pointed out. "You don't want Perrault poking through your dirty laundry and there's no time to look for another police chief. Even if you found one, I doubt anyone in his right mind would take the job with three open homicides—one of them his predecessor. So the choice comes down to me and Perrault and there's no contest. I'm the more experienced investigator, I already know a lot about the cases. I have the most incentive to find the killer, and best of all"—he allowed himself a smile—"I'm apolitical."

Talbot, who had been listening quietly, said, "Mr. Delaney, I'm sure you can appreciate that your request has caught us completely by surprise."

"Yeah. I hear you held meetings here all day yesterday. Did you come up with a solution?"

Sanborne rubbed his wire rimmed glasses furiously. "What we discussed in the privacy of these chambers is confidential and certainly none of your business."

Talbot put a restraining hand on Sanborne's arm. "Now, Whit, I'm sure Mr. Delaney didn't intend to pry. We'd like a little time to consider your request, Mr. Delaney."

"Well, he has my vote," Eleanor said smacking the highly polished desk with the flat of her hand.

"For heaven's sake, Eleanor," a red-faced Sanborne sputtered, "there are procedures to follow."

Talbot gave Sanborne's arm a cautioning squeeze. "Mr. Delaney, would you let us know where we can we get in touch with you later today?"

Delaney stood up. "That won't be necessary. I'll wait outside."

"Well, I'm afraid these deliberation may take some time."

Delaney decided it was time to bluff these rich country bumpkins into making a quick decision. "Just before I came over here, I was on the phone with a producer from *Behind the Scene.*"

The color drained from Royce Gardiner's pink cheeks. *Behind the Scene* was a cheesy, but wildly popular national TV show that had turned in-your-face ambush journalism into an art form. "My God, you... you didn't..."

"No, I didn't. She called to clarify a couple of facts about a messy society murder I handled last year. You ever wonder how hard it must be for those producers to come up with all those interesting stories week after week?" Delaney asked the would be secretary of commerce.

"I've never given it a thought." Talbot answered coolly, but Delaney saw that his expression had suddenly become guarded.

"She told me they're always on the prowl for a story," he continued. "She said murder and politics drive the ratings right through the roof. People can't get enough of that kind of stuff." He stood up, satisfied he's planted the hook. "I'll be outside."

As soon as the door closed, Sanborne slammed his fist on the table. "Absolutely not. I will not have that... blackmailing Neanderthal as the chief of police in this town. I'd rather have the State Police in here than that—"

"Easy, Whit," Talbot said. "Don't let your personal animosity cloud your judgment."

"Jonathan, the man is a fool," Sanborne shouted. "Have you forgotten that spectacle at the club?"

"Granted, the man is a buffoon," Gardiner said in a conciliatory tone, "but we agreed that we don't want the governor's hatchet men coming in here."

"I know everyone's concerned about the impact of adverse publicity," Sanborne said. "But how can you people seriously consider hiring this incompetent man?"

Talbot flicked the ash off his cigar. "Whit. I think you're being unreasonable. Everyone in this room, including you, has a vested interest in the wellbeing of this town. May I remind you that we all have extensive financial interests here. Through my contacts I've been able to keep the unfortunate business of these homicides out of the local newspapers, but how long can that go on? Sooner or later some enterprising bottom feeding reporter or, God forbid, someone from a program like that ghastly show *Behind the Scene* will hear about these murders and we will be on every program from *Dateline* to *Entertainment Tonight*."

"My God," Gardiner muttered, "Haddley Falls would become an instant ghost town."

"Exactly," Talbot said, crushing his cigar in an ashtray. "Who would want to spend their vacation in a town where three people have been murdered?" He patted Sanborne's arm. "Of course I'd rather have someone more suitable," he said in a mollifying tone. "But the detective has a point. Not only don't we have time to search for another police chief, it's highly doubtful that we could find someone who would take the job under these circumstances. We have to face the facts. Haddley Falls is a ticking time bomb and we must defuse it immediately."

Gardiner drummed his manicured fingernail on the polished conference table. "I think we should take a vote. Whit?"

Sanborne scowled. "Absolutely not."
"Eleanor?"
"Absolutely yes."
"Jonathan?"
"A very reluctant yes. And you, Royce?"
"I, too, reluctantly vote yes. All right. The vote is three to one. We will offer Mr. Delaney the position."

Delaney was summoned back into the room.

"We've considered your offer," Gardiner said, "and we're prepared to accept it. Of course there are a few details that must be worked out."

"Such as?"

"Well, salary—"

"Doesn't matter."

"Oh." Gardiner didn't know what to make of that. He'd never heard anyone say money didn't matter. "When will you be prepared to start?"

"Right now."

Gardiner tugged at his mustache. This was all highly unusual and his legal mind was reeling. He was used to protracted negotiations and written contracts. "Very well," he said with a shrug. "Then I guess you're hired."

As they started to get up, Delaney said, "Before you go, there are a few ground rules I'd like to cover." They all sat back down slowly, glancing uneasily at each other.

"Anyone ever hear the term 'good cop, bad cop?'"

"Yes, I have," Eleanor said excitedly. "I believe it's when one detective plays the good cop in order to gain the suspect's confidence and the other detective plays the bad cop in order to frighten the suspect into telling the truth."

"That's it exactly, Eleanor. When Tony Brunetta and I were partners, guess which part I played?"

Gardiner groaned.

"Sorry. I know there are a lot of influential people in this town, present company included. I'll do my best not to ruffle any feathers, but three people are dead and no one"—he looked directly at Sanborne—"is going to interfere with me. I expect you to cooperate with me fully, and I expect you all to run interference if anyone outside this room tries to get in my way. Agreed?"

They nodded, ruefully wondering what kind of man they'd unleashed.

Now that he saw he had their undivided attention, he said, "Mr. Sanborne, I'll want to interview you, your son, and anyone else who was in the house the night of the murders. What would be a good time this afternoon?"

"*This* afternoon?"

"Yes, sir."

"Stop stalling, Whit," Talbot said. "Give the man a time."

"Oh, very well. Three o'clock," Sanborne muttered.

Delaney smiled. He'd cleared his first obstacle. As he headed for the door, he said over his shoulder, "I'm on my way to the station house. Maybe someone should call ahead and break the news to Lt. Tucker."

As Delaney was driving to the police station, he saw JT and Clint Avery in a police cruiser in front of him. He pulled up beside them at a light.

"You are going to be my investigators," he said to the two shocked deputies.

JT grinned. "You took the job?"

"Yeah."

"Pete, I'm so glad you did. I'm sure—"

"Stuff the congratulations. I selected you two because you're the best in the department. God knows that's not saying much. You're going to have to learn fast and it's going to require all your time. You can forget about your personal lives until this is over. Anyone have a problem with that say so now."

"I have no problem," JT said, taken aback by his abruptness.

"No problem for me," Clint said. "I don't have a life."

When Delaney walked into the station house the receptionist who'd been gruff with him that first day looked up and smiled. "Welcome to the Haddley Falls Police Department, Chief Delaney."

Chief? He thought. I've spent my entire career busting the balls of bosses and now I'm one of them. God help me. Having a title before his name reminded him of the enormity of what he was undertaking. Now that he'd talked them into giving him the job, he wondered if he was up to it.

"Major Perrault is in Chief Brun— I mean *your* office," the receptionist said.

"What's he doing there?"

"I don't know, sir."

Major Chad Perrault was sitting behind Tony's desk when Delaney came in. Startled by the sudden intrusion, he tossed the report he was reading back in the in-basket.

"Get out of that chair," Delaney said evenly.

Getting caught snooping had flustered Perrault, but he wasn't about to be intimidated by this stranger. "Who the hell are you?" he snapped.

Delaney slammed the door behind him. "I'm not going to tell you again, fatso."

Perrault rose to his six-foot four-inch height and tucked his stomach into his sagging trousers. "I'm up. Now who the hell are you?"

"Pete Delaney, the new chief."

Perrault's pig-eyes widened. "They gave *you* the job?"

Delaney grinned. "That seems to be everyone's reaction."

The major recovered from his shock and stuck his beefy hand out. "Major Chad Perrault, the head of the State Police Homicide Bureau."

Delaney ignored the extended hand. "What are you doing here?"

Perrault pulled his hand back and scratched his belly. "I was waiting to talk to Lt. Tucker, but I guess you're the man in charge now."

"You still haven't told me what you're doing here."

"I've come to offer my help."

You made Chief Brunetta the same offer. What'd he tell you?"

"He said he was going to handle it himself."

"Tony was being too kind. What he meant was he didn't need a fat-assed political hack like you fucking up his investigation. I agree."

Perrault's moon face reddened. No one talked to him like that. He made a menacing move toward Delaney, but stopped when he noticed that Delaney hadn't blinked. He'd learned that men who were afraid blinked. The others you left alone. He jabbed a thick finger at Delaney. "You're another smart-assed big city detective who thinks he knows everything. But you're gonna find that you ain't as smart as you think."

Delaney slid behind his desk. "Don't let the door hit you in the ass on the way out."

Perrault slammed the door so hard, a photograph of Mayor Gardiner's stern face popped off the wall.

Delaney examined the contents of the in-basket. When he was satisfied that Perrault hadn't seen anything important, he buzzed the receptionist. "Would you ask Sergeant— Who is the clerical sergeant?"

"Charlie Tuttle. Right away, Chief."

An apprehensive Charlie Tuttle came in. He'd heard the door slam, saw the big major stomp out of the building, and figured he was in trouble. "You wanted to see me, Chief?"

Delaney motioned the sergeant into a chair. "Charlie, how long have you been with this department?"

"Four years, sir. Before that, I did twenty-five years with the Farnham PD."

"Why'd you leave?"

Tuttle tried a smile. I was getting too old for that job. Farnham can be a rough town."

"Charlie, did you let Major Perrault into my office?"

"Well, no... that is..." Tuttle shrugged. "He kinda said he'd wait there and... I guess I let him."

Delaney was pleased that the sergeant didn't try to bullshit him. "In the future, no one comes in to my office unless I say so."

"Yes, sir," Tuttle said, relieved that he was getting off so lightly with the new chief.

"Would you ask Lt. Tucker to step in here?"

As Charlie turned, he realized that he had a manila envelope in his hand. "Oh, I almost forgot. The forensic report from the State Police. It came in yesterday, but I didn't know what to do with it." He tossed it in the in basket.

A minute later, Tucker came in. The diffidence and politeness he'd shown yesterday was gone, replaced with icy hostility. Apparently, he'd heard the bad news. He stood in front of the desk and crossed his arms. "You wanted to see me?"

Delaney noted that Tucker couldn't bring himself to use the word "chief." He almost felt sorry for the poor bastard. He'd been passed over for the chief's job twice in one year. "Tucker, let's get something straight right up front. I'm the chief and you're not. Can you live with that? Yes or no?"

Surprised by Delaney's bluntness, he muttered a yes.

"Good. Here's my game plan. I took this job to solve three murders and then I'm outta here. In the meantime, I have a problem. I don't know diddly squat about being a police chief and I don't want to. So you're gonna run the day to day operations while I investigate these murders. Think you can handle that?"

Some of the wariness went out of Tucker's face. He'd come in here expecting to be fired. "Sure, I can handle that."

"Fair enough. You do a good job and when the time comes for me to leave, I'll put in a good word for you with the mayor."

Tucker nodded cautiously.

"Your first assignment will be to prepare a memo to everyone in the department reminding them that everything they do, see, or hear, is strictly confidential. They will talk to no one outside this department about police business without my permission. Word it anyway you want, but the bottom line is that anyone who violates that confidentiality will be shit-canned forthwith."

"I'll start on the memo right now." At the door he turned and said, "Welcome, aboard, Chief."

"Yeah, thanks, Walt.

When he was alone, Delaney sat back, cautiously pleased with himself. He was beginning to lose some of his buyer's remorse. In his first fifteen minutes he'd set the tone on how he wanted the department to run and it looked as though Tucker would be able to handle his end of the bargain.

He retrieved the forensic report out of his in basket and hefted the thick report in his hands and grunted. In his experience the thicker the report, the less useful information it contained. He tore open the envelope and flipped past the tests and procedures performed, and went directly to the fingerprint section of the report. His eyes locked on two sentences: *A thorough examination of the crime scene revealed no visible prints. An attempt was made to locate latent prints with negative results.*

"Sonofabitch!" He threw the report on the desk in disgust. No prints my ass. What about the murdered couple? Did they walk around their boat with rubber gloves on? He knew there could be only two explanations for no prints. Incompetence or sabotage. He hoped it was the former. An incompetent technician could be brought back to do the job right, but it was another matter if someone had deliberately screwed up the crime scene. He thought of Major Perrault.

He buzzed his clerical sergeant. "Charlie, find Clint Avery."

A minute later, the deputy called. "Yes, Chief?"

"Did the state forensic technician print you and Chief Brunetta?"

"I don't know about the chief, but no one printed me."

"That's what I thought."

Delaney had his answer. The technician wasn't incompetent. He never intended to find prints.

"Oh, by the way, Chief, I got the DOBs of Jeff Wallace and Madeline like you asked."

"Good. Get in here and run a record check."

While he was waiting for Avery, Delaney checked the title page of the forensic report and called Corporal Kyle Morgan, the State Police Crime Scene Unit technician who had conducted the investigation. The technician sounded young and inexperienced. Perfect for what Delaney had in mind. After a few pleasantries, Delaney got to the point of the conversation.

"Corporal Morgan, maybe you could do me a favor. I'd like to talk to you about how you guys handle crime scenes up here. I'm from New York and this is all new to me. How about we have lunch tomorrow?"

Morgan hesitated. "Gee, I don't think so, Chief. I'm real busy and—"

"Hey, I know. I'll bet they run you guys ragged. All I'm asking is an hour of your time."

"I don't think I can—"

"Mrs. Murphy's Chowder House on Main. Know where it is?"

"Yeah, but—"

"Good. I'll see you there at noon. Bring your appetite."

JT and Clint silently watched a disappointed Delaney read Jeff Wallace's rap sheet. The physical therapist had been arrested only once for possession of cocaine. Delaney had hoped to find a long list of arrest for violent crimes. Still, he reminded himself, a lot of ritualistic murderers had no prior records. You gotta start some place.

"What do you think, Chief?" Clint asked.

"Not good. I was hoping to see a pattern of violence." He didn't tell them, but the news wasn't all bad. He was certain that Sanborne didn't know about the drug arrest and he planned to use the rap sheet as leverage to gain the physical therapist's cooperation.

Clint read the printout. "Does this mean he didn't do it?"

"No, but it's not encouraging and I can use all the encouragement I can get right now."

"Any other suspects?" JT asked.

"Just Andrew."

Clint's eyes widened. "Wow! Mr. Sanborne's retarded son?"

"Let's get something straight right now. I don't give a shit about names or blood lines. We will follow this investigation wherever it leads us."

"Why do you suspect him?" JT asked.

"Opportunity for one thing. The cove's in his backyard."

"You think he's capable?"

"He's locked up in that big house for a reason. And he's got a big muscle-bound minder in the form of Jeff Wallace to contain him. Maybe Andrew's a homicidal maniac. Maybe he howls at the moon. You ever see him?"

JT shook her head.

"But Mr. Sanborne..."

Delaney held up his hands. "Clint," he cautioned, "don't say it again."

CHAPTER EIGHTEEN

Delaney's second visit to Sanborne castle was much more agreeable. This time Madeleine Crown invited him in with a smile, albeit a nervous one. Even the sullen Jeff Wallace was appropriately polite, which Delaney attributed to the presence of his grim-faced employer hovering in the background.

Delaney interviewed Madeleine first. She was the most vulnerable of the three and he hoped to pump her for some useful background information. In the solitude of Sanborne's study—a comfortable, dark-paneled room containing more books than he'd ever see outside of a public library—Delaney began with some general questions to make her feel at ease. Then he got down to specifics.

"Madeleine, how long have you worked for Mr. Sanborne?"

"Eighteen months."

Delaney's eye's swept the well-appointed room. "I can see why you'd rather teach here," he said out of the side of his mouth. "It sure beats the hell out of PS 21."

She smiled shyly. "And the money's a lot better, too."

Delaney was pleased by her response. It showed she trusted him. In his experience he'd learned that people were reluctant to talk to a stranger about money. "What do you teach him?"

"Not very much I'm afraid. Chronologically, Andrew is twenty years-old, but mentally, at least in some areas, he's five. What I try to do is stimulate his brain with simple games."

"That's gotta be tedious."

She rolled her eyes. "It is, unless the game has something to do with World War II."

"Huh?"

"Andrew has an astonishing knowledge of that war."

"How can that be? You said—"

"There's a term for it. They used to call people like Andrew 'idiot savants.' Now they're just called savants, which means a person who knows a lot about a limited area. Their knowledge can be impressive, but they have no real understanding of that knowledge."

Delaney nodded. "I've seen people like that on *60 Minutes*. Some of these people can barely tie their shoes but they can play Chopin etudes by ear or multiply complex series of numbers in their heads."

"Exactly."

"How did he lock in on World War II?"

"I'm told that when he was a child he started watching old episodes of *Victory At Sea* and became hooked on military documentaries. He absorbs anything to do with that war. He's fixated on it."

Delaney shifted the focus to Wallace. "How long has Jeff been here?"

"About two years."

"What's his job?"

"Makes sure Andrew get his daily workout in the exercise room."

"Andy pump a lot of iron?" Delaney asked.

"I really don't know."

"He a big guy?"

"Close to six foot."

Delaney began to see a profile emerging. "Muscular?"

She giggled, as though that was the silliest question she'd ever heard. "No, not at all."

Delaney grunted. Whoever butchered that couple would have to have been very strong. Still, it was possible that a skinny guy, fueled by the unbridled anger of a twisted mind, could cause the same damage.

"Madeleine, I'm going to talk to Andrew later. Do you have any advice for me?"

"Do you know a lot about World War II?"

"No."

"That's too bad. It would be a very good way to establish rapport with him."

"I'll fake it."

"I wouldn't advise it. You won't fool him and if he gets mad, he'll stop talking."

Delaney closed his notebook. "Okay, Madeleine, thanks for talking to me."

She looked surprised. "Is that all?"

Delaney grinned. "Yeah, that's it. I generally use thumb cuffs and toothpicks under the fingernails, but you were very cooperative."

She smiled hesitantly, not sure what to make of this strange man.

He walked her to the door. "If you can recall anything that seems a little strange or out of the ordinary, would you give me a call?"

"Sure, Chief Delaney. I will."

Wallace was sitting on a chair outside the study. Delaney put his hand on his shoulder and felt the taut muscles ripple. "Come on in, Jeff."

Wallace flopped down into a leather wing backed chair and casually tossed one leg over the arm. It was his clumsy way of saying he belonged here and Delaney didn't and he wasn't afraid of this interview.

"We got off on the wrong foot the other day," Delaney began. "What do you say we make a new start?"

Wallace ran his hands through his crew cut, a practiced move that gave him a chance to display his bulging biceps. "I don't want to make a new start," he said, staring at the wood-beamed ceiling.

"I'll tell you what," Delaney said, playing his trump card. "As a peace offering from me to you, I won't tell your boss that you've been busted for drugs."

Wallace's arms dropped to his side. "How'd you…"

"Jeff, I'm a cop. It's my job to know these things."

Anger flashed in the physical therapist's eyes. "I got my act together. I got a good job here. I don't need—"

"Jeffy, what'd I say? He'll never know."

"What do you want from me?" A wary Wallace asked.

Delaney reached over and smacked Wallace's high-top sneaker off the arm of the chair. "Sit up straight. Just the truth, asshole." The easy-going tone vanished and Delaney pinned the unnerved young man with hard, cold eyes. "If I find out you're jerkin' my gherkin, pal, I'll have you tossed out of here so fast your ears will pop." He sat back and grinned. "Now, can we talk?"

Wallace cracked his knuckles nervously. "Listen, man, I made a mistake a few years ago. It cost me a scholarship—maybe a shot at pro ball. But my life's back together. I need this job."

"I'm all in favor of the working man. Just cooperate and you'll have no problem from me."

"What do you want to know?"

Delaney spread a floor plan he'd gotten from a reluctant Sanborne on the desk. "Where's your bedroom?"

Wallace pointed to a room in the west wing, the side of the building that faced away from Crater Cove. Delaney hid his disappointment.

"Your job is to make sure Andrew gets his daily exercise?"

"Yeah."

"Sounds easy enough."

"The hell it is. All he wants to do is play with those damn toy soldiers all day."

"Were you home on the twenty-first?"

"Yeah."

"All night?"

"I went to a movie earlier."

"What did you see?"

"I don't remember."

Delaney sat back and studied Wallace. "Jeffy, Jeffy. I don't think you're clear of the concept. I'm the cop. I look for motive and opportunity. You're the suspect. You should be trying to establish an alibi. If you want me to believe you, I strongly suggest you remember the name of the movie."

Wallace screwed his face up in concentration. "I don't know. I don't care about movies. I go just to get out of the house." When Delaney said nothing, Wallace continued. "It was in that rundown joint just outside of town, the one that only plays old movies... It was something with James Cagney."

"What time did you get back?"

Beads of perspiration sprouted on Wallace's brow. "Jeez, I don't remember. I swear to God."

Delaney pressed. "After eleven, midnight, one?"

"Around midnight I think. I can't say for sure."

"When you got back, did you go right into the house?"

"Yeah."

"You hear anything, see anything?"

"No."

"What time did you go to bed?"

"Right after Letterman."

"After you went to bed, did you hear anything outside?"

"Naw. I sleep like a log. Not even thunderstorms wake me."

"You ever walk down to the cove at night?"

Wallace's body shuddered involuntarily. "Hell no. I don't like bugs or animals, especially at night."

Delaney grinned at the thought of this muscled man being afraid of frogs and snakes. "One more question. You ever go down to the cove with Andrew?"

"No way. The kid's scared shitless of the water. The first week I was here I took him down to the cove. I figured we'd go for a run on the beach. When he saw the water, he freaked out. The old man was really pissed. I was lucky I didn't get canned right then and there."

"Why was he afraid of the water?"

"Who knows." Wallace glanced over his shoulder as though he expected to see Sanborne standing behind him. "The kid's fucking nuts," he whispered. "Last week he was babbling about Omaha beach. Not for nuthin', but there ain't no beaches in Omaha-fucking-Nebraska."

"Jeff, Omaha beach was the code name for one of the landing sites on Normandy."

"Huh?"

"World War Two? Ring a bell?" He saw the blank look on his face and said, "Never mind."

Delaney was disappointed that his theory was going up in smoke. There was no way that anyone who was terrified of water would have swum or rowed out to that sailboat. He closed his notebook. Still, he had to cross his *T*s and dot his *I*s. "Time to talk to Andrew."

Wallace led Delaney through a maze of dimly lit corridors and up a flight of stairs. At the end of a long, gloomy corridor, he stopped at a massive oak door and unlocked it. "Go on in, I'll get Andrew."

Delaney stepped into a spacious room whose walls were covered with large maps of Europe, Africa, and the Far East. Every map was studded with multicolored pins and flags. A 12x12 table made of plywood sheets stood in the center of the room. Half of it was covered with rolled maps, the other half occupied by neat ranks of miniature toy soldiers. On a far wall thousands of toy soldiers and models of war ships lined floor to ceiling shelves. It also appeared that Andrew had the biggest collection of World War II videos that Delaney had ever seen outside a Blockbuster. There was everything from *Bridge on the River Kwai* to the complete set of *Band of Brothers*.

The triple arch-shaped casement windows offered a commanding view of the ocean beyond and a good view of Crater Cove through the trees. Delaney peered through a tripod-mounted telescope and sighted on a fishing trawler about a mile off shore. As he twisted the focusing wheel, a man on the stern smoking a cigarette came into sharp relief.

"*Don't touch that,*" a petulant voice said.

Delaney spun around to face a thin young man with translucent skin. He had the body of a man, but the open, guileless face was that of a child. His lower lip jutted out in a pout. This was not the face of a murderer.

Delaney stepped away from the telescope. "I didn't break anything."

Andrew stomped his foot. "No one is supposed to touch my things."

Delaney nodded to Wallace, who was standing in the doorway behind Andrew. "I'll call you if I need you."

Andrew's pout gave way to cautious wonder. "Who are you?"

"I'm a policeman."

Andrew's face registered disappointment. "You're not a soldier?"

"Well, policemen are kinda like soldiers."

The bright blue eyes widened. "Do you have a gun?"

"Yes."

"A Colt .45?"

"Browning 9mm."

Andrew frowned. "I never heard of it. A Colt .45 can fire ten rounds in eight seconds. Can yours?"

"I don't know," said Delaney, who knew next to nothing about guns.

The young man screwed up his face in disgust. "You don't know anything. What kind of soldier are you?"

"The kind that asks questions." Delaney sat down on the window alcove seat. "Can I ask you some?"

"Is this a game?"

"Sort of."

Andrew pointed his thin finger at the wall maps. "Ask me anything about World War II."

"Okay. When was Pearl Harbor attacked?"

Andrew rolled his eyes. "December seventh, nineteen forty-one. That's easy. Ask me a hard one."

While Delaney was trying to think of a better question, Andrew closed his eyes. "Dunkirk evacuation started May twenty-sixth, ended June fourth." His eyes popped open. "That's easy, too." He closed his eyes again. "Wake Island; December eleventh to the twenty-third. Palau Island; September fifteenth to November twenty-seventh." He opened his eyes and fixed Delaney with a smug smile. "You didn't know that."

Delaney shook his head in genuine amazement. "Wow, you really know your stuff."

The Cove

Andrew picked up a toy soldier and examined it. "I wish I was alive then. It was very exciting."

"It's a very exciting time now."

Andrew shook his head violently. "*No.*"

"Okay. Can I ask you some different kinds of questions?"

Andrew stuck his lower lip out, reminding Delaney that he was dealing with a five year-old mentality. "Tell you what, Andrew. I'll let you see my gun, if you answer some questions."

Andrew held out his hand. "Let me see."

Delaney ejected the clip and handed the gun to him.

Andrew brushed a wisp of thin, blond hair from his eyes and examined the automatic carefully. "It's kinda like a forty-five only smaller."

"Yeah, they're pretty much the same." He put his hand on the telescope. "This is pretty powerful. I bet you can see all kinds of things with this."

Andrew squinted down the barrel. "Gas operated."

Delaney was sorry he'd given him the weapon. Obviously, he couldn't concentrate on more than one topic at a time.

"Andrew, can I have the gun back now?" Reluctantly, the young man returned it. "Now, about this telescope. I bet—"

Andrew scowled at him. "I don't have time to talk now. I have to get ready for the invasion of Sicily."

Delaney nodded. "Okay. Sure." He'd done something to make Andrew angry, but he wasn't sure what. At the door he said, "Maybe we can talk again sometime."

But Andrew wasn't listening. He'd spread a map of southern Europe on the table and was studying it intently.

CHAPTER NINETEEN

JC Bryce was sitting behind the wheel of the Toyota when Delaney came out. "How'd it go?"

"Wallace is still on my suspect list, but Andrew is off."

"Why?"

"He's not strong enough, not clever enough, and he's afraid of water. Still, I can't help thinking he might have seen something that night."

"Why?"

"He's curious, his room has a good view of the cove, and he has a telescope." Suddenly Delaney remembered something. "When I went into the room the telescope was looking downward, toward the cove."

"Did you ask him if he saw anything?"

"I tried, but I said something that turned him off. I gotta figure a way to get his attention and keep it. Let's take a ride down to the beach."

As JT drove along the winding beach access road, Delaney filled her in on the other interviews. When they got to the beach, he told her to stay with the vehicle and he went for a walk along the beach alone.

Spending a lot of time at the crime scene was something he'd always done. Most of the cops he worked with, including Tony Brunetta, thought he was nuts, but he found it therapeutic in a weird sort of way. He believed that close proximity to the murder scene gave him a clarity of thought that he couldn't get anywhere else. There were even times, although not many, when he sensed an energy at the scene, and when he did, he did his best to tap into it. Brunetta called it insight, but to Delaney it seemed almost mystical, as though the victim had crept back from the dead to whisper secrets in his ear. He'd never confided those feelings to the cynical cops he worked with, not even Tony Brunetta.

It was almost five and an afternoon breeze was blowing in off the ocean bringing with it a pleasant fishy scent of sea and salt air. It was a welcome change after the stale, stuffy Sanborne house. As he walked along the beach, trying to sort out the growing jumble of conflicting bits and pieces of information surrounding the deaths of three people, he had to admit that Crater Cove was the most pleasant crime scene he'd ever seen. A far cry from the usual garbage strewn alleys and dark, putrid apartments he was used to.

He also had to admit, however reluctantly, that his theory of a ritualistic murderer wasn't holding up, especially after Tony's death. He had been leaning toward the notion that Tony had been murdered by the same lunatic who'd killed the couple on the boat, but the manner of his death—three bullets to the back of the head—simply didn't fit the pattern of a ritualistic murderer.

He stopped to gaze out across the water at the spot where the sailboat had been. Puffs of wind imprinted random cat paws on the glass-flat surface. An image of JT swimming ashore flashed into his mind, and he thought of something she'd said that day. He turned and hurried back to the car.

"JT, the other day you said strangers don't come in here."

"That's right. It's impossible to spot the opening to the cove from offshore and even if you do, there's a lot of rocks and shoals to navigate. It requires local knowledge."

"But two people from New Jersey came in here with no problem. How could they have done that? Luck?"

"No way. Especially in the dark." She thought for a moment and then added, "Unless they knew how to get in."

"How would they know?"

"Someone could have told them how to get in. Even then—"

"What if they followed another boat in?"

"That's possible. It'd be easy if you followed another boat."

Delaney squinted at the sun reflecting off the water. "But why would they come in here?"

"Lots of reasons. They could have been tired. The weather might have kicked up. Why is it important to know why they came in here?"

"Because if they planned to come in, they might have been meeting someone. And that's something I'd want to explore. On the other hand, if they came in because of one of the reasons you just mentioned, they might have seen something they shouldn't have seen."

JT's eyes swept the peaceful beach. "Like what?"

"Like I don't know. Is there any way to tell if this was a planned stop?"

She thought for a moment. "We could look at their charts. If they were experienced cruising sailors, they would have plotted their course, including changes and stops, on the chart."

Delaney jumped into the Toyota. "Lets' take a look at them."

JT spread the chart on the desk in Delaney's office and traced her finger along the penciled line. "This line represents their course. They started from Toms River up the East River into Long Island Sound to Block Island. Then—"

"JT, I don't need to know their whole itinerary. Get to Crater Cove."

She slid her finger up the chart. "Their final destination was Yarmouth, Nova Scotia. Notice their course line hugged the New England coastline."

Delaney studied the chart filled with numbers and wavy lines. None of it made sense to him. "Where's Crater Cove?"

"It's too small to see on this chart, but it's right about here." The penciled course line went past it.

"So you're saying that if they were planning to go into Crater Cove, it would be marked on the chart."

"Right. They marked all their other overnight stops.

Delaney said, "So if they didn't know about the cove, then they couldn't have gotten in there by luck, which means they probably followed another boat in."

JT folded up the chart. "That's the most likely explanation. And when they came in they saw something they shouldn't have seen," she said more to herself than to him.

"Right."

"So what did they see?"

"Something that got them murdered."

Charlie Tuttle came in and handed Delaney a manila envelope. "Dr. Bynum just sent this over. He said you wanted to see it right away."

Delaney ripped open the envelope, wanting, and not wanting, to read Tony's autopsy report. Forcing himself to remain indifferent to the clinical description of how his friend was murdered, he read Dr. Bynum's detailed report. The lab reports weren't back yet and most of what he was reading he'd already heard from Bynum. He was about to toss the report in his in basket when his eye caught a sentence. He reread it again. *Physical observation disclosed an area of lividity approximately 45 centimeters by 32 centimeters on the back of the deceased.*

Delaney snapped forward in his seat. "Lividity on the *back*?" he said aloud.

"What's lividity?" JT asked.

"When the heart stops pumping, gravity takes over and blood settles at the lowest point."

JT nodded, trying to follow. "So, after the Chief died, he must have been on his back for some time."

"Except that when I saw Tony, he was lying on his *stomach*. Tony was moved after he died. He wasn't murdered at Crater Cove."

"Why would the killer do that?"

"I don't know. Maybe it was a convenient place to dump the body. Maybe the killer wanted us to connect the murder with the other two. Maybe—" Delaney suddenly had another, more disturbing thought. "The killer didn't try to hide the body. Maybe he wanted us to find Tony's body right away. He had to know we'd search Crater Cove."

Recalling the location of the chief's body, JT said, "You're right. He was behind the dune, but there was no attempt to conceal him. But why would the killer want the chief's body found?"

Delaney said nothing, but a terrible, nagging question was beginning to form in his mind: *Was he being manipulated by the killer?*

Delaney tossed the report on the desk. "Tony knew his killer."

JT felt the hair on the back of her neck rise. If Delaney was correct, the killer was someone in Haddley Falls. Someone she might know. "How do you know that?"

"He was too good a cop to let a stranger set him up like that," Delaney said.

"Why would someone from Haddley Falls kill the Chief?" she asked.

"I don't know. Maybe he stumbled onto something. Maybe he put two and two together."

"Did the Chief tell you anything?"

"No. He was murdered before he got a chance to tell me who he saw at the diner." Once again, he was reminded that if he hadn't been drunk, he'd have gone with Tony and... And what? He shook the thought out of his mind. "JT, I've got an assignment for you. Check with the weather service and find out what the weather and sea conditions were like the night of the murders."

After JT left, Delaney made a careful search of Tony's office. Maybe Tony had left some sort of clue—a telephone number or a jotted note of some kind. He rifled through desk drawers, file cabinets, and calendar entries. An hour later, a disappointed Delaney slammed the last drawer in the filing cabinet. He'd searched everywhere and had found nothing.

CHAPTER TWENTY

The next day, at ten minutes before noon, Pete Delaney pulled into the small gravel-covered parking lot of Mrs. Murphy's Chowder House. The restaurant did a heavy dinner trade with tourists, but Charlie Tuttle had recommended it for lunch because that was when the locals—seeking respite from loud-mouthed, garish-clothed tourists, clicking cameras, and the ever present, and overpowering, smell of sun screen—ate there.

Inside, the converted rambling Victorian house smelled of polish and food mixed with the not unpleasant smell of musty carpets and drapes.

A gray-haired woman carrying a menu approached. "Good afternoon, Chief Delaney. "Your other guest hasn't arrived yet. Would you like to be seated or wait at the bar?"

Delaney had never laid eyes on the woman, but obviously she knew who he was, and he was reminded, once again, that news travels fast in a small town. "Are you Mrs. Murphy?"

She smiled. "Goodness me, no. He's in the bar."

He? "Would you show me where the table is?"

The broad planked oak floors creaked as she led him into the dining room. It was early and no one was sitting at the dozen or so maple wood tables scattered about the cozy room.

She nodded toward a table in the center. "Will this be all right?"

He pointed at a table next to a stained-glass window. "I'd rather sit there."

"That will be fine."

"I'll sit here"—he pointed at the chair against the wall—"and my guest will sit opposite me."

"As you wish," she said without surprise. Ever since a patron had insisted on being seated in a chair facing magnetic north, she'd become accustomed to strange requests.

Delaney went into the bar, a subdued room with a brass and stained-glass decor. There was only one customer seated at the small bar; a man with a homemade haircut and wearing a baggy brown suit and matching bow tie.

The bartender, a squat man with slicked black hair and an unruly mustache, stuck out a beefy hand. "Chief Delaney, good ta meet ya. Carmine Polli."

Delaney shook the wet hand. "Hello, Carmine. I thought Mrs. Murphy was tending bar."

"*I'm* Mrs. Murphy," he said out of the side of his mouth.

Delaney grinned. "Ah, a man of mystery. And judging from your accent, not from these parts either."

"Mulberry Street. Little Italy. When I decided to open a joint here twenty-five years ago, people told me an Italian restaurant wouldn't make it." He shrugged elaborately. "So, I called it Mrs. Murphy's Chowder House."

"What brought you all the way up here?"

Carmine looked around and whispered in a voice gravelly from too many unfiltered cigarettes, "I had a little trouble back in the old neighborhood, if you know what I mean."

Delaney smiled, developing a genuine liking for this man. "Aren't you afraid they'll come up here looking for you?"

"Yeah, in the beginning. But they're all dead now. They should rot in hell, the dirty bastards. What can I get ya?"

"Club soda."

Carmine tugged at his mustache. "*Marone!* They don't make cops like they used to. *Club soda?*"

"I'm on duty."

While Carmine was pouring the soda, the man in the bow tie said, "Any progress on the murders, Chief?"

Delaney scooped up a handful of peanuts from a bowl on the bar and popped them into his mouth. "It's progressing."

"Any suspects?"

Dear lord, Delaney thought, save me from sidewalk detectives. "No, not yet."

"You ask me, it was done by outsiders. You oughta take a look at the Cooper Apartments near the Interstate. Full of God knows what kind of trash. Don't think any of 'em work. Don't know where they're gettin' their money from."

Carmine placed a club soda with a lime wedge in front of Delaney. "Whaddaya talkin' about, Herb? They work fourteen hours a day in the hotels."

The man stuck his weak chin out belligerently. "Yeah, well what about off season?"

"After the season most of 'em leave." Carmine looked at Delaney and sighed. "He's a regular Perry Mason."

The man drained his martini and slammed the glass down on the bar. "Well, if you're so smart, Carmine. You tell me who did it?"

"How should I know? Another?"

"Yeah, and don't forget the three olives."

Carmine shook his head in exasperation. "Herb, you've been coming in here for fifteen years. Right? Have I ever forgotten the three friggin' olives?"

The man mumbled something unintelligible.

Carmine mixed the martini, made a great show of dropping three olives in the glass, and slid it in front of the man. "Take it easy, Herb. You'll get agita."

The man jabbed a finger at Carmine. "Don't make light of this, Carmine. If this town gets a bad reputation over these murders, you'll suffer just like the rest of us businessmen."

"What business are you in?" Delaney asked.

"I own the hardware store down the street." He took a gulp of his martini and his bowtie bobbed up and down. "The only good thing to come from these murders is business has picked up."

"How so?"

He cackled dryly. "I'm selling a lot more locks now. But I'll tell you, Chief. The people that come into my store are real scared."

"I should be selling shotguns instead of shots," Carmine said, drying a glass.

"It's not funny, Carmine. Suppose, just suppose someone in town did it. You know what kind of impact that could have on the economy of this town?"

Carmine chuckled. "Look at the bright side, Herb. If someone in this town did it, we'll be famous. Burning a couple of witches in Salem didn't do them no harm."

The man quickly drained his drink and pounded the empty glass on the bar. "All I'm saying is no one in this town did it." He scooped up his change and stared for the door. He stopped beside Delaney. "If I was you, Chief, I'd check out those Cooper Apartments. Dollars to donuts you'll find your killer there."

"After the man left, Delaney popped another peanut into his mouth. "Kinda hyper."

"He's all right. Like most of the people in this town, he's scared shitless about these murders."

"Tourist bucks?"

"Yeah."

"You don't seen concerned, Carmine. How come?"

"This is my third joint. I lost my first place back in the fifties because the neighborhood went bad. Then I opened a joint on Third Avenue. A year later they tore the el down and suddenly I'm in a high rent district and the landlord forces me out. So I lost one joint because the neighborhood was bad and I lost the other joint because the neighborhood was too good. Go figure."

"I got the impression your friend, Herb, would like me to charge one of people in the Cooper Apartments with the crime whether he did it or not."

"Like he said, this town will shit if it turns out one of the townies done it. He'd rather believe it was one of the transients from the Cooper Apartments." Carmine shook his head thoughtfully. "Now I think I understand how lynchings happen."

While both men were pondering that observation, the hostess came in and told Delaney his guest had arrived.

State Police Corporal Kyle Morgan, looking decidedly uncomfortable, was already seated in the chair Delaney had designated. His collar was too tight and his fleshy neck spilled out over the top.

Delaney slid into his seat, pleased with the seating arrangement. The bright light from the stained-glass window behind him shown directly into Morgan's face, causing the young corporal to squint uncomfortably. During an interrogation, Delaney always made it a point to make it as unpleasant as possible for the subject.

"Corporal Morgan," he said offering his hand. "Thanks for meeting me. What looks good on the menu?"

Morgan ordered the house special—a bowl of Mrs. Murphy's original clam chowder, a beer and the burger platter. Delaney ordered another club soda and a turkey sandwich.

The waitress brought the drinks first. While they were waiting for the food to arrive, they engaged in the small talk that men engage in when they're trying to feel each other out. Delaney learned that Morgan, born and raised in Farnham, had been with the State Police for three years, the last one as a forensic technician. Like most cops he liked the job, hated the hours, and complained about the low pay.

Delaney told Morgan enough war stories to convince the State Police officer that he was dealing with a very knowledgeable and experienced homicide detective.

As Morgan was taking a sip from his iced mug, Delaney said casually, "I met Major Perrault the other day. You know him?"

Morgan pulled the mug away from his lips with a jerk. "Sure. Everyone knows Major Perrault."

Delaney noted with satisfaction that the mention of the major's name evoked a fear response in the young corporal. "You work for him? I mean, is he somewhere in your chain of command?"

"No, well... sort of. He's the CO of the Homicide Squad, so he has a lot to say about the Forensic Unit."

Delaney squeezed the lime wedge into his glass. "Seems like an experienced man. He been in homicide long?"

"Gee, I'm not sure. I really don't know the major that well."

Delaney saw that Morgan was getting really uncomfortable about talking about Perrault and steered the conversation in another direction. "So you've been a tech for a year?"

"Yeah."

"Homicide work is really interesting, isn't it?"

"It sure is," Morgan said, warming up to the subject. "It's not like those bullshit CSI TV shows where they do everything but pull the switch on the electric chair, but it's an interesting job. Still, to tell you the truth, I'd rather be a homicide detective than..." He quickly took another sip of beer, and Delaney knew that was the carrot that Perrault was dangling in front of him.

The waitress arrived with the food. After she left, Delaney resumed. "I'll bet you accumulate a lot of experience in that one year."

"Oh, yeah. Of course we don't get as many cases as you guys in New York, but we get our share."

"I read your report. Very professional."

Morgan beamed.

Delaney sprinkled pepper on his turkey. "There is one thing that puzzles me, though."

Morgan ripped open a package of Oysterettes, crushed them in his hands and dropped them into his chowder. "What's that?"

"You didn't find any fingerprints."

Morgan shrugged. "Lots of times we don't find prints."

"Really? I guess you looked pretty good though, huh?"

"Oh, yeah. That's SOP."

"You always follow procedures, Kyle?"

Morgan, getting uncomfortable again, furiously stirred the Oysterettes into his soup and squinted at Delaney across the table. "Sure."

"Kyle, do you know what elimination prints are?"

Morgan ripped open another package of Oysterettes and dumped them into his soup. "Sure. You take prints of everyone who was at the scene. That way, if you find their prints, you can eliminate them."

Delaney took a bite of his sandwich. "You didn't take elimination prints this time," he said matter-of-factly.

Morgan frowned. "I didn't? I don't understand that. I always take elimination prints."

"That's what I figured. You're a professional. You wouldn't forget a thing like that."

"Right. I can't imagine what happened." Morgan thought he heard a note of sarcasm in Delaney's tone and tried to read the chief's expression, but the light from the damn window was shinning in his eyes and Delaney's face was in shadows.

Until now, Delaney's tone had been conversational. Now his voice turned hard. "I think I know what happened, Kyle. Perrault wants this case. He told you not to look for prints. Probably mentioned something about a future opening in the Homicide Squad for a good cop and maybe you could fit the bill. The reason you didn't take elimination prints from Chief Brunetta and Deputy Avery was because you already knew you wouldn't be lifting prints at the crime scene."

Morgan shook his head violently. "That's crazy. Do you think I would risk my job for something like that? I'd have to be nuts."

Delaney dropped his voice, but the hardness was still there. "You think you're a good cop? You're a scumbag." Morgan's head snapped back as though he'd been slapped. "Chief Brunetta was a good cop and he was murdered by the same guy who killed those two people in the sailboat. You tell me, Morgan. What kind of cop would deliberately withhold evidence that might catch a cop killer?"

Delaney looked down at the bowl in front of Morgan. While he'd been hammering the young cop, a nervous Morgan had been ripping open packages of Oysterettes and dumping them into his bowl. The soup had become thick enough to be spread on a piece of bread. "You must really like those things," Delaney said.

Morgan cleared his throat as if to say something, but nothing came out. He pushed the bowl away from him and looked ill.

Delaney knew he had him on the ropes and eased off. "Kyle, I don't think any of this was your idea. I think if it were up to you, you would do everything in your power to catch a cop killer."

Morgan face twisted in anguish. "If it were up to me, I would. It's just that..." He finished the sentence with a helpless shrug.

"I know," Delaney said sympathetically. "That's what makes it so bad. Some sonofabitch pressured you into doing something that you didn't want to do."

Morgan tugged at his too-tight collar. "Chief Delaney, Major Perrault is a very influential man. He's got connections right up to the governor's mansion. That's how he got his job. What could I do?"

Delaney said nothing. At a moment like this silence was the worst punishment for Morgan. It gave him the opportunity to dwell on his predicament.

Finally, unable to stand the silence any longer, Morgan said, "I'm...sorry. Okay? I wish it could have been different."

Delaney lit a cigarette and sat back. "You can have a second chance, Kyle. The boat is still secured at the marina. We can go back there and look for prints together."

Morgan shook his head. "I can't. Perrault will—"

"Don't worry about the major," Delaney said confidently. "As a matter of fact, he's going to call you tomorrow and order you to do it."

Morgan looked at Delaney askance. "Why would he do that?"

"Because I'll ask him to."

Morgan, flustered by the turn of events and bewildered by Delaney's positive attitude, pushed his chair away from the table. "I gotta go," he mumbled, standing up.

Delaney patted the distraught man on the shoulder. "Don't worry, Kyle, everything will be okay. I promise Perrault won't do anything to hurt you. He'll call you in the morning and direct you to reexamine the scene, and that will be that. I'll see you tomorrow. Don't forget your fingerprint kit."

"What... what if there are no prints?"

Delaney had thought of that slim possibility. "Maybe there won't be, but we'll give it one hell of a shot, won't we?"

Delaney sat in his car and watched Morgan pull out of the parking lot. After the car disappeared around a corner, he reached inside his jacket pocket and took out a small tape recorder. He rewound it, pushed the play button, and heard himself say: *"Corporal Morgan. Thanks for meeting with me. What looks good on the menu?"* and pressed the stop button.

CHAPTER TWENTY ONE

Delaney was waiting at a stop light when Blair Lowell pulled up alongside him in a purple Corvette.
"Congratulations on the new job," she called out.
"Thanks, I think."
"Doing anything tonight?"
"Working."
"All work and no play…"
"You've got a point there."
"My place tonight. Seven o'clock."
Before he could answer, she pulled away, tires screeching.

Back at the station house Delaney stopped at Sergeant Tuttle's desk. "Charlie, reach out for Major Perrault and tell him I'd like to see him ASAP."

As he was heading for his office, JT was coming out of the clerical office. "How'd you make out with the forensic technician?" she asked.

"Great. "We'll be going back to the boat tomorrow to look for prints. I'll want you there."

"Me?" JT had heard Clint Avery's graphic description of the scene in the boat cabin and wasn't anxious to see it, even without the bodies.

"Yeah, you're a sailor. I want you to look the boat over carefully. Maybe you'll see something that was overlooked."

"All right," she said half-heartedly.

"It won't be so bad, JT. Everything is dried up by now."

She knew he meant well, but his words only made her more queasy. "Thanks a lot," she said sarcastically. As she was walking away, she turned. "Oh, by the way, if you don't have any plans for tonight, why don't you come over to my place. One of my neighbors gave me some fresh fish and I'm going to make my famous fish chowder."

"Oh, I'd really like to, but—ah, I'm working." He would have preferred to spend the evening with JT and silently cursed himself for accepting Blair's invitation.

"Okay," she said, wondering why he was lying. "No problem."

Just as he was getting ready to go to Blair's, the receptionist called to tell him that Major Perrault was here to see him.

The major came in smiling. "So, I guess you've changed your mind."

Delaney motioned him into a seat. "No, but you could do me a favor."

Perrault squinted at Delaney suspiciously. "What kind of favor?"

"There must have been some kind of screw-up, but your forensic technician forgot to look for prints. I'd like you to send him back here first thing tomorrow morning. We'll do it again."

"I don't have the authority to order that."

"Oh course you do. You just don't want to."

"All right, you're right. I don't want to. I told you it wasn't going to be easy handling this investigation all by yourself, *Chief*."

As he started to get up, Delaney opened the desk drawer and took out a tape recorder and put it on the desk. "Chad, give me a moment. You just gotta here this."

Eying the tape recorder as though it were a deadly cobra about to strike, Perrault slowly sank back down in the chair.

Blair Lowell lived three miles up the coast from Haddley Falls and Delaney had no trouble finding the place. The cantilevered house, perched precariously on the side of a scrub-oak covered cliff, had a commanding, multi-million dollar view of the Atlantic Ocean. Delaney didn't know if it was by design or accident, but the sprawling stone and wooden-beamed structure appeared to be of indeterminable age. Neither old or modern, it could have been built a year ago—or thirty years ago.

A black woman, wearing a maroon dress and a white apron, let him in and led him out to a large deck overlooking the ocean.

"May I get you something to drink?" she asked.

"No, thank you."

After she left, he peered over the edge of the deck. Forty feet below, the ocean waved rolled up onto the beach spreading patterns of white foam. From this height the crashing waves made only a soft whooshing sound.

About a mile offshore, a sailboat, heeled over in the wind, was making its way south. When he and JT made the sail to Crater Cove, they must have passed this house, but Delaney couldn't remember seeing it. He thought about JT and, once again, regretted not being able to take her up on her invitation. But he couldn't pass up an opportunity to get inside information from one mover and shaker about the other movers and shakers in Haddley Falls.

At least that's what he told himself. What he didn't want to admit, even to himself, was that Blair was an attractive woman who was fun to be with. And she was refreshing. Unlike Talbot and the others who tried to downplay their wealth while at the same time flaunting it, she enjoyed her wealth without apology. He suspected she was a lot like him—a cynic who didn't take the world, or herself, too seriously. And best of all, there wasn't a chance of an emotional attachment to her.

A few minutes later, a smiling Blair Lowell made her entrance looking stunning in a simple emerald green silk dress that was two inches above the knee and clung to her firm, well-shaped body. The last time Delaney had seen her she was wearing a long dress. He'd guessed then that she had good legs and now his suspicions were confirmed. "Well, I see you found the place with no trouble," she said. "Didn't Alice get you a drink?"

"She offered, but I didn't want anything."

Blair walked behind a round marble-tiled bar that was as well-stocked as any gin mill he'd ever seen. Premium brands only. "What'll you have, Pete?"

What to drink? Delaney had promised himself he wouldn't take another drink until he'd found Tony's murderer. But he was dying to have just one scotch. "Club soda," he said.

She cocked her head. "Club soda? How depressing. I hate to drink alone."

"You been living here long?" he asked.

"A few years. Just summers. I can't take these yahoos more than a few months at a time."

He walked to the edge of the deck and looked south. Can you see Crater Cove from here?"

"No. It's a couple of miles away. Must you be a cop twenty-four-hours a day?" She was smiling but there was a hint of exasperation in her tone.

"It's in my blood."

"How is the investigation going?"

"It's going." He had no intention of giving her any information. He was here to *get* information not give it. "I had lunch at Mrs. Murphy's Chowder House today."

Her laughter was deep and throaty. "Did you meet Mrs. Murphy?"

"Yeah, he's a real character. So, what can you tell me about the Haddley Falls food chain?"

"Where to start?"

"How about Royce Gardiner?"

"He's actually a weak little man, but full of bluster—sort of like the guy behind the curtain in *The Wizard of Oz*. He snows most people in this town, but he doesn't fool me. When the chips are down, he does what Jonathan Talbot tells him to do."

"Sanborne?"

"Old money. Reclusive really. All I know is he's fiercely protective of his son ever since the accident."

"Accident?"

"I don't know much about it. Apparently when Andrew was a kid he almost drowned. He was underwater a long time and oxygen deprivation or something affected his brain."

Now Delaney knew why Andrew was terrified of water. "When I was in Mrs. Murphy's I met the guy who owns the hardware store in town. He's afraid the killer might be from Haddley Falls."

"He's not alone," Blair said, popping an olive into her mouth. "It hard to understand if you don't come from a small town. But here, everybody knows everybody, or at least knows *of* them. They might not like each other, but like the dotty aunt who shows up at weddings and funerals, we tolerate each other. It's an incestuous town. Everyone depends on everyone else in one capacity or another."

"And what drives the machine is the tourist economy?"

"Pretty much. With few exceptions everyone in this town is tied in some way to the tourist industry. That's why these murders are such a hot button. It could all come down like a house of cards."

"Is the town really on such shaky ground?"

"Read the papers. The tourist industry is suffering. Royce and some of the others have really been scrambling to bring in business. If Haddley Falls gets a bad reputation, it's toast."

"Still, three people were murdered."

"Yeah, and it's inconvenient as hell. She took his empty glass. "Are you sure you don't want a real drink?"

"Just club soda."

She took their empty glasses and went back behind the bar. "Gardiner and the others are hoping you find the right man."

He took his club soda. "The *right* man? Do you mean the guy who did it or some fall guy who will cause the town the least amount of adverse publicity?"

Before she could answer that question, the maid came out on the deck and announced that dinner was ready.

The dining room was an airy semi-circular alcove with floor to ceiling windows that offered an unobstructed view of the ocean. Delaney tapped the crystal wine glass with his fingernail and it rang. "Nice."

"Waterford. I picked up a set on my last trip to Europe. I broke the last set throwing them at one of my ex-husbands."

"You should use a frying pan. It's the weapon of choice in the ghetto and a hell of lot cheaper to replace."

"I'll keep that in mind." She held up a bottle. "From the wine cellar. Château Latour forty-five. One of my exes claimed it was a fantastic year."

She handed him the bottle and ran her fingernail across the back of his hand. "Pete, I don't want to talk police business anymore. Would you be a dear and open it?"

And that was Delaney's downfall. After opening the wine, she insisted he take a sip. He respectfully declined. Wine was not his drink of choice. All that pompous talk of vintages, wine regions and this grape is better than that grape was to him so much bullshit. But she insisted and he took a sip. One sip led to another, and then—*what the hell?*—why not have just one glass? How often do you get a chance to experience a rare Château Latour '45? And one glass led to another and soon the bottle was empty and that led to opening another bottle and after that—it all got fuzzy.

The next morning he awoke with a real head-banger. It took him a moment to orient himself and realize he was in bed beside a naked Blair. His face was just inches from her neck and he blinked to focus on an elongated scar.

He touched the scar and she opened her eyes. "What's this?" he asked.

She threw the satin sheets aside and got out of bed. "Time to get up, lazybones."

He saw another, different kind of scar on her butt. "What's that?"

"Bruises. Water-skiing. I'm so embarrassed. I'm supposed to be an expert skier, but I hit a tree branch or something. My God, I was black and blue for a month. How about some breakfast?"

Delaney looked at his watch with bleary eyes. It was almost ten o'clock. "Oh, shit," he said bolting out of bed, "I'm late."

CHAPTER TWENTY TWO

By the time Delaney got to the boatyard parking lot it was almost eleven and JT and Corporal Morgan were waiting for him.

Before coming, he'd taken a cold shower and downed copious amounts of coffee, but it was no use. He was still hung over and worse, he looked hung over. There was no coffee made that could conceal bloodshot eyes.

He saw JT studying him with a mixture of anger and disappointment. He didn't need her disapproval to make him feel any worse. Just three days ago he'd promised he wouldn't have anything to drink and he'd already fallen off the wagon. If he was going to find Tony's killer, he couldn't afford to do that again.

At least the befuddled look on the corporal's face cheered him up. He would have given anything to hear the conversation that Perrault had with the forensic technician.

Corporal Morgan, clutching his fingerprint case, said, "Major Perrault told me I should meet you here." There was wonder in his voice. "Just like you said he would."

"Yeah. Sorry I'm late."

With shaking hands he unlocked the shed and pushed the doors open. In the center of the dimly lit cavernous structure, the sailboat, up on blocks, looked mildly sinister. Both JT and Morgan studied the boat with mild trepidation.

"Okay," Delaney said, breaking the silence. "Let's get started. JT, you check out the boat. Corporal, let's look for prints."

An hour later, Morgan, under the watchful eye of Delaney, lifted several prints. When he was done, Delaney gave him his instructions. "Kyle, process those prints and get me a report ASAP."

"Yes, sir." As he was leaving, he turned to Delaney. "Sir, what did you say to Major Perrault to make him so cooperative?"

"Me? I didn't say anything. Professional courtesy, I guess."

JT was standing in the bow of the boat. "Pete," she yelled down. "Come up here and take a look at this."

Delaney climbed up onto the boat and joined her at the bow where she was studying a the frayed line. "What is it?"

"The jib halyard parted."

"So?"

"So without this you can't hoist the jib and you lose most of your wind power."

"JT, you know I don't know anything about boats. Speak English."

"This line—we call it a halyard—is used to hoist the jib. The front sail? Losing a jib is dangerous. If the engine quits, and engines always seem to quit just when you most need them, you have very little power, just the main. I checked the weather for that night. It was blowing over thirty knots. It must have parted under the stress. If that happened to me, especially at night, I'd want to pull in someplace and fix it."

"Like the cove?"

"Any port in a storm."

"And you think the only way they could have gotten into the cove was by following another boat in."

"Yep."

"So if you're right, they decided to seek shelter, they saw another boat come into the cove, and they followed that boat in."

"I can't think of another explanation."

"I can't either. So what else? You checked over the boat. Find find anything unusual?"

"Yeah, I did," she answered, a puzzled expression on her face. The boat is loaded with electronics. Down below there's a marine GPS, a VHF radio, a satellite communication system, a DVD player, and a CD player. Funny the killer didn't take any of those things with him."

"JT, the guy had murder on his mind, not larceny."

"Then why did he take the radar unit?"

He looked to where she was pointing. Loose wires hung from a mounting bracket at the stern of the boat.

"What does a radar antenna look like?"

"It's a big round thing. Furuno's a popular brand. You see them on most decent sized boats."

"How much would a thing like that cost?"

"A couple of thousand bucks. But that's the puzzling part. The satellite communication system alone is worth a lot more than that."

Delaney didn't know what to make of it. He knew ritual sex murderers often took personal items of clothing, but he'd never heard of one taking a piece of electronics. "Maybe he's not a ritual sex murderer," he said to a frowning JT. "Things are getting curiouser and curiouser."

Later that afternoon, Delaney and Clint Avery drove out to the Sanborne house. Delaney wanted to ask Madeleine and Jeff if they remembered seeing any other boats in the cove around the time of the murders.

As they rounded a bend on the coast road, they came upon a pack of bikers hogging the road. Delaney recognized them. They were the same bikers he'd seen hanging around the Flotsam bar the first day he'd come to town.

He tapped the siren. The last biker turned around, saw it was a police vehicle, and gave them the finger.

"I don't get no respect," Delaney said, hitting the accelerator and pulling within inches of the motorcycle's rear fender.

"Whoa!" Clint said, grabbing the dashboard. "I don't think you oughta do that, Chief. The Demons are a rough bunch."

"Clint, we're the police."

He tapped the bike's rear fender with his bumper and hit the siren. The surprised biker wobbled out of control. He turned and gave Delaney a dirty look, but he pulled over to let him by. Delaney pulled up to the next motorcycle and did the same thing. The rest of the bikers got the idea and pulled to the side, giving him the right of way. As he shot through the pack, they gave him hard looks. He waved back, like the Queen of England on her way to Buckingham.

Suddenly, he noticed something. He stomped on the accelerator and jumped ahead a hundred feet. Then he slammed on the brakes and yanked the wheel. The cruiser screeched into a controlled spin and came to a stop, blocking the road.

And it was ass pucker time for the wide-eyed bikers. Some slammed on the brakes, others flew off the road into a ditch, and a few went down. The ones with better reflexes and brakes screeched to a stop in front of the police cruiser amidst a chorus of curses and waving fists.

Delaney got out of the car. "You gentlemen have violated a whole bunch of traffic regulations. OK. Line up. Size places."

They looked at the crazy cop. And then chains and blackjacks appeared and they started to move menacingly toward Delaney.

Delaney heard a metallic sound and the bikers stopped. He turned and saw that Clint, standing right behind him, had cranked a round into his shotgun. In that moment Delaney's estimation of Clint went up several notches. I was right, he thought, this guy is going to make a good cop.

Delaney stepped up to the leader of the pack—a huge redheaded giant who would have looked like a demented Viking, if he wasn't wearing a German helmet.

"That a real German helmet?" Delaney asked.

"Yeah, what of it?"

"I'd like to buy it."

The redheaded giant looked down at Delaney and grinned showing a mouthful of missing teeth. "It ain't for sale." He turned around and grinned at his fellow bikers. "But you can fight me for it."

"I'd rather buy it."

The giant biker tossed his helmet to his biker queen. "Like I told you, it ain't for sale."

Delaney sighed. "Okay. Let's discuss the rules."

The giant folded his massive arms and smirked. "Dude, there ain't no—"

He never got to finish the sentence because, without warning, Delaney kicked the big biker in the nuts. As the man doubled over, Delaney drove his knee into the man's face. Before he hit the pavement, Delaney was on top of him. He grabbed the woozy giant's hair and pounded his head into the pavement until he saw the man's eyes roll up in his head.

He stood up over the unconscious man. "I believe I just won a German helmet."

The astonished biker queen tossed the helmet to him.

As Delaney moved toward the car, a nervous Clint covered him with the shotgun. "You all have a nice day," Delaney said, over his shoulder. "And remember to stay to the right and don't forget to signal."

And they drove off, leaving the bikers standing in the middle of the road staring at their fallen leader.

For a moment, Clint was speechless. Then, he said, "Chief, you are *crazy*... I never saw anything like that."

"You mean you never saw Butch Cassidy and the Sundance Kid?"

"Can't say I have."

"Good thing for me that redheaded giant didn't either. Paul Newman did that to a guy who wanted to take over his gang." He slapped Avery's knee. "Who says you don't learn stuff from the movies?"

"What're you going to do with the helmet?"

"It's a gift for a friend. Let's find someplace where I can buy wrapping paper."

An hour later, Delaney was in Andrew's room handing him the gaudily wrapped gift. Andrew tore the paper off. "*Wow!* A German helmet!"

"It's the real thing," Delaney said.

Andrew put it on and strutted around the room.

"Andrew, I couldn't tell you who I was before because it was a secret. But now I have permission to tell you."

That got Andrew's attention. His eyes widened. "What's the secret?"

"I'm with Military Intelligence," Delaney said in a confidential tone.

Andrew's eyes grew even wider. "You are?"

Delaney walked over to the telescope and peered through it. "We have information that enemy spies landed in the cove sometime last week. Do you know anything about that?"

Andrew shoved the detective Delaney away from the telescope. Delaney was sure he'd blown it, but then, Andrew put his eye to the telescope and, after a moment, said, "It was a small landing craft..."

Delaney forced himself to keep the excitement out of his voice. "A small landing craft. Like a clammer?" he asked offhandedly.

Andrew stomped his foot. "No! I said a small landing craft."

"Okay, okay. What else did you see?"

Andrew continued to stare into the telescope. "Another spy was waiting for him on the beach."

"Was he on a boat, too?"

"No," Andrew said in a tone that said it should have been obvious. "He wasn't on a boat. He came by truck. They loaded something into the boat."

"Was it a big truck or a—"

"Then a sailboat came in."

The hair on the back of Delaney's neck stood up. He held his breath, almost afraid to speak for fear of breaking the tenuous tread of connection he'd made with Andrew. "A sailboat. Were they spies, too?"

Andrew said nothing and continued to stare intently into the telescope and it suddenly occurred to Delaney that Andrew was playing the scene out in his head in real time.

"The sailboat came near the two spies on the beach. They spoke and then the sailboat went to the other side of the cove."

"What did the spies do then?"

"They went away in the small landing craft."

"They didn't go to the sailboat?" a puzzled Delaney asked.

Andrew turned away from the telescope. "No." He went to his table and began to rearrange his soldiers. Obviously, the conversation was over.

A disappointed Delaney started for the door.

Andrew was moving a toy tank into position in front of a line of soldiers. Then he said, "Later, they came back..."

Delaney whirled. "Andrew, look through the telescope again. Tell me what you see, now."

Andrew did as he was told. Looking through the telescope, he said, "The landing craft went to the sailboat... and... the spies went downstairs."

"Did you get a look at the faces of the men—the spies?"

Andrew continued to peer through the telescope. "After awhile one of them came up on deck. Then, the other came up and..." Andrew pulled away from the telescope, suddenly terrified. He began to scream, "*NO...NO...NO....*"

Jeff and Madeline rushed into the room. "What happened?" Madeline asked rushing to comfort Andrew.

Delaney shrugged. "I don't know."

"You'd better go," Jeff said.

Downstairs, Delaney waited in the foyer until Madeline came down.

"I finally got him quieted down," she said. "What set him off?"

"I don't know. We were talking, then all of a sudden he went nuts."

"The only other time I saw him act that way was the last time he saw his brother."

"Andrew has a brother?"

"An older brother named Keith. He came to the house one night last spring. I was bringing Andrew down to the kitchen to give him dinner and I heard Mr. Sanborne and Keith arguing about money. Then, Andrew saw his brother and he became terrified. He started screaming just like he did upstairs before."

"Do you know why?"

"No. Mr. Sanborne ordered me to bring Andrew back upstairs. He never said a word about it and acted as though the incident never happened."

On the way back to town, Delaney asked Clint, "Did you know that Andrew had a brother?"

"No. But the Sanbornes are a very secretive family. I don't think there are too many people in this town who knows much about them."

When they were a block from the station house Delaney spotted someone who might know all about the Sanbornes. "Clint, let me out here."

He caught up to Eleanor Haddley as she was getting into her fire engine-red Land Rover. "Why, Mr. Delaney," she said. "Oh, I should say Chief Delaney."

"Pete will do. I'd like to talk to you when you have some free time.

"About the murders?" she asked conspiratorially.

"Yeah. About the murders."

"I'd be delighted. Come by my house tomorrow morning. Eight o'clock.

At exactly eight o'clock the next morning, Delaney pulled up in front of Eleanor Haddley's home. It was a classical, if sprawling, New England saltbox house. Not as ostentatious as Blair Lowell's, but much more tasteful.

Before he could use the brightly polished doorknocker, the door swung open and Eleanor came out lugging a set of golf clubs.

"We have to hurry. We have an eight-fifteen tee time."

"Oh, I don't play golf."

Delaney addressed the ball on the first tee. He took a mighty swing and the ball dribbled off the tee. "See, I told you—"

"Nonsense. You're just out of practice." The octogenarian stepped up to the ball and whacked a beautiful two-hundred yard drive right down the middle of the fairway.

It wasn't until the fifth hole that he finally got the chance to ask her questions. She'd been giving him nonstop golf lessons for the first four holes, but to little effect. So far, he'd managed to slice, dub, snag hook, and shank his way to a forty-eight for the first four holes.

On the fifth green he stepped up to the ball that was a difficult lie fifty feet from the pin. "I hear Andrew had a near drowning accident." He took a swipe at the ball, hitting it too hard. It shot past the pin and came to rest twenty feet beyond.

Eleanor has a six-footer and examined the contour of the green carefully while Delaney prepared to take another shot.

"It was no accident I can tell you that. The poor thing. I told Whit he should put that boy in a home. There was something wrong with him from the start. That boy's pure evil."

Delaney prepared to putt, praying the ball wouldn't end up twenty feet too far in the other direction. He hated this game. He had visions of being out here till nightfall trying to make it through eighteen holes. "Andrew?" he said, addressing the ball, "he doesn't seem like such a bad kid."

"Move your feet closer together, Pete. No, not Andrew. His brother, Keith. He tried to drown Andrew and almost succeeded."

Delaney's head shot up in surprise as he swung his club and took a huge divot out of the green.

Eleanor looked at the crater he'd created. "Oh, dear," she said shaking her head, "the groundskeepers aren't going to like that one bit."

CHAPTER TWENTY THREE

Delaney barged into Sanborne's study with Jeff right behind him.

"I'm sorry, Mr. Sanborne," Jeff said. "He—"

"That's all right, Jeff. Leave us."

Sanborne, who was seated at an ornate antique desk, waited for the door to close before he reached for the telephone. "You have some nerve coming into my home like this. I told Royce you wouldn't work out and now I will demand that you be dismissed."

"All I want are some straight answers about your son, Keith."

Sanborne's head snapped back as though he'd been slapped in the face. Slowly, he put the phone down.

The Cove

The haughtiness and the arrogance drained from him. "How did you find out?"

"That's not important. Just tell me how Keith almost drown Andrew."

Wearily, Sanborne got up and stood by the patio doors, staring out at the ocean beyond. Below him the waters of the cove glistened through a stand of maples.

"After my wife left me—and the boys—I was determined to raise them myself. I might have been a failure as a husband, but I was determined not to be a failure as a father. After all, I told myself, if I could run a multi-million dollar corporation, I could surly raise two little boys." He tried for a laugh, but it came out a grunt. "But the task was infinitely more daunting than I ever imagined. Andrew was a joy, but Keith… Keith…" The pain of that memory was evident in his face. After a pause, he went on. "I took him to the best psychiatrists in the country, but all I got was a lot of psychobabble about personality disorder and anti-social behavior."

He opened the patio doors and stepped outside. Delaney followed. The sun had set and a pleasant breeze was blowing in off the ocean. Involuntarily Delaney's eyes went to the spot in the cove where he and JT had spent the night. It seemed such a long time ago.

"The Sanborne line goes back over two hundred years," Sanborne continued. "There has never been insanity or mental disorder in the family. Ever. I refused to accept their diagnoses. It's true that Keith had a mean, cruel streak, even as a boy. He hurt small animals. He destroyed things. He… Nevertheless, I couldn't—wouldn't—admit to myself that I could have such a son."

Sanborne cleared his throat. "Thank God I was home that day. It was midmorning. I went down to the cove to look for Andrew. I was going to take him to the office. He loved going there. "As I came onto the beach"—his voice cracked—"I saw Keith standing in five feet of water, holding Andrew's head under water. My God, Keith was only ten," he said in disbelief. "How could a ten-year-old even conceive of such a horrible thing to do to his brother? I carried Andrew out of the water. I had no idea how long he'd been under, but he wasn't breathing. I performed mouth to mouth and finally, he began to cough up water."

Sanborne turned away from the view. "I told everyone it was an accident. Andrew recovered, but the doctors said he'd been without oxygen for too long. They said he'd never be quite right..."

For the first time since he'd met this self-important and haughty man, Delaney felt sorry for him. He knew what it was like to lose a son. But he couldn't imagine what it must be like to have one son try to murder another. "What happened to Keith?"

"I shipped him off to a boarding school—boarding *schools*, I should say. My son is very smart, Mr. Delaney. Brilliant actually. An extremely high IQ. But for some reason he could not control his emotions. He was thrown out of one boarding school after another."

"Where is Keith now?"

Sanborne was once again in control and his expression had become inscrutable. "I don't know and I don't want to. He comes and goes. I see him when he needs money. Otherwise, I never hear from him and that's fine with me."

"Thanks for talking to me," Delaney said. "I know it's hard."

"Mr. Delaney, is Keith mixed up in any way with these murders?"

Delaney turned away from Sanborne's anguished eyes. "I want to talk to him. If you hear from him, let me know."

Back at the office, the clerical sergeant handed him an envelope from Detective Morgan of the State Police. Delaney ripped it open and his eyes went the summary of the amended fingerprint section of the report. *A second and thorough examination of the crime scene was conducted in order to ascertain the presence of latent fingerprints. After an exhaustive examination of the crime scene, only the prints of the murdered victims were found.* Delaney tossed the report on his desk. So the perps wore gloves. Not unheard of, but, still, it was unusual. Only professionals—or a very smart killer—would remember to wear gloves. What was it that Sanborne had said about his son: *Brilliant? Extremely high IQ?* With a sinking feeling Delaney suddenly realized that if Keith Sanborne was one of the murderers, he would not make any stupid mistakes any time soon. This investigation, he thought ruefully, had just gotten a hell of a lot more difficult.

JT and Clint came into the office and Delaney brought them up to speed on what he's learned. "So, the bottom line is," he concluded, "I think Andrew saw his brother in that telescope that night."

"Wow. What do we do now?" JT asked.

"Find Keith."

"How?" Clint asked.

"Have either of you ever seen Keith?" They both shook their heads. Delaney slid a photo of Keith that he'd gotten from Sanborne across the desk to Clint. "That's him. Clint, I want you to stake out the Flotsam."

"How come, Chief?" .

"The way Sanborne described his son, that's the most likely place he'll show up."

Clint checked his watch and yawned. It was almost twelve-thirty. He'd been sitting in his car parked up the street from the Flotsam for over three hours. Whenever someone came or went, he trained his binoculars on them, but so far he hadn't spotted anyone who resembled Keith. He was quickly finding that detective work was not nearly as exciting as the cop shows he watched on TV.

At this hour of the night, the Flotsam was jumping. An assortment of beach bums and bikers sucking on longneck beers had spilled out into the street. The deep thump, thump of the jukebox reverberated in the air giving Clint a headache.

A Mercedes pulling into a parking lot a block from the bar caught Clint's attention. Mercedes were not often seen in this part of town. He peered through his binoculars, but from his angle he couldn't see the license plate or the occupant. A scruffy man in his mid-twenties, who'd been standing in the street with a group of men, had also seen the Mercedes pull in. He broke away from the group and headed toward the car.

Watching through his binoculars, Clint saw a hand reach out the window and give the man an envelope. The man handed a small package back to the occupant. A shiver ran up Clint's spine. *He'd just witnessed his first drug sale.*

As the man faded into the darkness, the Mercedes made a U-turn and headed up the street toward Clint. Just as the car passed under a streetlight, he got a clear view of the driver. "*Holy shit!*" he said aloud as the Mercedes sped past him.

Delaney and JT were in the office reviewing the autopsy report when an excited Clint burst through the doors.

"Chief, you're never gonna believe this."

"Clint, sit down and catch your breath. You keep up this pace you're gonna get the big one before you're forty. You saw Keith?"

"No. You're not going to believe it, but I saw the *mayor* buy drugs."

"*Holy shit!*" JT exclaimed.

"That's exactly what I said," Clint said.

Delaney snapped forward in his seat. "Are you sure?"

"Yes, sir."

"Tell me everything. Don't leave anything out."

When Clint finished his story, a stunned JT said, "Do you think there might be a connection between the mayor and those murders?"

"Anything's possible," Delaney said. "All right, you guys want to be detectives, JT, tell me what you think we have so far?"

"Well, it would appear that the people on the sailboat were murdered because they saw something they shouldn't have seen. And from what Andrew described, it sounded like they may have inadvertently stumbled upon a drug transfer."

Delaney nodded. "Possible and plausible. Clint, why was Chief Brunetta murdered?"

The deputy shrugged. "Because he saw something he shouldn't have seen? Or maybe he found out something he shouldn't have known?"

"You're both right—to a point. When I start a homicide investigation, I always start with a working theory to explain the murder and I only discard it when the facts make it untenable. For example, Andrew was my prime suspect, but after seeing him there's no way he could have been the murderer. So that theory went out the window."

"What's your theory now, Chief?" Clint asked.

"That someone important in the town is behind these murders."

The two deputies looked at each other, staggered by the implication of what he was saying. It was hard enough to accept that a stranger had come into their peaceful town and murdered three people. But to imagine that the murderer might not only be a local, but in Delaney's words "someone important" bordered on the preposterous.

"Why would you think that?" JT blurted out.

"For openers, this is not a drug cartel operation."

"And how do you know that?" an exasperated Clint asked.

"Because big time syndicates bring drugs in on ships, not little boats. What we're talking about here are two-bit drug hustlers, and two-bit drug hustlers don't go around murdering people—especially police chiefs."

"So who murdered that couple and the chief," a confused Clint said.

"Here's how my theory plays out. From what you saw tonight, it would appear that Royce Gardiner has a drug problem. What would happen to the mayor if this came out?"

"He'd be finished in this town," JT said. "They're not real big on forgiveness around here."

"Right. I think those murdered people on the sailboat saw something that could have implicated Gardiner and he had them killed. Hell, he might have been one of the two men."

Clint shook his head. "I'm sorry, Chief. I just can't imagine Mr. Gardiner killing anyone."

"That's what the Bordens said about their nice daughter Lizzie."

"And what about the chief?" JT asked. "Why was he murdered?"

"That's where my theory makes even more sense. Tony was a sharp, experienced cop. There's no way he would allow himself to get setup for an assassination. When he went to that diner, I think he saw someone he knew. Someone he thought he could trust."

"*Royce Gardiner?*" the deputies said in unison.

Delaney smiled grimly. "I'll make detectives out of you two yet."

Clint exhaled sharply, trying to digest everything Delaney had just said. "Now what do we do?"

Delaney opened the desk drawer, took his 9mm out and shoved it into his holster. "Not we. Me. I'm gonna have a chat with the mayor."

Delaney did his best to hide it, but JT saw the fury burning in his eyes and it frightened her. She knew it was not a good idea for him to go there alone—not the way he was feeling. She jumped up. "We'll come, too."

"*No*," he snapped. "Amateur hour is over. I've got some serious business to do and I don't want you two getting in the way."

Before JT could protest, Delaney was out the door.

On the way over to Royce Gardiner's house, Delaney bitterly reflected on the ironic twist of events. In his twenty years in the NYPD, Tony Brunetta had survived getting shot, stabbed twice, and more brawls with fleeing felons than he could remember. He had to come to quiet, peaceful Haddley Falls to be murdered.

By the time Delaney pulled up to Gardiner's house, his anger was at a breaking point. But he reminded himself he had a job to do. First, he had to get Gardiner to tell him everything. There would be time for retribution later. Right now, it was important to stay in complete control.

He rang the doorbell of the darkened house. A moment later, the lights came on and Gardiner, with ruffled hair and striped pajamas, opened the door. "Chief Delaney? What in the world…"

Delaney pushed him aside and came into the house.

"Now just a minute," Gardiner protested. "What's the meaning of this…?"

"I have a few questions for you, Royce."

"Chief, it's after one in the morning for heaven's

sake. Can't this wait till tomorrow?"

Helen appeared at the top of the stairs. "Who is it, Royce?"

An astonished Delaney looked up at her. Even if he hadn't heard the slur in her voice he'd have known she was high as a kite just by looking at her. Her eyes sparkled and she had the dreamy look of someone who'd just had a cocktail of downers. *She* was the junkie in the family.

"Go to bed, Helen," Gardiner said curtly. "I'll handle this."

"Where's your stash, Helen?" Delaney shouted.

"What in the world are you talking about?" Gardiner said. He tried for outrage, but Delaney caught the fear in his eyes.

Delaney had promised himself he wouldn't lose control, but it was hard not to. Here were these two old rich people, who by day held themselves up as paragons of virtue and morality, but at night led a pathetic and sordid secret life that had led to the death of his friend.

Pushing Gardiner aside, he bounded up the stairs two at a time and grabbed Helen's thin wrist. "Where's the stuff, Helen? The bathroom?"

He dragged the confused woman into the bathroom. Now he was completely out of control. He yanked open the medicine cabinet. "Is it in here?" he shouted, sweeping pillboxes and jars of cold cream onto the marble floor. Shampoo and perfume bottle exploded on the floor and vanity.

"*What are you doing?*" a now hysterical Helen shrieked.

"I'm looking for the shit your husband bought at the Flotsam tonight. Where is it goddamnit?"

A terrified Royce Gardiner appeared in the door, pointing a gun at Delaney. "Stop right now or by God I'll shoot. I swear to God I will."

Delaney turned to face the terrified man. "You got the balls, Royce. Go ahead."

Gardiner thrust the gun toward Delaney. He tried mightily to pull the trigger, but he couldn't. His hand was shaking too much. "I can't," Gardiner muttered. "I can't..."

Delaney snatched the gun out of the old man's hand and slammed him against the door. "Is this the gun that was used on Tony?" he shouted, waving the gun in the mayor's face.

"Are you crazy?" Gardiner asked, genuinely bewildered by the accusation.

"It was about drugs, Royce, wasn't it? Those people on the sailboat saw something that could have destroyed your reputation. Then you lured Tony to the diner and killed him, too. Am I right?"

Gardiner shook his head violently. "No... no... Good God, do you honestly think I had something to do with Tony's death? That's insane."

A drug addled Helen, with mascara smudged on her face, crawled on the floor toward her husband.

"Royce... what's happening? I don't understand..."

Gardiner slumped to the floor and cradled her in his arms. "It's all right, Helen. It's all right..." Tears streamed down his face as he looked up at Delaney. "She's sick. She's been sick for a long time. What's the harm? A few pills... only at home... No harm... I don't know anything about what happened in the cove or about

Chief Brunetta's death. Mr. Delaney, you've got to believe me."

Suddenly Delaney saw the pathetic couple for what they really were—lonely, frightened people. And it snapped him out of his rage. He looked around the bathroom, ashamed of the wreckage he caused, hardly able to believe what he's done.

He knelt down beside Helen, but she cringed from his gentle touch. "Helen, I'm sorry. I didn't mean to frighten you. I thought..."

As his voice trailed off, it suddenly occurred to him that he'd made too many crazy assumptions, too many wild leaps of logic. And now he knew why. He'd committed the unpardonable sin of a homicide investigator—he'd allowed himself to become too close to an investigation. He'd made it personal and that had clouded his judgment. He'd allowed himself to react as Tony's friend and that was unacceptable. He might as well have JT and Clint handle the investigating and just go home. They couldn't screw it any more than he had. An investigation called for objectivity and clearly he had lost his ability to be objective.

Still, in spite of all that, he knew he would not—could not—quit until he had found Tony's murderer. Taking a deep breath, he willed himself to become once more a professional homicide investigator. "Royce," he asked quietly, "who's supplying you with the pills? I need his name."

Gardiner wiped the tears from his eyes. "His name is Wade. I don't know his last name..." An ashen faced Gardiner clutched Delaney's arm. "Chief," he said in a voice quivering with fear and despair, "if anyone finds out about this, I—we—are finished in Haddley Falls."

Delaney pried the frightened man's hand off his arm. "Just yesterday he'd felt sorry for Sanborne. And now, he was feeling sorry for the Gardiners. Maybe the rich weren't so different after all. Maybe behind the walls of their fancy houses and fancy lifestyles, they were just as pathetic as the rest of us.

"Don't worry, Royce," he said. "There's no need for anyone to know."

CHAPTER TWENTY FOUR

By the time Delaney arrived at the Flotsam it was closing time. Parked where Clint had been, he watched the last few stragglers stagger out of the bar. Just when he was beginning to think that Wade wasn't there, a man came out and stopped to light a cigarette. He was just as Clint had described him—short, muscle going to fat, a ponytail and an MIT tee-shirt. It was Wade.

The man climbed into a beat-up Chevy and pulled out of the parking lot. Delaney waited until the taillights were almost out of sight, and then he, too, pulled out and followed.

He was so intent on watching Wade's car that he didn't notice a figure standing in the shadows across the street watching him the whole time. After he pulled away, Keith Sanborne stepped out of the shadows, watched Delaney's car go down the road and ran to his pickup truck.

Delaney slowed down when he saw Wade's car pull into the driveway of a rundown bungalow. He pulled off the road, waited a few minutes and then with the headlights off coasted into the driveway next to Bowman's car.

He peeked in the kitchen window and saw Wade getting a beer from the refrigerator. He slipped around to the front of the house and knocked on the door.

When Wade opened the door, Delaney stuck his 9mm in the startled man's face. "Can we talk?" he said, backing the man into the living room.

"Yo dude, easy, man. Who the fuck are you?" Wade demanded.

"Rule number one…" He punched Wade in the stomach and the man crumbled to the floor. "Every time you lie, you get hit. There is no rule number two."

Delaney handcuffed him and pushed him onto the couch. "Where do you hide your stash, Wade?"

"I don't know what you're talking about."

Delaney slapped him across the face. Then he grabbed him by the neck and dragged him into the bedroom and threw him onto the bed. While a scowling Wade watched, Delaney emptied three bureau drawers and dumped the contents on the floor.

"Yo, you got a warrant or something?"

"Nope."

"Well, it's fucking illegal to search without a warrant."

"What's your point?"

Wade squinted at Delaney. "You really a cop?"

"Chief of Police. Can you believe that?"

He dumped the last of the drawers on the floor. "All right, I haven't got all night. Where is it?"

"Where's what?"

"Your stash. The stuff you sell to mayors."

"I don't know what the fuck you're talking about—"

Delaney backhanded Bowman, sending him sprawling off the bed with blood gushing from his nose. "You forgot rule number one again, didn't you?"

Wade had been hassled and busted by cops more times than he could remember, but he'd never met a crazier cop than this guy. "The floorboards under the rug," the terrified man muttered.

"Sit back down on the bed." As Wade awkwardly struggled to get off the floor, Delaney tossed a filthy rug aside and pried a floorboard loose, revealing a metal box the size of a shoebox. It was filled with pills and glassine envelopes.

"Okay, you're busted. Should I give you your Miranda or can you do it yourself?"

"All right you got my shit and you got me. Let's go."

An alarm bell went off in Delaney's head. *Wade was too anxious to go.* "Keeping rule number one in mind," he said, "is there anything else in the way of contraband that you should tell me about?"

The man shook his head. "No, dude. I swear to God." Clearly he was lying.

Delaney opened a closet door and saw Wade stiffen.

"There's nothing there, man. You got my shit. Let's go."

"It seems the drug dealer doth protest too much."

Delaney rummaged through the piles of dirty clothing and stacked boxes containing nothing of importance. He was about to give up. Then he noticed a large cardboard box on a top shelf. He pulled it down and inside was a radar unit with cut wires. And it all fell into place. Wade and Keith Sanborne were the two men in the boat. One of them, he was sure, had killed Tony.

In a rage, Delaney hurled himself at Bowman. They fell across the bed and dropped between the bed and the wall. Delaney jammed the barrel of his 9mm into the terrified man's cheek.

"You know what Russian roulette is, Wade? You put one bullet in a revolver, spin the chamber, and pull the trigger. Your chances of dying are just one in six. But I play Delaney style and I use an automatic. That's too bad for you because your chances of dying are a hundred percent."

The petrified man saw the murderous look in Delaney's eyes and believed he was about to die. "Don't do it, man," he sobbed. "Oh, Jesus… don't do it…"

Delaney picked Wade up and threw him on the bed.

"This radar unit came from the sailboat in the cove, didn't it?"

Wade nodded.

Delaney grabbed Wade by the hair and leaned real close to his face. "Keeping in mind rule number one, I want you to tell me the whole story from the beginning. Shine me on and this is your last night on earth."

Wade saw the wild look in Delaney's eyes and believed him.

"Okay, okay. I'll tell you whatever you want to know. But you gotta know it was Keith's idea."

Delaney felt a surge of adrenaline. *Keith*! His hunch had been right. Andrew had seen his brother in the telescope that night. "From the beginning, Wade, and don't leave anything out."

"It started when Keith asked me to help him get rid of a body."

"A body?" a puzzled Delaney asked. "What body?" He'd had assumed this was all about drugs. Suddenly all his carefully thought-out theories were coming apart. First Gardiner, and now this.

"I don't know who she was. Some prostitute. Keith ran a stable of girls. He told me something went wrong between the broad and a john. I don't know the details and I didn't want to know. Anyway, she was dead and he wants me to help him get rid of her."

"Why'd he pick you?"

"I got a boat."

"Go on."

"We waited until dark. Then I came into the cove with the boat. Keith was waiting for me on shore. He had the body in the back of his pickup. It was supposed to be real simple. And it would have been, if that goddamned sailboat hadn't come into the cove. The captain must have seen me come in and followed me. There's no way he could have gotten in on his own. Anyways, Keith sees the sailboat and goes bat shit and that scared the shit out of me."

"Why?"

"You don't know Keith, man. When that dude gets whacked out there's no telling what he'll do. I've seen him do some crazy shit."

"Go on."

"I'm, like, trying to tell him it's cool. All the while I'm praying that the sailboat go to the other end of the cove, but the sonofabitch comes right toward us. Keith threw a tarp over the body. There's two of them on the boat. A woman and a man. The guy told us he got some kind of equipment problem and he wants to anchor in the cove for the night. He wanted to know if the cove was deep enough and if there was any rocks and shit he should look out for. I tell him it's OK. I just want him to get the fuck away from us. "I look and Keith's got this crazy expression on his face as he watches the sailboat head for the other end of the cove. I've seen that expression before and I know that means trouble. I go, 'Keith, they didn't see nothing, dude. It's dark. There's nothing to worry about.'"

"What did he say?"

"He wasn't buying it. After we loaded the body into my boat, he says, 'take me out to the sailboat.' He still had that crazy look on his face and there was no telling what he might do. So I told him a lie. I told him we had to get out of the cove right away on account of the tide was going out and we could run aground. Thank God, he bought it. We dumped the body a few miles offshore."

"And then what?"

"I felt relief, man. We got rid of the body. The job was done. I just wanted to collect my two hundred bucks, go home and chill the fuck out on some fine weed. But then Keith says we gotta go take care of the people on the sailboat. I go, 'Keith, they didn't see nothing, man. Let's just leave well enough alone.' But he wouldn't listen. When Keith gets something in his head, there's no talking him out of it. He's like a damn dog with a bone. He opens his toolbox and takes out a tire iron and two knives. He hands me a knife. I go, 'Keith, I can't do no murder, man. Please, let's just forget about it. We'll go to Flotsam's and I'll buy you a drink.'"

"What'd he say?"

"He goes, 'if you don't do what I say, I'll cut your fucking heart out. You got gloves on board?' I say 'yeah,' and pull two pair out of a fish tackle box. He tells me to put on a pair and he puts on a pair. Now I'm really scared."

"So what happened next?"

"As soon as we come into the cove he tells me to cut the engine and we row over to the boat." By now Wade was sweating profusely. He wiped his face on his shoulder. "Man, don't make me go through this again," he pleaded. "I still get nightmares."

But Delaney had no intention of letting him off the hook. "You're breaking my heart, Wade. Keep talking." He nudged the man with the barrel of his gun. "And don't forget rule number one."

Reluctantly, the drug dealer continued. "We climb on board and sneak down into the cabin. They were both sleeping. Suddenly, the guy wakes up. He jumps up, but before he could do anything, Keith slashed his throat. Just like that. *Jesus…* I almost puked right there. The guy fell back on the bunk, gurgling in his own blood. I never saw so much blood in my whole life. Then the woman woke up. She never made it out of the bunk. Keith bashed her over the head with the tire iron. That was it. Just like that, they were both dead."

"Why did you mutilate them?"

"It wasn't my idea, dude, I want you to know that. I just wanted to get the fuck out of there. I was shaking like a leaf and I thought I was gonna hurl any minute. Then Keith gets this weird look in his eye and says, 'Wade, remember Charlie Manson?' *Shit*. Why did he have to mention that guy Manson? Wasn't he the dude with the girls that carved up that Sharon Tate broad?"

"The same. Go on."

"Keith says he wants to cover up the killings, make it look like it was done by some sex psycho or something. Next thing I know, he's cutting up the bodies real bad."

"What did you do?"

"Nothing. Well, at one point, Keith turns to me. He's *smiling*. Can you fucking believe that? Smiling. He goes, 'Wade you haven't done anything. Let me see you do something.' He had that crazy look in his eye again and I swear to God I thought he was going to do me like he did them. The woman was dead already, so I sorta stabbed her a couple of times. Just to satisfy Keith. I may be a doper, but I ain't no murderer. I did it because I was afraid Keith would kill me if I didn't."

"Save the excuses for the jury. Then what happened?"

"I got up on deck as fast as I could. When Keith came up he was carrying that radar unit. He cut away the antenna and hands it to me. 'What am I supposed to do with this?' I say. 'Maybe you get a few bucks for it', he goes. Then he tossed the tire iron into the water and we left."

Now came the hard part for Delaney. Asking the question that he'd been dreading. "Who killed Chief Brunetta and why did he die?"

"Hey, man. I had nothing to do with that. I swear to God."

Delaney grabbed him by the hair, savagely yanked his head back and jammed the gun barrel into his throat. "Remember rule number one?"

The terrified man started crying. "I'm telling you, man… I don't know nothing about that cop getting killed. I don't… I swear to God, you gotta believe me."

Delaney looked down at the man. Tears streamed down his face and he was trembling uncontrollably. Delaney holstered his gun. "I believe you. For now. But if I find out you lied to me about any of this, Wade, I'll kill you."

Delaney put the handcuffed man in the front seat next to him. "Why didn't you get out of town when you had the chance?" he asked Wade as they pulled out onto the road.

"It was Keith's idea. I wanted to go. I got family in Florida I could have holed up with. But he said if I left town, the cops would figure me for a suspect for sure."

"What about him?"

"Didn't matter. He comes and goes all the time."

"Did you know you sold pills to the mayor of Haddley Falls tonight?"

"No shit, that was the mayor? Damn. Well, I guess I'm not too surprised. I sell pills and shit to half the big shot townies on a regular basis."

Delaney was so intent on stitching Bowman's story into a coherent narrative that he didn't notice a pickup truck slowing overtaking them. Just as he was about to ask Wade if he knew where he could find Keith, the pickup roared alongside and slammed into Delaney's car. As Delaney fought to control the car, he glanced over and saw Keith yank the wheel again. The pickup slammed into him with a screeching of metal on metal. The side view broke off.

With one hand on the wheel, Delaney yanked out his automatic. As he tried to get a clear shot at Keith, the pickup slammed into him again. At that moment, Wade saw his chance to get away and kicked at Delaney and the steering wheel. Unable to deal with Keith's slamming into him and Wade's kicks, Delaney lost control. The car skidded off the side of the road smashed through a wooden barrier and plunged down a steep ravine, rolling over and over.

At the bottom of the ravine, the car stopped rolling, wedged upside down against a tree. For just a moment there was a strange, eerie silence. Then the car exploded into flames.

Releasing his seatbelt and using his elbow to smash the driver's side window, Delaney crawled out as the flames began to lick the interior of the car.

"*Help*! Wade screamed. *Don't leave me here!*"

For an instant Delaney was tempted to do just that. The piece of shit deserved to burn to death, but— not just yet. He still needed some answers. He ran around to the other side of the car. Shielding his face from the flames, he reached inside. "Give me your hand."

Wade grasped Delaney's hand in a death grip and his eyes were wide with fear. "I'm stuck, man. Don't let me die. Oh, please. *Get me outta here...*"

Delaney pulled on him, but he quickly saw that it was useless. The man's legs were pinned under the collapsed front firewall. Then he looked up and saw Keith making his way down the side of the ravine. He instinctively reached for his gun, but the holster was empty. Then he remembered he'd had the gun in his hand when they went off the road. It had to be in the car. He tried to peer into the car's interior, but the heat of the flames drove him back.

Suddenly, a shot whizzed by Delaney's head and thunked into the side of the vehicle.

Wade stretched out his hand. "*You gotta help me, man*," he pleaded with Delaney. "*Don't leave me here. Keith will kill me.*"

Another shot ricocheted off the car. This one closer. It was no use. Without a gun he was a sitting duck. He dove into the dark underbrush.

Keith, waving a gun in front of him, warily approached the burning car. He knelt down beside Wade.

"Hey, buddy, how you doing, man?"

"I didn't tell him nothing, Keith. I swear to God... Get me out of here..."

"You're a lying sack of shit." Without warning Keith raises his gun and fired two shots into Wade's head.

Fifty feet away, concealed by thick brush, Delaney watched helplessly as Keith murdered Wade in cold blood. He had to nail Keith before he got away. But how? He was unarmed and Keith had fired only two shots from his automatic. That meant he had at least five or six more rounds in the clip. Looking around, he realized that he might be able to use a stand of trees as cover to get around him. He judged he could get within fifteen feet of Keith—close enough to rush him before he got a shot off.

As he stood up, he stepped on a branch. Keith whirled and fired at the sound. A bullet kicked up dirt at Delaney's feet as he dove into a gully and rolled into the brush.

Slowly, Keith moved toward the sound of the noise. "I know you're there, cop," he shouted in a mocking tone. "Come on out."

Delaney was running out of options. If he stayed where he was, Keith would surely find him. If he got up and ran, he had no cover and he'd be an easy target. Then, somewhere nearby, he heard the gentle sound of running water. It had to be a steam or a river. He crawled toward the sound and found a stream. And now he was faced with two more choices—neither of them very good. He could stay on the bank and get shot like a fish in a rain barrel or he could slip into the stream and probably drown. He decided he'd rather drown than give Keith the satisfaction of shooting him.

Convincing himself that the stream was shallow—no more than a a few feet, he prayed—he slid into the water. The surprisingly cold water took his breath away. But the real surprise came when he tried to stand and found he couldn't touch bottom. In an uncontrollable panic he lunged for the bank with flailing arms, deciding that he'd rather take on Keith than drown after all. Then, mercifully, his feet touched the bottom. He grabbed onto an overhanging branch while he regained his breath and listened. Then, no more than forty feet away, he saw Keith standing on the edge of the gully silhouetted against the flaming car.

Keith slid down the ridge and started toward Delaney. Fighting to control his fear of the water, Delaney ducked under water. The cold, black, gurgling water enveloped him and seemed to be trying to suffocate him. He gasped, swallowing a mouthful of water. Fighting the urge to gag, he kept saying to himself over and over again, *You can do this… You can do this…*

Keith didn't know where Delaney was, but he assumed he'd gone into the stream. As he stepped forward to investigate, he heard the faint sounds of sirens in the distance. He hesitated, then, cursing, he pointed the gun toward the stream and emptied his clip into the water before he ran back up the hill to his pickup.

Still submerged, Delaney heard—and felt—bullets zinging and corkscrewing all around him. He concentrated on holding his breath. But then, there was sudden roaring in his ears and lights exploded behind his tightly shut eyes. He was losing consciousness. He shot his head out of the water gasping for air, fully expecting to see Keith on the bank, pointing a gun at him. Instead, over the soft gurgling stream and the sound of his own frantic gasping for air, all he heard was the welcoming sound of sirens in the distance. "Here comes the cavalry," he muttered, stumbling out of the water and collapsing onto the muddy bank.

Delaney stood on the road with JT and Clint and watched the paramedics carry Wade's charred body up the hill. Except for a nasty gash in his forehead and a badly strained arm—"It's only my drinking arm," he'd kidded an anxious JT. "Good thing I don't use it anymore."—he'd come out of the accident relatively unscathed.

"You sure it was Keith?" Clint asked.

"Yeah. I got a good look at his face before I went off the road."

"That dead prostitute may be the key to everything," JT said. "If we could just find her and ID the body—"

"That's a big ocean out there," Clint said, stating the obvious. "How're we gonna find her?"

"I don't know," Delaney said. "But I know who might know."

The next morning Delaney drove out to the Coast Guard station and found the commander on the dock supervising a training exercise. He turned when he saw Delaney approaching. "Yes, sir. What can I do for you?"

"Morning, Commander. I'm Pete Delaney, Chief of Police, Haddley Falls. I'm investigating a murder and I have a question for you."

"Sure, Chief. Fire away."

"If a body was dumped a couple of miles off Crater Cove, where do you think it would end up?"

The commander frowned. "That depends, Chief. If it's weighted down properly, never. But that's not usually the case. It'll most likely surface, but where it ends up depends on wind, current, and tide. We've had people drown off the beach at Haddley Falls and end up as far as a hundred miles up the coast."

"That's not real encouraging. You're saying it could end up anywhere.

"Sorry, wish I could be of more help."
"Me, too."

CHAPTER TWENTY FIVE

Back at the stationhouse, a disappointed Delaney summed up for JT and Clint where they were with the investigation: "Our best witness is dead and our best piece of evidence is somewhere in the Atlantic ocean. There's a technical term for this—we're fucked."

"And we still don't know who murdered Chief Brunetta," JT said glumly.

"Or why." And that bothered Delaney most of all.

"So what's next?" JT asked.

"I guess we should look for Keith," Clint offered.

JT was doubtful. "He's gotta be a hundred miles from here by now and still running."

"Maybe," Delaney said. "Or maybe not."

"You think he's still around here?" JT asked.

"Bad guys do some very stupid things. And psychotic bad guys do a lot of very stupid things. I want you both to go out and beat the bushes. Hit the Flotsam,

The Cove

the beach, the harbor, gin mills, motels—anywhere you think he might turn up. Ask questions."

As they were getting up to leave, he cautioned them, "Remember, if you come across him, don't try to take him on alone. That's what you have cell phones for." What he didn't tell them was that he wanted the pleasure of taking out Keith Sanborne himself.

It was late afternoon and Sanborne was in his study reading. Suddenly, he sensed something and turned to see Keith standing by the open French doors.

"What are you doing here? I told you—"

"I need money."

"I just gave you money."

"I need a lot more."

Keith crossed the room and slid a painting aside, exposing a safe. "Open it."

"Get out."

"Don't be so grumpy, Pop. I have good news for you. As of today, you have seen the last of me. What's that worth to you?"

Sanborne peered over his reading glasses and asked the question that he didn't want answered. "Are you involved in those cove murders?"

"I really don't have time for a father-and-son heart-to-heart just now. Open the safe, give me the money, and I'm outta here."

"No, I will not do that," Sanborne said firmly. "I've done enough for you and you've given me nothing but grief. I want you out of here, Keith. I know you're my son, but I don't ever want to see you again."

"You won't. that's what I'm trying to tell you. Just open the safe." Keith pointed a gun at his father. "I'm not going to tell you again."

Sanborne took his reading glasses off and wearily tossed them on the desk. He was tired of fighting his son and tired of protecting him. "Kill me and you'll never get the money."

Keith's eyes glistened with a wild hatred as he debated whether he should kill his father or not. For as long as he could remember, he'd always hated his old man, but he never could figure out why. He shook his head to clear that thought from his head. He didn't have time for this. "You've got a point, Pop. Instead of killing you, maybe I'll just go upstairs and finish the job I started with Andrew." He started toward the door.

"No... for God's sake..." Sanborne cried out. "All right. I'll give you what you want. Just leave Andrew alone."

As soon as Sanborne opened the safe, Keith pushed his father aside and took out stacks of cash. "That's what I like about you, Pop. You always have a lot of cash on hand. I don't know what I'd do if you were a credit card kind of father."

Sanborne sat down heavily. "Go. Just go."

Keith stuffed the rolls of money into his jacket pockets. "Oh, I'll need the keys to the Mercedes. My truck was in an accident."

"They're in the car," Sanborne said, too beaten down to argue.

"I wish I could say it's been great," Keith said, as he disappeared through the patio doors.

Sanborne stared at the open safe for a long time. Then he came to the most painful decision of his life and reached for the telephone.

"Haddley Falls Police Department. May I help you?" the dispatcher asked.

"I need to talk to Chief Delaney right away."

In his office Delaney picked up the telephone. "Delaney here."

"Chief... this is Whit Sanborne. My son... Keith... was just here."

Delaney stood up. "How long ago?"

"He just left. He took money and my Mercedes."

Delaney slammed down the phone and rushed out to the front desk. "What's the quickest way to get to the interstate from Sanborne castle?" he asked the desk sergeant.

The sergeant traced the route on a wall map. "Down the coast road to Holly Avenue, then west to the interstate…" He turned and Delaney was gone.

Delaney drove down Holly Avenue and made a left onto the coast road, hoping to intercept Keith. He prayed that the sergeant was right about the shortcut. He drove down the coast road, zooming past other cars at a speed of over a hundred miles an hour. He slowed only to look at the faces of the drivers in the occasional oncoming car. It seemed like every other car was a black Mercedes. Suddenly, a Mercedes blasted past him from the opposite direction. Delaney saw the driver's face for a split second, but he recognized Keith. He slammed on the brakes and made a screeching U-turn.

Keith looked in his rearview mirror and saw the police car make a U-turn. He stomped on the gas and the powerful auto surged forward.

Delaney had the accelerator floored, but his SUV was no match for the more powerful Mercedes' engine. To make up time he kept his foot on the gas through curves and bumps in the road. As he rocketed over bumps and skidded though turns, he was on the verge of losing control, but he did make up some distance.

He looked ahead and saw that there were no cars coming in the opposite direction. This could be his only chance. He couldn't let Keith make it to the interstate because he was certain he would lose him there. He unholstered his gun. It was a long shot he knew. He was too far away, he would be aiming at a moving target, and his bouncing SUV would make it difficult, if not impossible, to hit him. But he had to try. "Here goes nothing," he muttered, emptying a clip at the rear of the Mercedes. Then, to his amazement he saw the rear window shatter.

When the rear window exploded, Keith felt a sharp sting in the back of his head. He didn't know if he'd been shot or it was a shard of glass. He touched the back of his head and felt a trickle of blood. That momentary distraction was enough to allow the car to start drifting off the road. When Keith realized what was happening, he cut the wheel to compensate, but he over corrected and the car began to fishtail. Keith fought to stay on the road, but there was too much momentum and the rear end skidded off the road. When he tried to get back, the wheels caught in the uneven edge of the road and whipped the steering wheel out of his hands. Totally out of control, the car made a sharp lurch to the left and the car rolled over.

Delaney watched the Mercedes roll several times and he skidded to a stop in a cloud of dust twenty feet behind the upside down car. Through the dust, he saw Keith crawl out of the car and take off into the woods. He aimed at the retreating man's back and pulled the trigger. *Click.* The gun was empty. The he remembered—*he'd fired the entire clip at the Mercedes.* Cursing, he jammed a fresh clip into gun and ran into the woods after Keith.

Bleeding from a gash in his forehead, Keith staggered through the trees and ran up a hill. He came to a clearing, rushed to the edge, and stopped. A hundred feet below the roaring ocean crashed onto jagged rocks. He has nowhere to go but back the way he'd come.

He turned and saw Delaney coming toward him through the trees. He crouched down and took aim. When Delaney stepped into a clearing, he fired.

The round kicked up dirt at Delaney's feet, but he kept coming. Keith fired another round and leaves from a branch over Delaney's head fluttered to the ground. *The sonofabitch won't stop.* Furious, he fired three quick rounds that went wild, and then—*click. The gun was empty.*

Delaney kept coming. "Give it up, Keith," he shouted.

Keith backed toward the cliff.

When Delaney was less than thirty feet away, he stopped. "I've got questions. You've got answers." Keith had a wild, evil grin on his face. It was the look of a psycho, a look Delaney had seen many times before.

"Okay, Delaney," Keith called out. "You want to play questions and answers? What do you say we play *Jeopardy*? I'll be Alex Trebek and you'll be the contestant. Ready? Here's the answer: Pete Delaney. For one million dollars, what's the question?"

Delaney shrugged, not knowing where this was going. "You got me, Keith. I give up."

Keith grinned manically. "Oops, I just heard the sound of the buzzer. Sorry, no million dollars. The question is: What was the name of the man who was setup to take over the investigation after Brunetta was out of the way?"

It took a second for Delaney to get it. "Me..." he said softly.

"Correct. My client paid me to off Brunetta so a drunk like you would take over the investigation, knowing you'd fuck it up."

Delaney felt a knot forming in his stomach as he realized the implication of what Keith was saying hit him. *Tony Brunetta had been murdered so he could be manipulated into taking over the job.*

Keith saw the anguish in Delaney's face and grinned. "You're not very good at this game are you? Then again, you've not been very good at finding out who was behind your buddy's murder either. Maybe *Jeopardy* is too hard for you. I'll tell you what, let's play an easier game. How about *The Price Is Right*? Pick the right door, Delaney, and I'll tell you the name of the client who hired me to kill Brunetta."

Delaney said nothing. He wanted nothing more than to blast the miserable sonofabitch off the cliff, but first he had to know the name of the man who ordered the death of his friend.

Keith started laughing manically. "Give up? Want to know the client's name? *Come on down*," he shouted. And then, without warning, he turned and dove straight off the cliff.

Delaney rushed toward him. "*No*—!"

He reached the edge of the cliff just in time to see Keith's body bounce off the jagged rocks below.

"You *sonofabitch*..." Enraged, he aimed his gun at Keith's broken body and emptied his clip into him.

The next morning, at Royce Gardiner request, Delaney appeared in his office to brief him and Jonathan Talbot on the results of his investigation. Sanborne had been invited, but, understandably, declined to come. Eleanor Haddley was out of town.

Delaney, sitting at the conference table across from Gardiner and Talbot, concluded his report. "And so, Keith murdered the couple because he thought they saw him with the body and could ID him."

Talbot shook his head in dismay. "My God. And he murdered Tony, too?"

Delaney nodded.

"Do you have any idea who hired Keith to kill Chief Brunetta?" Gardiner asked.

"No, I don't."

An image of Keith diving off the cliff flashed in his mind. All last night he'd relived that moment in a reoccurring nightmare. In the nightmare he'd been able to reach out and pull Keith back from the brink. But every time he asked Keith who his client was, Keith simply laughed in his face.

He looked across the table at Gardiner and Talbot, wondering if one of them could be the client. But maybe the client was a woman? Blair Lowell? Eleanor Haddley? Or maybe it was someone he'd never even met. After all, at the country club he's demonstrated to an awful lot of influential people in Haddley Falls that he was a certified drunken buffoon. But what did it matter? All the speculation in the world wasn't going to tell him who ordered Tony's death. Because he didn't know—would never know—he could trust no one in this town.

"Well, what's next, Chief?" Talbot asked.

"That's it. I'm done."

"But what about the dead prostitute?" a startled Gardiner asked.

"What about her? Maybe she'll bob to the surface someday. Maybe not. What's the difference? It won't bring Tony back or those two people."

Talbot stood up. "Regrettably, I believe you're right, Chief. I think it's time we put this unfortunate matter behind us. You've done a great job for our community. Thank you very much," he said, shaking Delaney's hand.

Gardiner walked Delaney outside. As they stood on the steps outside his office and watched tourists streaming in and out of gift shops, Gardiner said, "Thank you for not bringing up that… that matter, Chief."

"It's no one's business, Royce. Just get her help."

"I already did. She left yesterday to visit a 'sick aunt' in Ohio. It could be sometime before she comes home."

Delaney studied the busy flow of traffic on Main Street. "And I thought small towns had no secrets."

"Not true, Mr. Delaney. This town, like any other, is full of deep, dark secrets."

Delaney was sorting out the case files, his last act as police chief, when Lt. Turner came in.

"I spoke to Gardiner," Delaney said. "He's agreed to make you the new chief."

Turner frowned. "I don't know if I want the job."

"Why not?"

"I couldn't have investigated these murders. I would have been in way over my head."

"Welcome to the club."

"Would you consider staying and keeping the job?" Turner asked.

"I thought you wanted the job."

"I did. But I kind of like the arrangement we have now."

Delaney was genuinely touched. From the first time he'd met Turner at the cove, he was sure they were going to have it out someday. One more person I've misjudged, he thought ruefully. Perhaps I'm not the greatest detective in the country after all. "I can't, take the job, Walt. There's something else I have to do."

Turner offered his hand. "Well, OK. Good luck, Chief."

Delaney shook his hand. "Good luck to you, too, Chief."

When Delaney came out of the stationhouse, JT was waiting for him in the parking lot. "Well, I guess that's it?"

"Yeah. I put the case files in my—in Turner's office."

"So he's going to get the chief's job?" She didn't sound enthused at that prospect.

"He's not that bad. If there are no more murders in this town, he should do fine."

"Pete, why don't you come over for dinner tonight. I mean, that is, if you're not busy."

"I'd like to, JT, but there's something I have to do tonight."

The truth was, he would have liked nothing better than to take her up on the offer, but he did have something he had to do—something he'd promised he'd do as soon as the investigation was over.

"Is it Blair?" she blurted out. "Oh... I'm sorry," she said, reddening. "I shouldn't have said that. It's none of my business."

Since he'd first met her, JT had always displayed a fierce self-confidence, but now she was showing another side of herself, a more vulnerable side, and he found it appealing.

"It's nothing like that, JT," he answered, feeling a sudden wave of unbearably sadness come over him. "It's something I have to do alone."

"Pete, you shouldn't be alone tonight. We all feel terrible about what happened. It's so frustrating when there are loose ends..."

"Tony always hated loose ends." The sadness was about to overwhelm him. He had to get away. "I gotta go. You take care."

"Yeah, you, too," she said, puzzled at his sudden abruptness.

She stood in the parking lot and watched him drive away in his old, beat-up Honda, feeling, herself, a terrible sadness.

CHAPTER TWENTY SIX

It was time to finish what he'd started the night of Tony's funeral. On the way back to the house, Delaney stopped at a liquor store and bought a bottle of scotch. The owner recognized him and thanked him profusely for solving the murders and saving the town from economic ruin. Delaney, already in despair because he'd been unable to find out who ordered Tony's murder, mumbled a thank you and left quickly. The guy was a civilian and there was no point in telling him that as long as the man who ordered Tony's death was still at large, Tony Brunetta's murder was not solved.

By the time he got to the house, it was almost nine o'clock and darkness had descended on the surrounding woods. He took the scotch and his gun out to the back porch and sat down on a worn wicker chair that gave off a mild sent of mold and mildew. He poured a drink and stared at the amber liquid, wondering how something so beautiful could be so devastating.

Booze had become the central part of his life—his life support system—after Kitty and little Peter died. It was a conscious choice—and the only thing that eased the pain. He'd always believed that when and how much he drank was nobody's damn business. He hurt no one but himself. Or so he'd thought. It never occurred to him that his drinking could hurt another human being. But his drinking—being a *drunk*—had cost his best friend his life. He would never forgive himself for that. But, of course, in his case "never" wouldn't be for very long.

He swished the scotch around in the glass, wanting to drink it down, to feel the sharp taste of liquor, to start the numbing process that would make the hurt go away. But he couldn't do it. Not just yet. He had to live with the pain a little while longer. It would be his way of expiating his guilt for what he had done to Tony.

He put the glass down on the table next to his gun. Somewhere in the distance, a whippoorwill started its mournful song.

At the same time Pete Delaney was listening to the whippoorwill, Bobby Collins was steering his skiff across a calm ocean illuminated by an enormous full moon that carved a shimmering silver streak across the surface of the water. Bobby played his flashlight across the water in front of him. In the distance, a Clorox bottle he used as a float for his lobster pots glowed dimly. He gunned the motor and pulled alongside. He grinned as he pulled the pot aboard. This had been one of the most profitable nights in a long time. Every pot had given up at least two hefty lobster. This one yielded four.

As he was headed toward his next pot, he saw something white and shapeless floating about a fifty yards to starboard. Curious, he turned the bow toward it and gunned the engine. In his seven years of harvesting lobsters, he'd come across the damnedest things out on the water—everything from a bale of Mexican Gold marijuana to a life preserver from a US warship.

He was almost upon it, but he still couldn't tell what it was. It was long and very white. *Maybe a dead baby Pilot whale.* He's seen plenty of those, too. Sometimes the inexperienced young whales, confused or terrified by the sound of propeller screws, failed to get out of the way and were run over. As he came along side, he poked at the blob with his boat pole. The formless shape rotated slowly and the bloated face of woman, tangled in a mass of hair, stared up at him, pale and eerie in the soft glow of the moon.

Delaney still hadn't touched his drink. He'd decided he would wait until the whippoorwill stopped singing. As if on cue, the bird stopped as suddenly as it had begun.

"A sign from the gods," he said to the woods and picked up the glass. He stared at the scotch and then, just as he was about to take a sip, the phone rang. He let it ring—he had no intention of picking it up—but then he stiffened when he heard Tony's cheerful Bronx-accented voice: *"This is Chief Brunetta. Please leave your name and number. I'll get back to you as soon as I can."*

The answering machine beeped and he heard JT's voice, "Pete, are you there? Pick up the phone. We found the dead prostitute."

Delaney closed his eyes, wanting her to stop talking, wanting her to leave him alone.

"Will you pick up the damn phone?"

He put the glass down, stomped into the kitchen and grabbed the phone. "Where is she?" he snapped.

"The county morgue."

"You should go see her."

"What about you?"

He turned toward the porch door and saw the full glass and the gun on the table. "I'm out of the cop business," he said, hanging up.

In the stationhouse, JT slammed the phone down. "Shit."

Clint was standing next to her. "What did he say?"

"He doesn't work here anymore."

"So what should we do now?"

"Go take a look at the body I guess."

"What for?"

"How the hell should I know? We should just look. That's all."

Pete settled back into the wicker chair. He picked up the scotch and sniffed it, savoring its smell, remembering how alcohol had helped him get through so many tough times. "I need you just one more time, buddy," he said to the glass. " Just to.. just to…" Suddenly, he slammed the glass down on the table. "Goddamn it," he muttered He snatched up the gun and headed for the door.

Five minutes later, he pulled into the hospital parking lot. He found Dr. Bynum in the autopsy room about to begin his work. Bynum glanced up when Delaney came in. "I'm getting way too much practice at this, Chief."

Delaney pulled the sheet away. Mercifully, the putrid smelling body gases had dissipated, but now the body smelled like rotten fish. She looked like a typical floater—bleached white, flabby skin, bloated extremities. Fish had nibbled parts of the flaccid flesh. It was impossible to tell if she'd been pretty in life. One eye was missing and the other was almost gone.

What could a dead prostitute tell him about Tony's murder? He was on a fool's mission, he told himself. Just as he was about to turn away, to go back to the house and finish what he had started, he noticed a mark on her neck that looked familiar. He leaned closer. And then he remembered where he had seen a similar mark. "Doc, help me turn her over."

He examined her buttocks. Again, the same marks he'd seen on— "Blair..." he muttered.

Bynum looked up. "Who?"

Delaney was already out the door.

JT pulled into the hospital parking lot less than a minute after Delaney had pulled away. She turned off the engine.

"What are we doing here?" Clint asked, nervously licking his lips.

"Clint, we're the police."

"Oh, right. I keep forgetting."

When they came into the autopsy room Bynum was conducting a physical inspection of the body and dictating into a tape recorder. JT and Clint made it a point of looking everywhere—except at the table where the body was.

Bynum switched off the tape recorder. "Are you here to see the body, too?"

"What do you mean, *too*?" JT asked.

"Chief Delaney was just here, but he lit out of here like his hair was on fire."

"Pete was here? Where did he go? What did he say?"

"I don't know. He mentioned someone named Blair."

JT raced for the door. "Clint, you stay here."

"All I know is I'm retiring right after this and moving to Florida," Bynum said to a perplexed Clint.

Delaney screeched to a stop at the front door of Blair Lowell's house and was out of the car before it stopped rocking. He ran up the steps and pounded on the door.

A moment later, Blair opened the door. "Well, well. What a surprise—"

Delaney pushed her inside.

"*Pete*, what the—"

"Where did you get that mark on your neck?"

"What mark?"

Delaney ripped her high-necked blouse open and dragged in front of a hall mirror. "That mark." He had his hand around her neck, squeezing. "Where did you get it?"

"Pete...I...can't...breath..."

"So help me, Christ, I'll kill you if you don't tell me. Where?"

"*Jonathan...*"

Staggered by what she'd just said, he let her go and she slumped to the floor, gasping for breath.

"Jonathan Talbot?"

"It's the way he enjoys sex..."

He helped her off the floor and tried to rearrange her torn blouse. "I'm sorry..."

She pushed him away. "Get the hell out of my house, you crazy bastard. What right do you have to come in here like this and—"

He grabbed both her shoulders and shook her. "Listen to me, Blair. I just saw marks like that on a body in the morgue."

Blair paled. "Oh, my God..."

He led the shaken woman into the living room and sat her on a couch. "Tell me everything he did."

She wiped her eyes, smudging her mascara. "Pete, I need a drink."

He tossed a couple of ice cubes into a glass and filled it with vodka. "This is important, Blair. Don't leave anything out."

"God, this is so embarrassing. Jonathan got off on bondage. It wasn't my thing of course, but I'm always willing to try anything once. He tied my hands behind my back with a silk rope. Then he ran the rope up around my neck and tied it to the bedpost."

Delaney handed her the vodka.

"Aren't you having one?"

"Maybe later." He sat down next to her. "Go on."

"Then he used a whip. That's how I got the marks on my butt. He said a little pain heightens the pleasure. Well, he kept hitting me and it started to hurt. I told him I'd had enough and to let me go. But he kept hitting me and the more I struggled, the more the rope tightened around my neck. I told him, enough was enough. I told him that I couldn't breathe. Well the stupid bastard wouldn't stop and I actually passed out and... Oh, my God... I could have been asphyxiated."

Delaney pulled out his cell phone and punched in a number.

A receptionist said, "County Hospital—"

"This is Chief Delaney. Put me through to Dr. Bynum."

A moment later, Bynum picked up. "Bynum here."

"She didn't drown, did she?"

"Why, no, Chief, she didn't. There was no water in her lungs. But how'd you know—"

"Her windpipe was collapsed. She died of asphyxiation."

"Why, yes, that's right. But how did you—"

Delaney hung up and rushed out the door.

CHAPTER TWENTY SEVEN

Delaney had never been to Jonathan Talbot's home, but he could have guessed that he'd have the biggest house in the most exclusive part of Haddley Falls where mansions hid behind twelve-foot hedges trimmed to a millimeter of plumb by an army of illegal aliens.

He rang the doorbell and was relieved when Talbot answered the door. He didn't want any witnesses to what was about to take place.

Talbot tried to mask his surprise. "Mr. Delaney, what brings you here?"

"Loose ends. May I come in?"

Talbot led Delaney into his den. "Grab a seat. Pete, you've got to try this." He went to the bar and poured scotch into two tumblers. "I know you're a man who can appreciate a good drink." He handed Delaney a tumbler. "This is the finest single malt Scotland produces. It cost three hundred dollars, but I got it from a grateful client."

Delaney took a sniff and put the glass down.

Talbot frowned when Delaney didn't take a drink, but he didn't say anything. He downed his own drink and quickly poured another, wondering why the troublemaking cop was here.

"Where's Mrs. Talbot?" Delaney asked.

"Off on a shopping spree in New York. For the life of me I can't imagine what she does with all the crap she buys. Women. Who can figure them out? Wasn't it Freud who said, 'What do women want?' God, I wish I knew. Well, anyway I'm a bachelor for the weekend and that's not all bad," he said, winking at Delaney.

Good for him, but not for some poor prostitute. Delaney could imagine Talbot tying up yet another prostitute this weekend. Would this one die, too, or survive his pathetic perversions? "When I debriefed you and Royce, I didn't tell you everything," he said.

"Really?"

"Before Keith did a swan dive off the cliff, he and I had a chat."

Talbot gulped his drink, poured another, and sat down trying his best to appear calm.

"He told me you were the one who hired him to get rid of the prostitute," Delaney said casually.

Talbot tried to chuckle, but it came out more like a cackle. "That's preposterous. Besides," he said, studying Delaney carefully to see if he were bluffing, "if you had that information, why didn't you use it before?"

"I didn't have the body then." He saw Talbot stiffen. "I just came from the morgue, Jonathan. She's so bloated her own mother wouldn't recognize her. But the bruises are real clear. Rope marks on the neck. Whip marks on the buttocks. Typical S&M stuff. Hardly the kind of thing a future Secretary of Commerce should be involved in."

Talbot slammed his empty glass on the table. "If you are suggesting that I am into some kind of kinky sex and murdered that girl, you are out of your mind."

"That's not what Blair says."

Talbot looked as though he were going to be physically ill. He poured himself another drink, sloshing most of it on his hand. "Blair Lowell is a fool and a slut who'll sleep with anyone. Apparently, even you."

Delaney was enjoying Talbot's discomfort. "You know what, Jonathan? Gardiner was wrong about this town. There are no secrets here. Sooner or later someone talks."

"Why did you come here?" Talbot demanded.

"Just trying to tie up loose ends."

Talbot stood up abruptly. His mounting panic was making it hard for him to think clearly. Should he run? Should he bluff it out? How much did Delaney really know? He regretted gulping down those drinks. He was beginning to feel dizzy, just when he needed to have all his wits about him.

He moved toward his desk. "Do you like cigars, Mr. Delaney?" He opened the brass and mahogany humidor and removed a tray of cigars. At the bottom of the box was a loaded nine-millimeter Berretta. "These are Cubans," he said, pleased at how calm he sounded. "They're truly excellent and you must try one." He stared down at the gun, calculating his chances. Could he get the gun out before Delaney could react? What if Delaney got the gun away from him? Hell. What choice did he have? He snatched up the gun and fumbled with the safety not remembering if the safety was on or off. When he looked up, Delaney was pointing a gun at him.

"I think they call this a Mexican standoff, Jonathan." Delaney was grinning, but there was a cold, deadly gleam in his eyes. "But you know what? I have the advantage because I'm suicidal." Pete moved to the center of the room and dropped the gun to his side. "Go ahead, Jonathan. I'll give you the first shot. But swing the barrel over, you're pointing way too far left."

A horrified Talbot looked into Delaney's eyes and saw absolutely no fear. "You're insane..."

"I'll buy suicidal, but I'm not so sure about the insane part."

Talbot's finger tightened on the trigger. He wanted nothing more than to snuff out the life of this meddlesome policeman. But he didn't have the nerve to pull the trigger. He dropped the gun to the floor.

In a blur, Delaney was on him. He jammed his automatic into Talbot's neck and forced him to the ground. "Do you know what Russian roulette is, Jonathan?" Delaney whispered. "You put one bullet in a revolver, spin the chamber, and pull the trigger. Your chances of dying are just one in six. But, bad news for you. I play Delaney style and I use an automatic. And that means your chances of dying are a hundred percent."

"*Stop*! For the love of God! What do you want?"

"You can start with the truth."

"All right. All right. I'll tell you everything."

Delaney dragged Talbot to his feet and shoved him into a chair. "From the beginning."

When Talbot regained control of his breathing, he began. "It was an accident for God's sake. I didn't mean for that girl to die. When it happened, I didn't know what to do. Obviously, I couldn't call the police. I called Keith. He's the one who got me the girl in the first place. You've got to believe me, I had no idea that maniac would murder those people on the sailboat. He was just supposed to dispose of the body. That's all. Damn him."

Delaney asked the painful question. "Why did you have Tony killed?"

"I didn't mean for that to happen either. I convinced Gardiner and Sanborne that we couldn't afford to have the state police come in because—well, as I pointedly told them, we all had skeletons in our closet. That was just an excuse, but it was enough to scare them into accepting my plan. I let them believe I was afraid of state police involvement because of my pending cabinet appointment. But the truth was, I was afraid that a professional investigation by the state police would discover my involvement with the girl."

"*Involvement*? You certainly have a way with words. Jonathan, you killed her."

"You can quibble over semantics, but the point is, it was an accident. That's all it was. In any event, I convinced Gardiner and Sanborne that Tony should handle the investigation."

"That was another mistake, Jonathan. Tony was the best homicide investigator in the NYPD. Perrault and a dozen of his asshole investigators couldn't find granite in New Hampshire."

"I will concede that Tony was a good policeman back in New York, but without the proper support I didn't think he had a chance of getting to the bottom of it. Then, the night of the dance, I asked him if he could solve the murders alone. He said he could and I believed him. He was so confident, it frightened me. At that moment, I knew I'd made a tactical mistake. But what could I do? Then, later that night, when you crashed onto my table in a drunken stupor, I realized *you* were the solution to my dilemma. Chief Brunetta had told me that you two were very close, like brothers. If something happened to Brunetta, I was fairly certain you would insist on running the investigation. I would see to it that you did handle the investigation. With you in charge, I knew I wouldn't have to worry about a drunk getting to the bottom of these murders."

Delaney's mouth went dry and pinwheels floated before his eyes as he was reminded once again that *he* was the cause of Tony's death.

Delaney fought mightily to contain his rage. The matter of fact way Talbot was telling the story, he could have been talking about an exceptionally good golf game he'd had last Saturday. He could feel his finger tightening on the trigger. He just wanted to kill Talbot and get it over with, but he had to hear the whole story first, no matter how painful it might be. The sequence of events was painfully clear to him. He didn't need Jonathan to spell out what he already knew, but he had to hear it from his mouth.

"So you hired Keith to murder Tony, knowing I would insist on taking over."

"Keith and I were waiting for Tony behind the diner. As soon as the chief got in the car, Keith jumped up from the back seat and…" Talbot shrugged.

It was all becoming clear to Delaney. It was as he suspected. Tony would never have gotten into a car and left himself open like that unless he knew who was in that car—Jonathan Talbot. "And you had Keith leave

Tony's body at the cove so we'd be sure to find him right away."

"Exactly."

The sonofabitch almost smirked, Even now, Delaney realized, he can't help being proud of how well he'd planned everything.

"And, as I expected, you came in demanding his job."

"But you didn't count on me sobering up."

The half-smirk vanished. "No, I didn't. May I have another drink?"

"Go ahead."

"One for you?"

"No, I'm sort of on duty."

"As you wish." Talbot poured another drink, sniffed it appreciatively, and took a sip. "You really should try this. It's truly spectacular."

Delaney noticed that Talbot had suddenly regained his composure, and he wondered why. "So the bottom line, Jonathan is that five people are dead because you tied a knot too tight," Delaney said.

"Well, if you must put it that way. I suppose it's true. In any event, it was all most unfortunate."

"You don't seem all that concerned."

"I'm a very pragmatic man, Mr. Delaney. The Commerce job is gone of course. I realize that, but at least there's no capital punishment in this state."

"What's your point?"

Talbot smiled. "Parole. I know an awful lot of influential people in this state. Your evidence is flimsy at best. Keith is dead. And you certainly can't use what I've said against me. I believe coercion is still against the law. Even assuming I'm found guilty in a trial, with my record of philanthropy and community involvement, I won't do more than a couple of years in minimum security."

"You don't get it, do you, Jonathan? You've just had your trial."

Talbot suddenly understood what Delaney was saying. He dropped his glass and it hit the soft pile with a muffled thud. "You... you're not going to arrest me?"

"No."

" Certainly you can't kill me?"

"Now you've got it."

"But that's *insane*. You're bluffing... You could never get away with it."

"That's the point, Jonathan. I don't have to get away with it. After I kill you, I'm going to kill myself." He saw the astonished look on Talbot's face and added, "In retrospect, Jonathan, I think you'll have to agree you couldn't have picked a worse guy for Tony's job."

Delaney raised his gun and pointed it at Talbot's chest. This was what he'd been waiting for since the day Tony was murdered—to find the man who murdered his best friend and exact retribution. As a bonus, he took some consolation in knowing that he wasn't the failure that he thought he was. He had, after all, found Tony's murderer. Now it was time to let it all go. To find peace.

"Goodbye, Talbot. See you in hell…"

"Pete—" JT stepped into the room, nervously pointing her gun at Delaney. "Put the gun down. This man is my prisoner."

Delaney continued to hold his gun on Talbot. "Go away, JT. This doesn't concern you."

"I heard everything. Talbot's a murderer. We can convict him. What you want to do is wrong, Pete. Let a jury decide."

"Get out of here, JT."

"Not without my prisoner."

"Then you'll have to shoot me to get to him."

"You can't do this to the people who believed in you. What about Tony? What about your wife? Your son? Me? What about every goddamn deputy in the Haddley Falls Police Department?"

"Get the hell out of here," Delaney shouted.

He didn't want to listen to her anymore. He didn't want to listen to reason or logic. Why was she even talking that way? Couldn't she see? Couldn't she understand? There was a perfect symmetry to what he was about to do. Talbot murdered Tony. He would murder Talbot. He would kill himself. They'd be no trial, no high-price lawyers to obfuscate, to twist the facts, to fog the jury's mind. He had seen too many murderers get off in the past. In the beginning, he'd been enraged. *Where was the justice?* Then, as he became more experienced, he realized that the courtroom was nothing more than the theater of the absurd. If the defendant had enough money he could always buy the "right" lawyer who would believe anything—or pretend to believe anything. He could buy an "expert" witness—or insure that there was no witness. Christ. Hadn't the whole world witnessed the O.J. trial? Delaney was not about to let that happen. Not this time. Not to the man who murdered Tony Brunetta.

JT's muffled voice came through his heated thoughts first soft and indistinguishable, then, finally, loud and insistent. "What would Tony say?" she shouted at him. "For the love of God, Pete, you're about to commit murder. That's something you and Tony spent your whole lives fighting."

Delaney was aware of his finger on the trigger. It would, he knew, take less than five pounds of pressure to squeeze off a round. And the trigger, he also knew, would travel less than a third of an inch and then it would be all over.

JT's voice echoed in his head. *"What would Tony say?"* Delaney hesitated. He knew exactly what Tony would say, because he'd said it so often in the past: *"Pete, our job is to find the perp, collect the evidence, make a case and the let the courts decide. New York City is not a Banana Republic."*

Delaney lowered his gun. Jonathan Talbot's nascent smile died aborning when Delaney stepped forward and slammed the barrel of his gun into the side of Talbot's temple. He fell back, against the liquor cabinet, spilling the entire bottle of his very expensive Scotch malt liquor.

CHAPTER TWENTY EIGHT

The next day Delaney was in the office clearing out the few personal possessions he had when Clint came in waving a newspaper.

"Look at this, Chief."

The newspaper's headline read: *Jonathan Talbot, Nominee for Secretary of Commerce, Arrested for Murder.*

Clint shook his head. "You know, it's unbelievable, Chief. My cousin works for the Chamber of Commerce. She tells me they're swamped with calls from tourists. It seems the whole world wants to stay in Haddley Falls, the scene of the crime."

"P.T. Barnum was right, Clint. No one ever went broke underestimating the intelligence of the American public. The masses are asses."

Clint picked at an imaginary thread on his sleeve. "Um, Chief. The guys were wondering... I was wondering... are you gonna stay on?"

"Naw. I'm not the boss type."

"Oh, that's too bad."

Delaney shook the young deputy's hand. "Clint, you have the makings of a good cop. Fight the good fight."

Clint's face lit up. "Really? You think so, Chief?"

"Yeah, really," Delaney said, heading for the door. "You take care, now."

#

Back at Tony's house, an air of sadness hung in the air and Delaney hurriedly packed, wanting to get out of there as quickly as possible. As he zipped up his bag and took a last look around, there was a knock at the door.

It was JT on the other side of the screen door, looking lovelier than ever. Delaney had been hoping to get out of town without seeing her. It wasn't that he didn't want to see her, it was just that... Just what? He didn't know the answer to that question.

"Can I come in?"

"Sure."

There was a long, awkward moment of silence, then JT said, "Well, I see you're all packed."

"Yep."

"Great. Um, so what now?"

"Back to the big city.

"Can you get your job back?"

"I'm sure Lt. Weber has already changed all the locks, but I'm gonna give it a shot. What else can I do?"

"You could stay here."

Delaney looked into her eyes, trying to read where she was going with this. But he saw nothing. She had the makings of a good cop, too, he thought. Never express your emotions. Never let the other guy see what you're thinking.

"What would I do here?"

"Royce wants you to keep the chief's job. So does Walt. So do I... I mean, you know, me and all the other guys in the department."

Delaney, not trusting himself to look at her, turned away. He was surprised—and uneasy—to feel the old familiar stirrings that he thought had died with his wife and son. What was it? Love? The thought of caring for someone again? The thought of someone caring for him? It was all very exhilarating and scary and wonderful *then*, but he couldn't deal with that now, not ever.

He pushed the troubling emotion back deep inside of him. He couldn't go through that again. He couldn't love someone and risk having that person taken away from him. He was better off the way he was. Alone. With no one to worry about and no one to worry about him. It'd be better now, since he'd come to his senses about suicide. At some point, while he was pointing the gun at Jonathan Talbot's chest, it occurred to him that suicide was the coward's way out. He was many things, but being a coward wasn't one of them. No, he would not think again of taking his own life. He would not let this world defeat him. He would survive. Alone.

"I could teach you to sail." JT blurted out.

Caught off guard, Delaney allowed the wonderful possibilities to race through his mind. It was tempting, but.... "Thanks, JT," he said. "But it wouldn't work. I can't swim."

Delaney tossed his bag in the trunk of the Honda and turned to JT.

"Well... I guess that's it."

JT held her hand out. "Well, OK. I guess it is. It was nice knowing you Chief Pete Delaney."

Delaney took her hand in his and it was like electricity coursing through his body. The only two other times he'd touched her was when he'd helped her back onto the sailboat and then that embarrassing moment in the cabin. He didn't want to let her hand go. "And it was nice knowing you Deputy JT Bryce."

JT dropped the "hey-see-you-around" act and concern clouded her eyes. "Pete, are you going to be okay?"

"Yeah, I'll be fine. You know, I think I've finally done something useful here. I'm not feeling sorry for myself anymore.

They looked into each other's eyes, wishing one of them would say the right thing, but neither of them knew what the right thing was.

Delaney backed the Honda out the driveway and honked at JT. She waved as he pulled away.

On the road out of town, Delaney slowed to take one last look at the Talbot Meat Packing building. Further on down the road, he passed the Flotsam Bar. A cluster of bikers and beach bums were standing outside drinking beer out of long neck bottles. The red-headed giant was among them, glowering at him. Delaney waved as he passed. Through his rearview mirror, he saw the man give him the finger. He pulled off the road and slammed on the brakes. The way the man dropped his bottle and fell up the stairs and dove into the bar made Delaney smile.

He sat there looking at the Flotsam Bar through his rearview mirror for a long time, remembering how he'd seen it the first day he'd come to town and then the night he'd tailed Wade to his bungalow. Nothing much had changed. There were still the bikers, the pros, the drugies, and the rest of the flotsam and jetsam of Haddley Falls. Something should be done about that bar.

Then he started the engine and made a U-turn.

JT was standing in the Police Department parking lot, talking to Clint and two other deputies when Delaney pulled in. She looked up, saw him, and walked toward him.

Now that he was here, he didn't know exactly why he'd come back. He sat in the Honda, both hands clutching the steering wheel, Then she was there, standing beside him, saying nothing, her arms folded. He drummed his fingers on the steering wheel. He cleared his throat. He looked at the temperature gauge which was reading hot. He turned the engine off.

"Maybe you could teach me to swim first."

The End

ABOUT THE AUTHOR

Michael Grant is a retired lieutenant with New York City Police Department. He lives on Long Island with his wife Elizabeth and their Golden Retriever Jack. Mr. Grant has written three novels, *Line of Duty*, *Officer Down* and *Retribution*.

Mr. Grant can be contacted at *mggrant08@gmail.com*

Made in the USA
Lexington, KY
07 August 2017